THE
BRIEF

This book is entirely a work of fiction. The names, characters and incidents portrayed in it are entirely a work of fiction. Any resemblance to actual persons, living or dead, is entirely coincidental.

Copyright© Caroline Blake 2024

All Rights Reserved
No part of this book may be reproduced in any form,
by photocopying or by any
electronic or mechanical means,
including information storage or retrieval systems,
without permission in writing from both the copyright owner and
the publisher of this book.

First published January 2024

Instagram @carolinemelodyblake

www.carolinemelodyblake.co.uk

Dedication

This book is for all the self-published authors out there and for all those fabulous readers who support them. Cheers to you all! This book is dedicated to all of you.

I know that asking someone to buy a book with their hard-earned cash is difficult enough. But when that author is completely unknown and isn't backed up by a large publishing company, well, it seems like there is a mountain to climb. Self-published authors don't have a massive marketing budget and often rely on friends and family to spread the word, together with the wonderful Bookstagram followers and I am immensely grateful to anyone who takes a chance and buys a book by an indie-author.

I am even more grateful to those of you who share your purchases and reviews on social media and who take the time to write reviews on Amazon and Goodreads. It means a lot and it really helps to show other readers that it is a book worth reading

This book is also dedicated to my lovely friend, Eleanor, who is always my biggest cheerleader. Eleanor has been my friend for over thirteen years, since we met at a law firm in Manchester where we both worked. Back in the day, she was single-handedly responsible for the fact that I spent most of my wages on shoes, makeup and coffee, as she was my lunchtime shopping companion.

In addition, I like to thank Eilidh Locherty from Chaptered Vine Studio for her amazing proofreading and editing skills, and for showing me where commas and semi-colons should correctly be placed.

I'd also like to thank Whites of Garstang, who allowed me to sell my books in their shop at one of their special Christmas events. They made me feel so welcome, and fed me chocolates and tea all day long. Whites Chambers is named after them.

Caroline x

BTW, if you are struggling to get to know all the different characters in this book, turn to the back pages where you will find my character studies. These are the notes that I made before making a start on writing the book. I find it easier to write if I can get the characters clear in my head first.

You won't find all the facts about the characters in the book, but you might find them interesting to read.

Other Books by Caroline Blake

Just Breathe
Forever Hold Your Peace
Unexpected Storm

Prologue

Whites Chambers has occupied the narrow, three-storey Victorian building on the corner of St John Street in Manchester for a hundred and thirty years.

The busy chambers reverberate with activity in the afternoons. Barristers return from court triumphant that they have done their best for their client, whether or not that is, in fact, the case. Any mistakes which may have been made are quickly forgotten. Nobody has time to dwell on past cases and anything that may have gone wrong; a witness who didn't quite perform as expected; a closing speech that could have been a little more persuasive or a prison sentence that may have been too lenient or too harsh.

The clerks keep their resident barristers in constant and lucrative work. Their well-structured diary system means that the best legal brains on the Northern Circuit (according to their recently updated website) are constantly put to the test, defending or prosecuting the unfortunate beings who find themselves at the mercy of the English criminal legal system.

There is always another case waiting; its depositions wrapped in luxurious cream paper, the accusations held tightly within the traditional pink ribbon of the brief. In an occupation where a brilliant mind is paid for by the hour, the demand to leave any regrets behind and move on to the next case is always pressing.

And so it was on that particular Friday afternoon.

The heavy wooden door leading to Whites Chambers was pulled open by James, one of the junior clerks, who was rushing out for his daily sandwich, almost two hours later than usual, after a particularly busy morning. His journey was momentarily halted by three or four returning barristers (later, when questioned by the police, James was unable to remember the exact number) chattering animatedly about their morning in court. As he held the door open, he didn't notice the stranger behind them, who was able to enter the chambers without having to use the intercom system. The man, dressed in a black suit with a crisp white shirt and a black and grey striped tie, and carrying a leather briefcase, merged into the small crowd perfectly. If anyone had taken the time to look down at his shoes, however, they may have noted that they were old and scuffed at the toe. If anyone had taken the time to look closely at his face, they may have noticed the sheen of sweat on his upper lip and the tightness of his jaw. But after a busy day in court, the barristers were focused on getting back to their desks and to their next awaiting case.

Therefore, he went unnoticed.

James smiled politely and reverently and waited until his path was once again clear. Then he walked quickly down St. John Street, onto Byrom Street and down to Quay Street to his favourite sandwich shop. By the time he was ordering his bacon, lettuce and tomato on granary bread, he was well out of earshot of the unusual activity in St John Street.

His older colleague, Imran, head to one side, with the phone held between his ear and shoulder, concentrated on his computer screen. He was trying his best to juggle commitments and find someone who might be free to do a sentencing hearing next Wednesday. He vaguely noticed the group entering the building. The flapping of coats, the shaking of umbrellas and their loud voices annoyed him. The phone line to the instructing solicitors wasn't a particularly good one, and he was finding it hard to hear what was being said. But he smiled politely and professionally and then once again, stared at his computer screen.

"I'll have to put you on hold for a second," he said, "while I speak to Miss Kershaw. If we can move her conference to later in the day, then she'll be free to do the hearing for you."

The doors to the lift opened and the noise in the reception area diminished as they closed and took the group upstairs. The clerk put the solicitor on hold and listened to the ringing of Miss Kershaw's phone. He was irritated that she wasn't answering when he knew she was in the building.

"Miss Kershaw isn't at her desk at the moment," he said. "But leave it with me, I'll put the hearing in the diary for you. If she can't do it, for whatever reason, I'll find someone who can."

As he chatted to the young solicitor, laughing and flirting, which he did with everyone, he thought that he heard something that sounded like gunshot. But the traffic on St John Street was always busy, so he told himself that it was a car back-firing, although the hairs on the back of his neck and his arms told him that he was wrong. The noise seemed to have come from upstairs.

A few seconds later, when the doors to the stairs at the side of the lift flew open and a tall thin man wearing a black suit and scuffed shoes ran into the reception area, the clerk knew from the man's crazed look, his frightened eyes and the sweat running down his face that something was terribly wrong. The screams from upstairs could now be heard quite clearly through the ceiling and he knew that, whatever had happened up there, this man was responsible.

He had to stop him before he got to the door.

"Oi, what's going on?" he shouted, dropping the phone. He ran out from behind the long reception desk. Maybe the man would stop and calmly explain that everything upstairs was fine.

Nothing was going on. There was nothing to worry about. Yes, he had heard the car back-firing too. Or was it a motorbike? They would laugh and the clerk would then ask him his name and who he had come to see. He would ask him to take a seat. Would he like a tea or a coffee while he waited?

Deep down, the clerk knew that the chances of that happening were zero.

He had to stop him.

The man didn't say anything. He was walking now, almost running, to the door. He was seconds away from his freedom. But Imran was there first and blocked his way, his arms outstretched and his back to the door, ready for any altercation that may be forthcoming. He had been working at the chambers for nearly twelve years and he had met thousands of criminals in that time and, although they didn't usually wear suits, the clerk knew one when he saw one. He knew that this man didn't have an appointment and he shouldn't be in chambers. None of the barristers had a conference arranged until after four o'clock.

The continued screaming from upstairs disturbed him and although all of the clerk's instincts called out to him to get out of the way, to let the man go, he stood his ground.

The man stopped and stared at him for a moment. The clerk thought that he saw the tiniest flicker of regret in his eyes, a second before he raised his right hand and pointed the gun directly at his forehead.

Don't people say that your life flashes before your eyes in the moments before death comes to take you? That wasn't so for Imran. He didn't see his past life. Rather, visions of his future life zipped through his mind. In what must have been only a second, or two at the most, he saw his wife standing over his grave, sobbing and falling to her knees as his coffin was lowered into the ground and splattered with handfuls of soil thrown by the gathered mourners. He saw his daughter walking down the aisle on her own on her wedding day, fighting back the tears that would ruin her carefully applied make-up. He saw his unborn grandchildren playing in the back garden of the house he had bought with his wife just before they got married; the house where their daughter had grown up. He saw his wife spending her retirement alone, going on cruises where she sat with strangers at dinner and pretended to be happy.

He wasn't ready to die yet. There were so many things he hadn't yet done, so many places that he hadn't yet visited. He hadn't been to Cuba or seen the Grand Canyon. He had never eaten in a sushi restaurant. He hadn't finished the John Grisham book he had been reading for the past month. He liked to take his time with a book, reading a few pages each night before he went to sleep. Now it seemed that he would never know the ending. He hadn't even had time to pay off his mortgage. How would his wife manage without him?

He had always thought that he would saunter into retirement.

But complacency, it seemed, was not for everyone.

Fate had decided that his time was up, and he was willing to die like a man.

He closed his eyes and waited for the bullet that would propel him from this world into the next.

When he heard the front door open and felt the cool wind rush into the reception area, he prayed that it wasn't James, his young colleague, returning moments too early, clutching his expensive and carefully wrapped artisan sandwich. It wasn't fair for them both to be gunned down at work. If anyone was going to be the sacrificial lamb, then it should be him, surely. He was older, he was the senior clerk and, well, he couldn't think of any other reason, except that it would be a pointless waste of another life. Goodness knows what damage this man had caused upstairs, but he didn't need to kill another two people, just because they were in his way.

He waited for the sound of his colleague's startled voice, but when it didn't come, he opened his eyes, slowly and reluctantly.

The reception was empty.

The gunman had gone.

Chapter One
Eleven Days Before the Shooting - Monday

As Samantha dotted the foundation around her face and gently rubbed it in with her fingertips, she looked at her husband and smiled to herself. The door to their ensuite was open. She loved to watch him shave. Was that odd? There was something very masculine about it. The way he lifted his chin and dabbed the badger hair shaving brush over his neck, and then gently wiped the foam off with his silver-handled razor, ending the routine by splashing his face with cold water. As she curled her eyelashes and covered them with two layers of black mascara, she wondered whether he liked to watch her as she applied her makeup. The feminine equivalent of his shave. He had never said. So, probably not.

Even after ten years together, she still pinched herself every day when she woke up next to Alistair. She had confided in her best friend, Jamilla, shortly after their wedding, that she didn't think she was good enough for him. Too much gin had loosened her lips on a girls' night out and she confessed that she was worried that he would stray, sooner or later. Jamilla told her not to be so stupid - he had chosen her, hadn't he? But the words came from one who was blessed with natural beauty and curves that only dreams are made of. Nevertheless, Samantha worried. She told herself that there must be something about her that he loved, otherwise he wouldn't be here. She had heard something somewhere about men not wanting their wives to be too beautiful, so they didn't have to worry about them being constantly chased by other men. Maybe that's why he chose her. Whatever the reason, she was grateful.

She finished her makeup by adding golden bronzer and pulled her unruly curly hair into a tight ponytail. Alistair went into the shower as she went downstairs to the kitchen, where she made two coffees and poured them into stainless steel takeaway cups. They wouldn't have time to sit and drink coffee this morning. The traffic into Manchester was always crazy on a Monday and today's forecast for rain wouldn't help. Nobody seemed to want to get the tram at the slightest hint of inclement weather.

She popped a slice of bread into the toaster and then ran back upstairs to get dressed. She would have to eat it in the car, which Alistair wouldn't be happy about, but so be it. He hated finding crumbs on his leather upholstery.

"You know my trial starts this morning, don't you?" he said, curtly, as she walked back into the bedroom. "Why are you still in your dressing gown?"

He was already dressed in his self-imposed barrister's uniform of a navy blue three-piece suit, with a white shirt and blue tie. A thick white pinstripe ran through the jacket and trousers. There was nothing subtle about Alistair.

She grabbed his tie and straightened it for him. It didn't need straightening, but the opportunity to be near to him, if just for a second or two, was too much for her to resist. She didn't know why he bothered with it; it would soon be replaced by the white stiff wing collar for court, but he wouldn't dream of walking through chambers without a tie. Not for a second.

He batted her hand away. "Leave it. I've just put it on. I'm quite capable of sorting out my own tie."

She stepped back, away from him and turned to her wardrobe, so that he wouldn't see the start of tears.

"Can you just get dressed? Quickly," he said.

She took a deep breath and told herself that it wasn't personal; he was always grumpy on the first day of a trial. Although, as most of his trials lasted a week or less, he was grumpy most Monday mornings and she was getting a little tired of it. She didn't tell him so. It was just part and parcel of being married, especially to someone who had a stressful job. Surely, she had some annoying foibles that he had learned to live with over the years. She knew it irritated him when she picked the gel from her nails, and she never stuck to the shopping list at the supermarket. She always came back with a bag or two of extra groceries. There were probably other things that he had never mentioned. But nobody's perfect, are they?

She hung her dressing gown on the hook on the inside of the wardrobe door, took a black shift dress off the hanger and stepped into it.

"Okay, I'm ready," she said, pulling the side zip closed and turning to give Alistair a big smile to defuse the building tension. He was still scowling. She grabbed her work shoes, sensible and black with a low heel (boring as hell) and put them on.

"Come on, I thought you said you had a trial. Let's go," she said.

It was almost seven a.m. and she knew that he planned to leave at seven, to be in chambers for seven forty-five, so, today at least, she couldn't be blamed for making him late.

"Fine," he said, checking the time on his Tag-Heuer watch. "You'll have to finish your makeup in the car."

She ignored his last comment and followed him down the stairs and into the kitchen.

"I've made you a coffee," she said, nodding to the two cups. She picked up the toast, which had popped out of the toaster and was lying on the worktop and began spreading it with peanut butter.

"Aren't you meant to be giving up gluten?" said Alistair, as he took a large gulp of his coffee. "Fuck me, that's hot."

"I've just made it, that's why," she mumbled. She followed him out of the house, closed the door and walked to the car.

"What?"

"Nothing," she said, taking a bite of her toast and climbing into the passenger seat of their Jaguar F-Pace.

"Did you put the alarm on?" he said. He held onto the driver's door and peered at her, accusingly.

"Yes, I think so." She honestly couldn't remember. She was thinking about her busy diary and wondering whether James, their junior clerk, had managed to move her conference that was planned for tomorrow afternoon. As she left chambers on Friday, he had been on the phone to the instructing solicitor, promising that he would do his best. It wasn't the end of the world if he hadn't managed it, but she could do with a free afternoon to catch up with paperwork.

"Well did you, or didn't you?" Alistair stared at her for a second, not waiting for her to answer. "Right, I'll check it myself."

She watched him stamp back to the front door and open it. She could hear the beeping of the alarm and watched him stab the code into the panel, before stabbing it again to re-set the alarm.

"I told you I'd done it," she said, as he climbed into the car and started the engine.

"No, you didn't," he said. "You weren't sure. I don't know why you're incapable of remembering something that you did literally less than a minute ago, but there you are." He drove down the driveway and onto the road, quickly reaching a speed that was far too fast for a residential area.

Samantha didn't want to start her week with an argument. Not again. So she pretended to be engrossed with Radio Four, as they sat for the rest of the journey in silence.

Chapter Two
Monday

Sebastian Thomas arrived at chambers at a few minutes to eight, as he did every day and as he had done for the past thirty-five years.

"Good morning, James," he said, as he shook the rain from his umbrella. He held open the door to chambers with his back, until James ran across the tiled reception floor and held it for him. "Did you have a good weekend?"

"Yes, lovely, thank you, sir," said James.

Imran, in his position as senior clerk and self-confessed legal dinosaur, had insisted that all the barristers in Chambers were addressed by their surnames, or sir or ma'am. Modernity wasn't welcome in the legal profession and especially wasn't welcome in Whites Chambers.

"Did you have a good one?"

"Excellent, James, thank you very much," said Sebastian. "Today's trial is a non-starter, which meant I had lots more free time than I'd anticipated. Much to my wife's dismay." James laughed politely, as he helped Sebastian out of his raincoat and took his umbrella, which he placed in the tall ash wood stand next to the door. "A good friend of mine is the instructing solicitor. He had a last-minute telephone call with the defendant on Friday evening and he told me that he intends to plead guilty today, although until I hear him say the word 'guilty' with my own ears, I'd better be prepared for the alternative."

The lift doors opened, and Sebastian stepped in and pressed the button for the second floor. He tried to squash the thought that he should be taking the stairs. The diet and exercise regime that his wife was trying to instil could start tomorrow. Mondays were bad enough, without having to endure hummus, beetroot and lettuce wraps and thousands of unnecessary steps. He knew that she meant well and was looking out for him as he approached his sixtieth year, but the walk from the car park just now - via his favourite deli, where he had picked up a bacon and cream cheese bagel - and the walk to court and back would be enough for him today.

He pushed open the door to his office and settled down in his high-backed bottle green leather chair. He unwrapped his bagel, which was warm and steaming, and took a large bite.

Despite the fact that he had received the good news about today's defendant intending to plead guilty, (which was absolutely the right decision, as Sebastian had always felt that the evidence weighed too much against the defendant, despite his insistence that there was a perfectly good explanation for his fingerprints being found at the scene of the burglary) which had resulted in a leisurely weekend, Sebastian's energy levels were still low. He needed a holiday. Desperately.

He took his phone out of his jacket pocket and sent a text to his wife.

Laila darling, I need a holiday. I'm sure you do too. Caravan in Whitby or 5 star in The Maldives? X

He received a reply immediately, *Such a tough choice. Leave it with me. I'll do some research and we can chat tonight x*

Sebastian knew that Laila would make the right decision and would choose the perfect holiday destination for them. She always did. He put his phone back inside his jacket pocket and picked up the landline on his desk. He dialled zero for the clerks' desk. Imran answered on the second ring.

"Good morning, Mr Thomas," he said.

"Good morning, Imran. How are you?"

"Good thank you, sir. You?"

"Yes, very well, thank you." In all the years that Sebastian had worked with Imran - ten, fifteen, he could never remember - they had never had a proper conversation. They never seemed to get over the barrier of professional politeness. It was a shame. He seemed like a nice man. Maybe he should invite him out for lunch one day. Get to know him properly. Not this week though. Now that his diary was about to empty, he was looking forward to having a few days off later in the week. "Imran, I've been informed that today's trial is possibly going to be a guilty plea this morning. Please could you ring Monson and Co and double-check that is still the case and, if so, give the prosecutor the heads up?"

"Yes, sir, consider it done," said Imran.

"Thank you," said Sebastian, putting the phone down.

"Morning, Dad," said Jamilla, opening his office door. "Are you busy?"

"I've always got time you for, darling. How are you? You look troubled."

Sebastian met his daughter with a huge hug.

"I'm alright," said Jamilla. "I just wanted to see you, that's all. That bacon smells good."

"Don't tell your mum."

"I won't," she said.

Jamilla sat down in one of the tub chairs facing her father's desk. He pushed his bagel towards her with a conspiratorial wink and she took a small bite.

"I can tell when you're upset, but I won't press you on it if…" He was interrupted by his office door crashing open. "Robert! Please! How many times have I asked you to open the door gently? There are so many dents in that bookcase, it will be fit for nothing but firewood very soon."

"Well, whose stupid idea was it to put a bookcase right behind a door?" Robert peered behind the heavy oak door and rubbed at the bookcase, where the door handle had crashed into it. "No damage done," he said.

"Which is more than can be said about you," said Sebastian. "What have you done to yourself?"

Robert reached up his hand and touched the graze on his left cheekbone. "I walked into the cupboard door in the kitchen," he said. "Morning, Jamilla."

Jamilla ignored him.

"Mmm, somebody's fist more likely," said Sebastian.

Robert shrugged. That was a possibility. Highly probable, in fact. Thankfully, whoever had done the damage hadn't put much force behind the blow, or maybe he had managed to dodge out of the way in time. Who knew? But thankfully, he had managed to avoid a couple of black eyes. They would have been more difficult to explain away.

Sebastian shook his head. "You look a state, man. Have you shaved?" Robert rubbed at his chin, feeling the stubble that had grown overnight. "Don't answer, on the grounds that you will most definitely incriminate yourself."

Robert stood in front of Sebastian's old-fashioned mahogany desk, taking the admonishment like a recalcitrant schoolboy. How many times had he stood in front of the head teacher's desk like this? Too many to remember. If someone had told him that history would repeat itself at work, he would have chosen another profession. One where there weren't so many rules.

"I didn't get much sleep last night," he admitted. "I pressed the snooze button on the alarm one too many times, I'm afraid, so I didn't get time to shave. It won't happen again."

Robert's head teacher used to tell him that a little contrition wouldn't do him any harm. Despite him telling her that he was sorry for whatever transgression he had committed that particular week, she said that he needed to learn the meaning of humility. And whilst he was at it, he could take that stupid grin off his face. Right now, Robert tried to appear humble and contrite. Whether he managed to pull it off, he wasn't sure. What he was sure of was that he was holding onto his position in chambers by his fingertips. He was nine months into his twelve-month pupillage as a trainee barrister and in no time at all, the decision would be made as to whether he would be given a permanent position. This year, there was no competition. He was the only pupil. So, in theory, the tenure was his. All he had to do was to reach out and take it. So why did he keep fucking it up?

"Go and get yourself a coffee and use this," said Sebastian. He opened the top drawer of his desk and retrieved an electric razor, which he held out to him. "Don't look at me like that. It's clean. No shave, no court attendance." Robert took it from him. "And I'll have a tea, please. Nice and strong. We leave for court in forty minutes, okay?"

Robert clicked his heels together and saluted with his right hand. "Sir, yes, sir." Then, "Okay, okay, I'm going. Don't throw anything at me. I know you want to. Jamilla, can I get you anything?"

Jamilla turned to look at him, and shook her head, making no attempt to hide her disdain. He left the room.

"Why do you put up with him, Dad?" she asked. "He's a useless waste of space."

"I take it you two have had a spat?"

Jamilla's tears appeared suddenly and fell down her carefully applied make-up before she had time to stop them.

"I hate him," she said.

Sebastian rushed over to her, and she buried her head in his chest, as he stroked her hair with one hand and her back with the other. He didn't know what to say. He had told Robert only last week that he was on shaky ground, and he needed to work harder, on his appearance, on his attendance and on his attitude. And he certainly needed to work harder on his relationship with Jamilla. The sooner she ended it with him, the better, as far as he was concerned.

Chapter Three
Monday

In the kitchen on the ground floor, Robert filled the kettle with water and waited for it to boil, while he poured himself a black filter coffee from the large jug which was prepared by one of the clerks every morning. He tried not to move his head too much, hoping that his headache would at some point subside. Another Monday, another hangover.

He knew that Jamilla was mad at him. He was hoping that at some point today, he would remember why.

Robert's iPhone alarm had woken him at seven o'clock this morning. The incessant beep beep beeping reverberated around his head painfully. After fumbling around on his bedside cabinet, his eyes still tightly pressed shut, he had located the phone and pressed the stop button. As he lay back down on his pillow, his fuddled brain calculated that he had only had four hours of sleep. Maybe not even that. But he knew that the pounding in his head would force him to get up. He needed water and paracetamol.

He still couldn't remember the finer details of the previous evening, but he knew that he had been out longer than he had intended. A meal with Jamilla and an early night had been the original plan. He had invited her to stay at his apartment in Castlefield, just a short walk from the restaurant, but he couldn't remember whether she had said yes or not. He had reached his hand across the bed this morning and felt a cold space where her warm body should have been.

"Jamilla?" He had shouted. His voice was hoarse and croaky. He had cleared his throat with a cough that made his brain hurt. He tried again. "Milla, are you there?" No reply. He didn't hear the shower running or any activity in the kitchen. Where was she? His bedroom door was open, but he couldn't see her. He didn't have the energy to shout out for her again. He had closed his eyes, hoping that she would bring him a drink and some painkillers soon. She must have heard his alarm going off. But she wasn't there.

Now, pictures of last night flashed through his brain. A bottle of wine in the restaurant. Another bottle. Jamilla storming off to the toilet. Her pizza untouched. Had they argued? A wet pavement. A stumble into the road, car horns beeping. The roulette table, spinning. He remembered that he had lost. Again. Piles of red and blue plastic chips being swept away. The croupier's blank face.

After that, he remembered nothing.

He rested his elbows on the worktop and held his hands over his eyes, trying to blank out the awful shattered pieces of memory that jumbled in his head. Another night in the casino. No wonder Jamilla hadn't been by his side when he had woken up. He had promised her that he wouldn't go there again. Only a few days ago, she had held onto his hand and begged him never to step foot inside any gambling establishment ever again.

"Just for clarification," she had said earnestly, "That means casinos, betting offices and the shitty little places in Blackpool where they have those machines where you can win two pence pieces that you knock into a plastic cup." He had laughed and told her that he hadn't been to Blackpool since he was six years old. "You know what I mean," she had said, with tears in her eyes. "If you loved me, you wouldn't do it." He assured her that he loved her. He had kissed her cheeks, kissing away the salty tears, and promised her with all his heart that he would 'sort himself out'.

He had tried to explain to her that it was just a hobby, but she didn't get it. An argument about 'reigning in his spending' had ensued. She questioned whether he really needed his Porsche. Was it absolutely necessary? He could walk to work from his place in less than ten minutes, so if he returned the car and put the money into a savings account, they would have enough for a house deposit in no time. Robert had bitten down on his tongue. It was alright for her, with rich parents to subsidise her lifestyle. Nobody had bought him a car or paid for his rent. Unlike her, he paid his own way in life. But he hadn't said that, of course, because he loved Jamilla, and he knew that she would eventually be his wife. Hopefully.

The kettle boiled. He poured hot water over the teabag in Sebastian's favourite mug and stirred it around. While he waited for it to brew, he contemplated how he could make it up to her. He took his phone out of his pocket and tapped 'Interflora' into the browser. A flower delivery would do it. But then again, she would moan at him for not making it personal. At lunchtime, he decided, he'd go to the florist on Deansgate, choose her a huge bunch of flowers and take them to her office himself. Remorse and love, wrapped up in fragrant petals. Public displays of affection always went down well. He'd be back in her good books in no time. She knew which side her bread was buttered.

"What the fuck have you done to your face?" It was Alistair. The smug prick. He waltzed into the kitchen in the same way as he waltzed into any room - as though he was King Dick.

Robert tried not to let his true feelings show on his face. "Good morning to you, too," he said, with a false smile. He lifted the teabag out of the cup and went to reach for the bin, but

Alistair stood in his way. Drips of tea landed on the clean tiled floor.

"Aren't you meant to say something witty like 'you should see the other guy'?" Alistair laughed at his own pitiful attempt at humour.

"I didn't get to see him," said Robert. "He was taken away in an ambulance."

"Ahaha, yes, good one," said Alistair, braying like a donkey.

Robert wondered what time he could take his next paracetamol.

Imran appeared at the open door. "Mr Mallory, phone call for you. Line two."

"Fill the kettle up, will you, there's a good chap," said Alistair as he walked away.

Fuck you, thought Robert, as he poured milk into Sebastian's tea. He emptied the water from the kettle down the sink, picked up Sebastian's tea with one hand and his coffee with the other, and quickly left the kitchen.

Sebastian's room was empty when he got there. The smell of bacon lingered in the air. Robert stuck his nose into his coffee cup and tried to keep a lid on his nausea.

Further snippets of memory from last night were slowly but surely becoming clearer. He couldn't remember whether Jamilla was by his side at the time, but he remembered kicking a can of Coke and shouting, "Goal!" Where the goal was, he had no idea. The can staggered into the road, bumping noisily along on the tarmac. It finally came to rest in the gutter, its journey halted by a discarded bottle of beer. The colours of the red can and the green bottle mingled as they rolled into fallen blossoms from a nearby cherry tree. Robert had nearly fallen over its root, as it bravely struggled through the concrete paving slabs. He tripped, steadying his fall by holding onto the trunk. He saw that chunks of the tree's bark had been ripped away and someone had tried to carve initials within a heart. The artistry was half finished. The culprit had probably been caught by an over-enthusiastic community support officer.

Robert's inebriated brain had stared at the can and the bottle. Litter. The middle-class, well-behaved, well-educated boy within had wanted to pick them up. He remembered thinking that he didn't want to live in a place where littering was commonplace. But it wasn't his litter. So, he'd left it where it was.

Then someone bumped into him from behind. The memory was hazy. Was it a man? Sorry mate. Pats on the back. Far away words and laughter. Heels clip-clopping on the pavement, fading away.

He remembered looking down at his feet. When he managed to work out that they were his feet, he made a huge effort to put one foot in front of the other.

A cycling Deliveroo driver swore at him, and almost knocked him over. "Get off the road, you stupid twat!"

He hadn't realised that he was on the road.

Oh God! It's no wonder that Jamilla isn't talking to him.

Chapter Four
Monday

Samantha met Jamilla in Pret a Manger on the corner of Crown Square just after nine. As often as their work schedule allowed, they met for coffee on a Monday morning, away from chambers. A chance for them to dissect their weekends, before their working weeks began. Jamilla was just collecting the coffee and making her way over to a table when Samantha arrived.

"I've already got you a coffee," said Jamilla, handing Samantha a skinny latte.

"You're a darling, thank you." Samantha took the cup and drank from it immediately. "I'm meant to be cutting down on dairy, but -"

"Dairy? I thought it was gluten that you were giving up?" Jamilla wasn't a fan of abstinence.

"Yes, that as well. Alistair thinks - "

"No, no, no," said Jamilla, putting her hand up to block any further words. "Don't tell me that this is his decision? Since when has he been in charge of what you can and can't eat?"

Samantha smiled and shrugged. She didn't need to explain. She knew that Jamilla wasn't Alistair's biggest fan. Jamilla tolerated him for the sake of their friendship, but she had made her views about him known on more than one occasion. In her opinion, Samantha could do better, and Jamilla was biding her time, waiting for her friend to come to the same conclusion on her own. Alistair was a first-class prick. It wasn't that Jamilla hadn't forgiven him for kissing Jennifer Maxwell at last year's Christmas party, it was the way he had dealt with it. His arrogance and egotism had rubbed salt into Samantha's wounds. There was no denial - there couldn't possibly be, because too many people had seen them together - and there was no apology. He had justified his actions by insisting that Jennifer had been the instigator; that they had both had too much to drink and at least he hadn't harboured any intention of sleeping with her.

"Everyone has a cheeky little snog under the mistletoe," he had slurred, ignoring the tears that were beginning to fall down Samantha's face. "That's why they call it a Christmas kiss. It even has a name!" The claret in his glass sloshed around as he gesticulated to various groups of men and women around the room, none of whom were snogging at that particular time. Jamilla couldn't remember seeing any mistletoe, for that matter. His argument was lost, along with any respect that Jamilla may have had for him. She had followed Samantha into the bathroom, where she hugged her and passed her a handful of tissues to mop her tears.

Within days, Samantha had forgiven Alistair and they had never spoken about it again.

"So, how was your weekend?" asked Samantha, anxious to divert the subject away from Alistair.

Jamilla shook her head. "It was pretty good until last night. But then I went out with Robert."

"Ah," said Samantha. She was aware of the troubles between Jamilla and Robert; his drinking binges and frequent trips to the casino were usually at the heart of them. She didn't know why Jamilla didn't nip their romance in the bud. They had only been dating for seven or eight months. But apparently, she loved him. And who was Samantha to judge? "It amazes me how long it takes for men to grow up. Do you want to talk about it?"

"In all honesty, no." Jamilla looked at her watch. "I don't want to give him any head space right now. Tell me about your new murder case instead, it sounds much more interesting than my failing love life. What are your initial views?"

"Well, she definitely killed him, there's no doubt about that," said Samantha. "But I'm not happy about her pleading guilty to murder."

"Really? Tell me about it," said Jamilla.

Olivia Stevenson, a tragic case of a thirty-year-old woman who had killed her boyfriend when she threw an extremely heavy lamp at his head during an argument, had played on Samantha's mind all weekend, since the brief had landed on her desk last Friday morning.

"I just don't think there's enough evidence to prove malicious intent. It was a horrible accident during a heated argument. One of those split-second moments that can change someone's life forever. She called the police immediately and admitted what she had done, but I'm sure she didn't mean to kill him. She was distraught."

"Have you listened to the call?"

"No, not yet, but I've read the transcript. Thankfully, her solicitor had the sense to advise her not to answer any questions throughout the police interview."

"The poor woman," said Jamilla. "She must be terrified."

"Yes, she is. The brief says that afterwards, in the police station cell, Olivia told her solicitor, in a torrent of tears, that she knew she was guilty, and she deserved to go to prison for the rest of her life. I talked to Alistair about it and his view was that she must have known that when she picked up the huge heavy lamp and threw it at her boyfriend's head that it would do some damage."

Jamilla rolled her eyes at the mention of Alistair's name.

"Whether or not she thought, or intended, the damage to lead to his death, well, I doubt that very much. It was an accident, pure and simple."

"Yes, I agree," said Jamilla. "Hopefully the jury will too."

"That's exactly it," said Samantha. "I'll advise her of her plea today, but her solicitor says that she wants to plead guilty, and she doubts that we can change her mind. She's pretty adamant about what she wants to do, apparently."

"Well, I hope you can get through to her. My morning isn't half as interesting. My defendant is accused of handling stolen goods. Bang to rights. Dozens of watches, bracelets and rings were found in his spare bedroom upstairs."

"Maybe he's just a very generous man who likes to buy jewellery for the people he loves," said Samantha, laughing.

"Yes, maybe. Let's find out if the jury think that, shall we?"

They drained their coffees, collected their bags and made their way to court.

*

Ten minutes later, Samantha and her instructing solicitor were sitting side by side in a tiny interview room in the bowels of the court, waiting for the defendant to be brought to them. Samantha had never represented a murderer before. She wasn't naive enough to think that all murders were cut and dried, but this case was more complicated than she had hoped.

The door to the interview room was opened by a civilian guard who gently pushed Olivia into the room. "Olivia Stevenson," said the guard. "Let me know if there is anything you need and in case of emergency, press the red button."

"Thank you," said Samantha. "Olivia, pleased to meet you. Come and sit down." Samantha stood up and held out her right hand, which Olivia took and shook gently. "My name is

Samantha Mallory and I'm going to be representing you in court today for your plea hearing."

"I'm pleading guilty," said Olivia, firmly.

Samantha nodded. "I understand that is your intention, but if you wouldn't mind, I'd like to go through the evidence. You might change your mind after you hear my advice…"

"I want to plead guilty."

"Well, let's discuss it first, shall we? Then we *both* might be satisfied that a guilty plea is indeed the correct way forward. Okay?" Olivia nodded and studied a stain on the table in front of her. She licked her finger and tried to wipe it away, giving up after a few seconds when it was clear that she wouldn't succeed. "So, in your own words," continued Samantha, "Can you explain to me what happened?"

A look of terror flashed across Olivia's face. She didn't want to relive the nightmare of that night, again. It seemed as though she had spoken about it dozens of times, to various people – the person who answered the 999 call, the police who attended her house, the detective who interviewed her, her solicitor. But she knew that she didn't have much choice. If this was her penance, then so be it.

"We'd been out with some friends," she said, still staring at the stubborn stain. "We got back home, me and Tim, that is, about half eleven and then, out of nowhere, we were arguing. We'd had a really good night, but Tim was a jealous person and lately, our arguments had become more intense. His jealousy was fired up every time my phone pinged. The sound of an incoming message seemed to ignite something inside him, and he became a different person. A jealous monster."

"Go on," said Samantha. "You had an incoming text message that started the argument, is that right?"

Olivia nodded. "WhatsApp," she said. "He tried to snatch my phone out of my hand, but I was quicker. I lifted my arm high in the air out of his reach. This just made him more angry and he slammed his hand down hard on the arm of the sofa, knocking his coffee cup to the floor."

"Did he ask you who the message was from?"

"No," Olivia looked up and met Samantha's eyes. "He didn't really get the chance."

"Tell me what you did next."

"I laughed. I don't know why. Maybe I was trying to defuse the situation or maybe I was just too drunk to take it seriously. But it was like a cartoon. The way he banged his hand on the sofa and the cup just flew into the air and landed on the floor. It just made me laugh. I said something like, 'It's a good job I've got wooden floor, or that would have made a right mess.'"

"What did he say to that?"

"He shouted at me. He said, 'Is that all you can think about? Our relationship is on the brink of collapse and all you can think about is a fucking coffee stain?' Sorry for swearing." She held her hands up to her mouth.

"It's okay," said Samantha.

"I mean, it wasn't even a problem because, like I said, I've got wooden floors." She shrugged and rubbed at the stain on the table again with her index finger. "What is this?" she asked.

"I'm not sure," said Samantha. "Ink maybe?" She put her hand over Olivia's to stop the rubbing. Olivia pulled her hand away and clung to it with her other one. "What happened next, Olivia? Take your time and tell me in as much detail as you can."

"I got annoyed then. He was ruining another night, and I was sick of it. In my head, I was giving him one more chance and then I wanted to end it with him. I couldn't cope with his moods, one minute laughing and then the next minute accusing me of chatting to people and flirting behind his back. I didn't do any of that. I was completely faithful to him."

"What happened next, Olivia?" repeated Samantha, softly.

"I got up from the sofa. I was going to go into the kitchen and get a tea towel or something. There was coffee all over the floor. But he got up too and blocked my way. He put his arms out across the door like this." She held her arms out to the side, her hands facing down towards the floor. "I couldn't get past him. He asked to see my phone. He wanted to know who the message was from."

"Where was your phone at that time?"

"I think it was in my jeans pocket."

"Who was the message from?" asked Samantha.

"My friend, Heather, who we'd been out with, just saying something stupid like she'd had too much to drink and felt sick, something like that."

"And did you tell him that? Did you tell Tim that the message was from Heather?"

"No."

"Why not?"

"Because I hadn't done anything wrong. It was just a message from a friend." Regret floated around Olivia like a dark fog, choking her, making it difficult for her to breathe.

"So why didn't you tell him that? He was upset, and getting angry and you could have made him feel better by telling him the truth. The argument would have been defused, wouldn't it?" Samantha knew that she was goading her client, but she wanted to see whether she became angry, whether her true personality would peep through the shell of the person sitting in front of her.

"I don't know, maybe," said Olivia. Her right hand rested on her heaving chest, as she took deep breaths. "If I had, I wouldn't be where I am now, would I?" The tone of her voice didn't change. She didn't become angry and snap. She didn't cry, weep and wail. She didn't show any emotion at all. She was completely defeated. Her life was in shattered pieces, and she didn't have the energy to attempt to pick them up and put them together. "I threw the lamp at him. Then he fell onto the floor and didn't get up."

"What went through your mind when you picked up the lamp? Were you angry? Did you want to hurt him?" asked Samantha.

"No. Nothing," said Olivia. "I don't know." She licked her forefinger and rubbed at the stain on the table again.

Samantha let her sit with her thoughts for a moment, waiting for her to speak.

"I was angry," she admitted, raising her head. "And he was in my way. I needed to get to the kitchen, so I could mop up the coffee."

Samantha looked across at the young solicitor, whose head was down, writing everything her client said.

"So, when you picked up the lamp, and you were about to throw it at him, was the intention to hurt him?"

"No, of course not," said Olivia. "I just wanted him out of my way, and I thought that if I threw it at him, he would move." Tears then streamed down her face and dripped from her chin. She didn't wipe them away. Samantha reached into her handbag and pulled out a tissue, which Olivia took and scrunched up in her hand. "I can't believe that this is my life. Why is this happening to me? Just take me back to my cell. That's where I deserve to be." She lifted her chin, sat back and folded her arms across her chest. "I'd like to go back to the cells now please."

Chapter Five
Monday

"How did your plea hearing go?" asked Robert, when Samantha arrived back in chambers at lunchtime.

"All good in the end," she said. She put her soft leather Chloe tote bag (bought for herself from the money that Alistair had given her for her last birthday) onto her desk and sank down in her swivel chair. Her office, even though it was one of the smaller ones in chambers, had two desks and was shared with Robert for the duration of his pupillage. "She pleaded not guilty, but I know I've got an uphill battle on my hands. She insists she wants to plead guilty, and I'll be very surprised if the trial ends up going ahead."

"Such is the system," said Robert. He wasn't the sort of person to get emotionally involved in the court cases he had attended, but then again, he hadn't represented any of his own clients yet.

"Aren't you meant to be in a trial with Sebastian today?" she asked.

"Last-minute guilty plea," said Robert. "It's been adjourned for sentencing reports, so I'm free for the rest of the day. I've got some heavy-duty grovelling to do. Jamilla's not speaking to me, you might have gathered."

Samantha laughed. "Possibly, but I haven't heard your side. What have you done this time?" Robert's tumultuous love life would have been something she looked forward to hearing about on a Monday morning if his girlfriend was anyone other than Jamilla. After what seemed to be a promising start, it was a rare weekend if he and Jamilla managed to get through it without an argument of some sort.

"I'm not sure," said Robert. "I can't honestly remember, but I think it involves a copious amount of alcohol and a casino."

"Classic. And, don't tell me, you lost a bit too much money?"

"Something like that," said Robert. He didn't want to admit that he shouldn't have been there at all. Losing too much money had just been another nail in the coffin of his and Jamilla's relationship. "I'm going to get her some flowers. Shall I bring them to work? Or leave it until tonight, maybe?"

"Neither," said Samantha. "Flowers are for happy occasions. You shouldn't buy them because you feel guilty. Why don't you go round to hers tonight, or try and catch her when she comes back from court and tell her how sorry you are. Then give her some flowers next time you see her, as a sign of love, not as a sign of guilt."

"Yes, good idea," said Robert. A notification from his banking app this morning had told him that he was reaching the bottom of his overdraft, so in all honesty, the flowers would have to wait. He would call his parents later this evening and ask whether they could send him a few hundred pounds to tide him over until payday.

"I'm going to make some tea," said Samantha. "Do you want one?"

"No, thanks," said Robert. "I've got water."

As Samantha approached the kitchen, she could hear someone already in there, clattering crockery about.

"Alistair! What are you doing here?" she said. She walked over to her husband, her arms outstretched to hug him. He ignored the gesture, turned his back to her and walked over to the fridge.

"One of the prosecution witnesses wasn't well, so we adjourned early for lunch," he said. He picked up a bottle of milk from the fridge and poured some into his tea. Samantha didn't pursue the hug. She knew that, even though they were married, he liked to maintain a professional distance between them at chambers.

"Can I have the milk please?" she asked, as he went to put it back in the fridge. "Thank you," she gave him a quick kiss on the cheek as she took the bottle from him. "Don't panic, there's nobody here. I'm allowed to kiss my own husband." She ignored his frown. "Have you got time for some lunch? Gino's is usually quiet on a Monday."

"I picked up a sandwich on my way in," he said, sitting down at the large wooden table in the middle of the room. Samantha hadn't noticed the paper bag from the deli around the corner. "I didn't get you one, because I wasn't sure what time your hearing was."

"Don't worry," she said. "I'll pop out and get something later." She was pretty sure that she had told him that her hearing was in the morning, but she couldn't blame him for forgetting. On the first day of a trial, he had so much to think about. She made herself a cup of tea and sat down across the table from him. She fought the urge to reach over and touch his hand. "My defendant pleaded not guilty."

"And was that the correct advice, considering the circumstances?" asked Alistair.

"Yes, I think so. It was accidental. I think the jury will see that."

"Mmm," said Alistair. "It's manslaughter at best, Samantha. You might wish to reconsider."

Samantha disregarded his pomposity and told herself that she had done the right thing. Jamilla agreed too.

"I don't think she meant to hit him on his head," she said. "She was completely shocked when he fell down. I can't imagine what she would have been thinking at that point. The absolute dread when she realized that her boyfriend was dead must have been overwhelming." Alistair looked up from his sandwich and Samantha could see disapproval in his eyes. She went on, "The 999 call is harrowing, you know. Thankfully she had the presence of mind to call for an ambulance immediately. She told the operator that he wasn't responding when she called his name. She shook him and his eyes didn't move. The operator had asked her if the patient was breathing and she had cried and screamed Tim's name half a dozen times before she stopped and told the operator that she had never seen a dead person before, but she knew for certain that he was dead. Isn't that awful?"

"Well, she killed him, so of course he was fucking dead," said Alistair.

"Alistair!" said Samantha, "Don't be so harsh. She didn't mean to kill him."

"Bollocks," said Alistair, taking a large bite of his sandwich. Mayonnaise and lettuce dripped out of the side and onto the napkin in front of him on the table.

"Alistair, she didn't mean it," repeated Samantha, as gently as she could. She could feel an argument brewing between them and wished that she hadn't discussed the case with him at all. Initially, she had wanted a second opinion from a prosecuting barrister, but a quick summary of the case wasn't the same as reading all of the evidence and speaking to the defendant in person, so she couldn't expect Alistair to feel as strongly about the case as she did. "I told her that we needed to discuss in detail whether her actions amounted to manslaughter, but today wasn't the time to do that. I need to review all the evidence again and meet with her when I have more time."

"She lost control, Samantha," said Alistair. "No jury in the land will let her off. She threw the lamp at him knowing that it would cause injury. You need to listen to me on this one." He finished the last bite of his sandwich, and stood up, dabbing at his mouth with his napkin. "Okay, I'm going back to court. I'll see you later." He breezed out of the room without giving her a second glance. His tea was left untouched on the table.

As soon as the door closed behind him, it opened again and Robert rushed into the room, his face ashen.

"What's wrong," said Samantha. "Are you alright, Robert?"

"Yes, I'm fine, thanks," he said. He was holding an empty glass in his hand which he held under the cold water tap. He took a long drink before he spoke. "I'm in a bit of trouble, actually." He put his glass of water on the table, got his phone out of his jacket pocket and opened it up. He sat down at the table and showed Samantha a text that had arrived a few minutes ago. The sender was Quay Street Casino.

You have reached the end of your credit limit with Quay Street Casino. Under the terms and conditions of your credit agreement, as you have missed the last two payments, we hereby request payment in full within the next twenty-four hours. Please contact us to make a payment of £10,500.

Chapter Six
Ten Days Before the Shooting - Tuesday

Over the course of his thirty-five-year legal career, Sebastian had seen hundreds, if not thousands, of prison interview rooms. They continued to depress him. Windowless, airless boxes where disappointing lives are dissected and deliberated. Grey, soulless rooms where dismal walls bear witness to dire situations caused by previous bad choices. A place where lies are told, and truths are hidden.

A thin silver pipe ran along the bottom of the wall from the radiator. Dust and detritus had gathered underneath, undisturbed by the cleaner's mop. It seemed to have been there for so long that the dust had blackened the already morbid coloured walls, giving it an almost deliberate effect.

Sebastian pulled out the flimsy plastic chair for his instructing solicitor. In this age of equality, he had still not quite managed to shake the habit. His wife loved his chivalry, but he made a mental note to restrict it to her in the future. Ambitious young women these days could seat themselves. Their chairs scraped on the tiled floor, as she and Sebastian settled themselves across the table from the defendant.

The tabletop was sticky, although with what, he had no idea. Food wasn't allowed in these rooms, so it couldn't be the result of sticky fingers that had spent too long rummaging in a bag of sherbet bonbons. Delights such as those were miles away, far from reach for the unfortunate beings that inhabited rooms such as these. Jay Harris was one such unfortunate being. Sebastian's brief, which had landed on his desk yesterday afternoon, a consequence of his collapsed trial leaving him with unexpected free time, informed him that the defendant was on remand in Manchester Prison, awaiting trial for an aggravated burglary and a particularly nasty assault. The purpose of today's meeting was to meet his client, advise him on the evidence and discuss his upcoming application for bail.

Harris was the middle child of a single parent, born and raised on Manchester's largest council estate in Wythenshawe. Although Sebastian hadn't previously met him and hadn't yet asked him any questions, he knew what his defence would be. Of course, he would say that his ex-girlfriend, the victim of the alleged assault, was exaggerating. They always did. It wasn't an assault. Not really. Things just got out of hand. Harris would tell him that he was a good person at heart. He had got in with the wrong gang at school. He had been bullied for wanting to do his homework, and as peer pressure was a stronger pull than education, he had left school with no qualifications. A life of crime awaited him. It wasn't his fault. Sebastian had heard the same story too many times.

"Good afternoon, Jay," he said. "My name is Sebastian Thomas. I've been instructed to represent you at your hearing on Friday." Sebastian didn't reach out his hand. He wasn't sure when the defendant had last washed.

"You gonna get me out, yeah?" asked Harris, who remained seated. His social skills didn't stretch to salutations.

"I will try my best," said Sebastian. "But I did tell your instructing solicitor earlier this morning, that your chances of getting bail are slim, in my view."

"What d'ya mean, slim?" Aggression was never very far from the surface in people like Jay Harris, in Sebastian's experience. He was used to treading carefully, choosing placating words in potentially difficult conversations.

"I mean that it is unlikely that you will be granted bail, at least without the most stringent conditions."

"I need to get out of here, man. I've been in here a week, yeah, and I was told I could get bail."

Sebastian looked at the young solicitor at his side, who shook her head. "I didn't tell you that you would definitely get bail, Jay," she said. "I said that you could make an application, but that..."

"For fuck's sake, man!" Harris's raised voice caused the prison officer standing outside in the corridor to turn around and peer at them through the glass door. Sebastian held up his hand, indicating that all was well. Managing expectations wasn't something that young solicitors were great at. In his view, the bail application shouldn't be made at all. There was zero chance that this man should be released before his trial. The evidence was overwhelming, and he had a long history of violent crime. He was likely to be going to prison for a considerable length of time.

The fact that his girlfriend had dumped him one day and was then seen with another man the next day is no excuse for breaking into her house in the dead of night with a machete and shouting that he was going to 'kill the bastard' who she had been seen with.

"Let's try to stay calm, Jay. I can't discuss your case with you if you're going to get irate," said Sebastian.

Harris leaned back in his chair, forcing the two front legs off the floor. Sebastian tried not to sigh. He really was desperate for a holiday. Everything seemed to be grating on his nerves this week. The beginning of the week had started well yesterday. His client had pleaded guilty, having been persuaded by his solicitor that it was the right thing to do. Being found guilty after a trial would only have meant a harsher sentence. The client was happy, having got away with just a fine, albeit a considerable one, and some community service. He had virtually skipped out of court. But as soon as Sebastian arrived back in chambers, he was presented with this new brief. In a working environment where quiet time was unheard of, he should have known that his diary would not remain empty for long. To top it all, Robert had left a message on his voicemail in the early hours of the morning saying that he had a stomach bug and wouldn't be able to make it in today. The thin ice that Robert was skating on was melting by the day.

"I never touched her, you know," said Harris, rocking his chair backwards and forwards. "She's lying, man."

Sebastian knew that, in all probability, he was the one who was lying. He had seen a photograph of his ex-girlfriend's leg. A large purple bruise around the ankle was evidence that someone had held onto her tightly. Her statement said that that person was Jay Harris. She hadn't seen his face, but she had heard his voice as he thundered up the stairs. She had jumped out of bed and pulled her bedside cabinet across the bedroom door, so he couldn't get in. The man who she says was Harris hammered on the door and then began to chop at the wood with the machete. She managed to scramble under the bed but within minutes, he had broken into the room. She then felt a hand grab at her ankle. She prevented herself from being pulled out from the safety of the bed by clinging onto the wooden slats underneath the mattress. Harris was eventually chased off by the next-door neighbour, who had heard her screams and called for the police. He was arrested within the hour.

"The bail application isn't a trial hearing," explained Sebastian. "But the judge will look at the evidence in the case and, I'm sorry to say…"

"Don't fucking say that, man!" Harris jumped up from his chair, sending it rocketing out behind him. It came to rest against the wall. He quickly turned around and kicked it; the force causing it to bounce off the wall.

"Jay, sit down!" Sebastian forced himself to remain seated. If he stayed calm, then Harris would stay calm. In theory. Or did that just work for puppies? In any event, it was too late. Harris's composure was already lost.

Someone had pressed the alarm button. Sebastian wasn't sure who. Maybe it was the prison officer. Maybe it was the terrified young solicitor by his side. But in a second, the room was filled with a deafening siren. The door was thrown open. A prison officer rushed over to Harris, who was still intent on kicking the life out of the plastic chair. In a practised movement, the officer grabbed his right arm and held it tightly behind his back.

"Be careful, please," said Sebastian quietly, without the slightest hint of zeal.

The prison officer looked at him for a second and defiantly squeezed the prisoner's arm further upwards, causing him to scream profanities at the guard. Another officer rushed into the room and grabbed his left arm. Together, they pulled him out of the corner of the room, towards the door.

"You're fucking dead, man!" Harris screamed at Sebastian as he was manhandled out of the room. "Fucking dead! You no good …Ahh, get off me….You're dead! Dead!"

The angry words disappeared down the corridor. The alarm stopped and the room was filled with sudden silence.

"My God," said the young solicitor. "I've never seen anyone kick off like that before."

"Are you okay?" asked Sebastian.

"Yes, I'm fine, thanks," she said, blinking back sudden tears. "Just a bit shaken, that's all."

"The joys of being on the defence team," said Sebastian. "To be fair, it doesn't happen very often. Rarely, in fact. Usually, the defendants are as good as gold when in the company of someone who is potentially going to keep them out of prison."

"Yes, that's what I thought. He's different though. You can tell by his eyes. He's got a screw loose."

Yes, I couldn't agree more, thought Sebastian.

*

Later that evening, as Sebastian drove home, he tried to convince himself that the episode with Jay Harris hadn't bothered him. But it had. A great deal. In his younger days, he would have laughed it off. He would have told everyone in chambers that he had had an 'interesting' afternoon. A glimmer of something eventful for them to chat about over coffee in the kitchen, before everyone returned back to their offices and their waiting briefs. But he wasn't in the mood to discuss it. He didn't want to give it any more thought. He was getting too old for this. He never thought that he would see the day when the criminal world didn't excite him any longer. But now that his rose-tinted spectacles had finally fallen off and were well and truly trampled and smashed, he saw it for what it was. An insalubrious underworld full of people who didn't deserve his representation. He was more than happy to leave them to their own devices from now on.

As he pulled up outside his house, he knew that he was making the right decision to step down. Early retirement and the golf course were definitely beckoning. He had been thinking about it for weeks, but today's events had cemented the idea.

He turned off the car engine and reached over to the passenger seat for his briefcase. Suddenly, his car door was pulled open. For a second, he thought it must be Laila, welcoming him home. But the space was filled by a tall man, blocking his exit. Menace and threat oozed from his every pore. The large hood of a black sweatshirt covered the top half of his face. His gloved hands gripped the car's door frame, making it impossible for Sebastian to get past him.

Sebastian had never been mugged before. He assumed that his position as one of the most notable defence barristers in Manchester had protected him somehow. He remembered that his mobile phone was at the bottom of his briefcase, out of reach. Although, even if he could reach it, who would he call? The police would take an age to arrive.

He hoped that Laila hadn't seen his arrival. He didn't want her to come outside, not now, with this lunatic around.

"Sebastian Thomas?" asked the man in a low whisper.

"Yes," said Sebastian. "Who are you?" How did he know who he was? Why did the mugger want to rob him in particular? There were plenty of well-off people in the neighbourhood – bankers, flashy footballers and even a pop star or two. He wasn't like them. He was discreet. He didn't wear his Rolex for work, and he never carried cash these days. He wasn't the sort of person who should be mugged.

"I know where you live, yeah."

Sebastian almost laughed with the absurdity of it. Of course, you do, he thought, you're right outside my house. He put his right foot on the driveway and attempted to get out of the car. The man's heavy hand pushed him back into his seat. It was then that he saw the knife. Not a huge chopping knife. But a tiny one. A sharp one. One that would do damage to soft skin.

"You better get Jay Harris bail on Friday, yeah," he said. Sebastian could smell stale cigarette fumes on his breath and lingering in the unwashed fabric of his clothes.

"It's not up to me to make that decision. You know that. Jay knows that," said Sebastian, keeping his eye on the knife, which was being pointed in his direction, precariously close.

"Don't make me use this." The man pushed the sharp pointed blade suddenly towards Sebastian's neck. "If he doesn't get bail, you're dead."

For what felt like minutes, but was probably just a few seconds, Sebastian stared into the eyes of the second person that day who had told him that he was 'dead'.

Chapter Seven
Tuesday

The individually styled houses of Barry Rise, each with a minimum of five bedrooms, sat comfortably within the coveted postcode of SK9. Built between 1910 and 1950, they were originally homes for the swiftly expanding upper middle class; those who had made their own fortune, with the help of a good education, grit and determination. Silver spoons were in the minority in the Georgian north-west of England. Hard work, rather than heritage, was the money-maker.

By the end of the twentieth century, most of the handmade wooden sash windows had been replaced by dreadful UPVC double glazing. The ubiquitous black paint was a stark contrast to the white render, which now covered the beautiful original brickwork. The ornate wrought iron gates and narrow footpaths that had originally led to each of the houses had been replaced by paved driveways. Where there used to be square front lawns and hydrangea-filled flower beds, there now sat Ferraris, Porches and Jaguars.

At number 6, Robert had spent most of the day in the second-largest bedroom of his parents' house, nursing a hangover of gigantic proportions. He had told his mother that he wasn't feeling well and in her much-loved capacity as mother-hen, she had spent the day running up and down the stairs with fresh supplies of coffee, hot buttered toast and homemade chicken soup. She probably knew that he wasn't unwell at all and that his symptoms of apathy and self-pity were purely self-inflicted and undoubtedly linked to the smell of stale alcohol in the room. She hadn't said anything, but the speed at which she opened the window was a clue. His mother wasn't stupid. But she loved her son and welcomed him back home.

Yesterday afternoon, after receiving the text from the casino, he had panicked and showed it to Samantha. He wished he hadn't. He begged her not to tell Jamilla and she promised she wouldn't, but he knew where her allegiance lay. Her advice, too, was next to useless. Talk to them, she had said. Tell them who you are. You've got a good job. You can come to some arrangement and set up a direct debit. Samantha was a lovely woman but what she knew about the real world you could write on the back of a postage stamp. He had thanked her for her advice, grabbed his coat and rushed into the bookies on Market Street, where he promptly lost two hundred pounds on Dare to Dream at Newmarket. The odds of ten to one would have given him a good return, but he should have known that the mare wasn't a sure winner. He just had a feeling that she was the one. The red and white checked shirt of the jockey, the chestnut mane and the shiny coat were all signs that she was a winner. Except she wasn't.

The next race was half an hour later. Robert had stared at the monitor high on the wall in the bookies, running his eyes down the list of runners, waiting for a name to jump out at him. The obvious winner. But in truth, he didn't know one end of a horse from another and simply chose the one in the middle of the list. Secret Squirrel had odds of five to two. That sounded more like a winner, didn't it? He went over to the desk and handed over the carefully filled-out betting slip. His handwriting was neat and small. He tucked his blue and silver Montblanc fountain pen back into his inside jacket pocket. A coveted gift from his parents when he had been offered the position of pupil at chambers.

"I'll have one hundred pounds on this, please." He wiped a bead of sweat from his upper lip surreptitiously.

The staff member didn't flinch at his request. Robert had expected a lecture about spending too much money, especially after he had just lost a significant amount. A questioning raised eyebrow, at least. But nothing. He's just doing his job, thought Robert, with a flash of altruism. If it wasn't for people like me, he'd be out of work. I'm doing him a favour.

"Your card's been declined."

"I'm sorry, what?" said Robert.

"Your card…"

"Yes, yes, I heard you. Try again please. Do I need to put the pin number in?"

The staff member didn't reply. With his head down, he tapped his fingers over the card machine and handed it to him again. Robert silently took it from him, pushed his card into the little slot at the top and entered his pin number. The staff member took the card machine from him and stared at it for a few seconds. Robert could feel his heart beating faster with every passing second. Adrenalin-fuelled sweat began to drip down his back.

"Declined again."

"Thank you," said Robert, taking his card out of the machine and walking away and out of the door with as much dignity as he could muster. He knew there was no point in trying another card. He had reached his credit limit on all three of his credit cards and was now at the limit of his overdraft on his current account. He took his phone out of his jacket pocket and sent a message to Lucas, his oldest friend. "Fancy a drink later?"

"Always, mate," Lucas replied within minutes.

Lucas ran his own mortgage and financial advice company in Alderley Edge. Wealth management it was called. The people of Alderley Edge liked to be told that they had wealth. His years of dedication to his business had rewarded him well and a couple of months ago, he had moved into his own five-bedroomed detached house, close to Robert's parents.

Before Lucas suggested an expensive meal out, accompanied by even more expensive wine, Robert sent him a message back. "Shall I come over to yours? I'd love to see your new place."

Lucas had been only too delighted to invite him over and Robert had been only too delighted to take advantage of his friend's well-stocked wine fridge. As a consequence, for the second day running, Robert's head felt like it was going to explode.

Now, as he lay on his parents' sofa, hugging a mug of coffee, and waiting for the start of The Chase on ITV, he was beginning to feel almost normal. His headache was gradually subsiding, but it would take a little longer for him to recover from the sickness in the pit of his stomach. Every time he remembered the text message from the casino and the state of his finances, he felt sick again. How on earth had he got himself into this mess? He thought that he would be able to confide in his parents. Their love for him would instantly boost him and all his worries would melt away. His dad would transfer some money into his bank account and he would promise to pay it back, although both of them would know that he didn't have to. But when it came to it, he couldn't tell them. He couldn't deal with their disappointment too. The burden of the cloud of Jamilla's disappointment was already too much for him to bear.

He still hadn't heard from her today. As he left chambers last night, he had left her a voicemail, telling her how much he loved her and begging for forgiveness. And now he didn't even have enough money to buy her the flowers that he so wished to buy. She loved flowers. He wanted to stand on her front doorstep with a huge bunch in his arms. He wanted her beautiful face to light up and smile, knowing that he had paid over-the-odds for the exotic flowers just because he loved her. Then they could hug and kiss and everything would go back to normal.

But what was normal these days? Hangovers, arguments, mounting debt? When had this started to happen? He had no idea how it had got this bad. A ten-pound bet on the Grand National sweepstake; a scratch card here and there; an hour or so a day on Sports Play, his favourite betting app. Tiny steps towards his downfall. The membership at the casino had been a relatively recent addition to his repertoire.

His phone rang. He debated ignoring it. Reluctantly, he sat up, put his coffee cup down on the small coffee table that his mother had very kindly moved within arm's reach for him, and picked up his phone.

"Hello," he said.

"Am I speaking to Robert Brierly?" asked a male voice that he didn't recognise.

"Yes, how can I help you?" For a moment, he wondered whether it was a solicitor, calling him for advice on a particularly tricky case. Although he knew that would never happen. He wasn't yet a qualified barrister and he wouldn't trust a single word of his own advice right now.

"I'm ringing about your debt with Quay Street Casino."

Robert jumped up and closed the living room door. He could hear his mother in the kitchen, singing along to an old Duran Duran song. Her Spotify playlist was full of their stuff.

"Yes, how can I help you?" said Robert, doing his best to sound nonchalant.

"Are you in a position to make the full payment?"

"Well, not right now, but I was going to call…"

"It's okay. I can help you."

Robert flopped onto the sofa, relief instantly relaxing his tense shoulders. "Help? What do you mean? Who I am speaking to?" He accentuated his private school accent and wondered whether he should have said 'to whom am I speaking?' Although he didn't want to sound like an arse.

"My name's Frankie. You can call me your financial guardian angel." He laughed, but Robert didn't feel like joining in. "I can help you with your, how shall we say, your predicament with the casino," he continued. His accent was broad Mancunian, although Robert could tell that he was trying to tone it down. "I'm in the finance business. I run a loan company. I can lend you what you need and then come to some arrangement with you about the repayments."

"So, I can pay monthly, you mean?"

There was the tiniest of pauses. "The repayments are weekly. I'd advise you to take the loan if you want to get the casino off your back. That is, before they go down the legal route."

Robert thought about Lucas and his wealth management company. He knew that Lucas would tell him to steer clear of this man. Get from off his radar. Right now. He's a loan shark and you'll never be rid of him, Lucas would say. Robert knew that was right. Legitimate loan companies didn't ring your mobile phone and offer you money. They might send a marketing email or flash up an offer on your banking app, but they didn't operate like this. However, although the warning bell in Robert's head was ringing, it wasn't loud enough. Or was it that the ringing had become so constant that he was unable to tune it out?

"Yes, that would be great," said Robert.

Chapter Eight
Tuesday

"I know I love her more than I should," said Samantha. "But she's just so cute." She rubbed her cat behind her ears and kissed the top of her head.

"How did you know what I was thinking?" said Alistair, without looking up from his phone.

Samantha was stirring a mushroom risotto on the hob and Alistair was sitting on a tall stool at the marble-topped island in the middle of the kitchen. The small TV on the wall was showing the Sky News channel. Samantha had turned the sound down low so that she and Alistair could talk. She was trying her best to snap him out of his mood. Again. She knew that she was giving him too much latitude lately. His moods and the stilted silences were beginning to irritate her. It used to be just Mondays when Samantha had to walk on eggshells. Now, every day was the same. A perpetual tiptoe around Alistair's needs and wants.

"I could feel you watching me," said Samantha. She didn't want to add that she could feel the disapproval from across the kitchen. "But what can you do, my beautiful little Fluff? When Cupid strikes, you just have to take the hit and feel the pain." She laughed at her own metaphor and snuggled further into the cat's soft fur. Fluff purred in response.

"Or get your armour on."

"What?"

"Nothing," said Alistair.

She had heard him, but she wanted him to explain, even though she knew that asking him further questions would antagonise him. Arguments with him weren't pretty. "You're like a terrier," he had said to her, just last week after a particularly big one, the cause of which Samantha couldn't recall, other than that it was something and nothing. "You can't accept when you're wrong and you pick and pick at me until I give in, tell you that I'm sorry and then you can walk away from the argument, victorious. Triumphant. Smug."

She had never been triumphant or smug after an argument, ever. They always left her defeated and upset. She would lock herself in the bathroom and run herself a bubble bath, where she could lick her wounds in private until she was ready to face him again.

Why was it that Alistair had a gift for ruining her good moods? He was guaranteed to bring her down whenever she felt excited about something. Her happiness always seemed to be reliant on him and, therefore, short-lived. Once, Jamilla had asked her whether she had any suspicions that he was having an affair, as though that was usually the root cause of a man being moody - the fact that he was missing his sexy new girlfriend whilst simultaneously being wracked with guilt about deceiving his loyal and loving wife. Of course not, Samantha had said, although the truth was that she worried about it constantly. She told Jamilla that he didn't have time for an affair. They were together most of the time. She knew his every move. What she didn't say was that Alistair kept his phone close to him at all times. Jamilla had shrugged her shoulders and said that if she was married to Alistair, she would have an electronic tag attached to his ankle and a tracker fitted to his car, for double measure.

Alistair put his phone on the island, face down, and took another sip of his gin. The ice cubes tinkled against the glass.

The sound of a party. Except in this case, it was the sound of alcohol soothing whatever troubles Alistair was keeping to himself. He moved over to the window. "What exactly are we paying that gardener for?" he said. "Have you seen the state of the lawn?"

"It's not a golf course, Alistair," said Samantha. "There's bound to be a few weeds here and there. It's nearly summer. They grow. That's what happens." She was speaking softly, with a gentle coaxing to her voice, as though speaking to a child who was about to have a massive meltdown. The toddler within Alistair had made far too many appearances lately. She put Fluff gently down onto the floor and walked over to Alistair. She put her arms around his waist and rested her head on his back. "What was that you were saying about armour, my hero?"

He shook her off. "I'm not your knight in shining armour anymore, Samantha. The armour is dull and battered and broken."

"Alistair?"

He turned quickly and she stepped out of his way. He grabbed his phone and put it in his trouser pocket. "I'm going out," he said.

"Where to? Alistair! Talk to me! Dinner's nearly ready."

Samantha listened to his receding footsteps down the hall. The front door slammed shut and he was gone.

*

Shortly afterwards, Alistair pulled up outside a large, detached house on the edge of Chorlton, partially hidden by two tall, black iron gates and a cluster of ancient oak trees. A new black Range Rover Velar with private number plates was parked on the gravel drive, confirming to Alistair that the man of the house was inside. He wasn't the type to go anywhere without his car - his status symbol. Alistair pressed the buzzer on the wall at the side of the gate, announced his arrival and waited until the gates opened slowly. He drove inside and parked next to the Velar.

By the time he had turned off the engine and climbed out of his car, the man was waiting for him on the doorstep. The front door - solid steel, painted an angry vermillion red - was wide open, showing the expansive hallway beyond. The white tiled floor glistened with rainbow sprinkles of light thrown from a gaudy crystal chandelier that hung from the ceiling.

"How's the trial going?" asked the man, with an air of someone who already knew. He took a drag on his cigarette and blew the smoke forcefully in Alistair's direction, with a slight tilt of his chin and a smirk playing around his mouth.

"It's going fine," said Alistair. "Just as planned."

"Good, good," said the man, nodding. He took another drag of his cigarette and waited for Alistair to speak.

"It will be fine tomorrow, too. Just closing arguments and then the jury will be going out. Everything is going as planned," repeated Alistair. He wiped his sweating palms on his trouser legs.

"What if it doesn't go to plan tomorrow? I'm relying on you; you know that don't you?"

"Yes, of course. Don't worry about it."

"Don't fucking tell me what to do." The man's movement was sudden, but not entirely unexpected. He stepped forward and grabbed Alistair's neck, pushing him up against the wall on the porch. Alistair didn't push him off. It was futile. Violence led to violence in most instances. In this case, with this man, it was one hundred percent guaranteed. "I don't need this shit. You should have sorted it. What do I fucking pay you for?" He spat whiskey-soaked words into Alistair's face.

Whether this was a rhetorical question, or whether he was expecting a response, Alistair wasn't sure. The less he spoke, the better, he deduced. But as the man's fingers began to tighten around his windpipe, Alistair had no choice but to explain himself. "Look, Frankie, this has never happened before, you know that it doesn't usually get as far as a trial." The grip loosened slightly. "It will all be over by tomorrow, I promise."

Frankie let him go. Alistair coughed and spluttered and sank down, resting on his heels. Frankie pulled him up, both hands on the collar of his jacket. "Stand up, you fucking girl." Alistair stood, straightening his collar.

"What do you want?" said Frankie.

"I've come for half a gram," said Alistair. "It's been a tough day."

Frankie laughed and patted Alistair's shoulder with his huge bear hand, as though a minute ago he hadn't been trying to bring about his premature death by strangulation. He disappeared inside, leaving Alistair standing on the step. Within seconds he returned with the white powder in a tiny plastic bag. "Here's a gram. I'll knock it off the balance."

"Thanks, I'll - "

"Yeah, you'll sort it tomorrow. Right." It was a command, rather than a question.

"Right," said Alistair.

"Yeah, well we'll see about that. I'll be in court tomorrow to see for myself."

Alistair pocketed the cocaine and walked to his car as nonchalantly as possible. He reversed quickly and drove out of the driveway and onto the road. He couldn't wait to get back home. He needed a line of coke to calm his nerves and give him some thinking space.

What the fuck was he doing? How had he got himself involved with these people? It had been a massive mistake, and he desperately needed a get-out plan, but right now, he couldn't think straight. After the trial, he would have a word and tell Frankie that he no longer wanted to be involved. It would be fine. He would tell Frankie that this trial was going to be his last job working for him.

It wasn't as though it was a serious crime. He didn't know why Frankie was so concerned. The defendant wasn't his family. He was just one of the doormen at his nightclub in Manchester. He doubted whether he was even a friend. But Frankie liked things to be in order. He liked to be in control and when one of his staff was arrested, it didn't look good. He had a reputation to maintain.

The doorman had been accused of assault with the intent to cause grievous bodily harm. It was potentially serious, but he had been on bail since his arrest, which Alistair told Frankie was a good sign. If a custodial sentence was likely to be handed out, then the man would have been kept on remand while he waited for the trial.

Jonty O'Connor had fought with another doorman on a night out. He had worn the metal knuckle duster on his right hand all night, prepared for the time when an old score could be settled. The fight had started in the bar and finished outside in the street upon the arrival of the police in two vans and a patrol car. Jonty was arrested and the other doorman was taken to hospital in an ambulance. Although there were dozens of people in the pub, dozens of potential witnesses, only one was sober enough to have any credibility. A taxi driver, waiting in his vehicle across the road, had seen everything. He was new to Manchester. He had never heard of Frankie Bryne or his employee, Jonty O'Connor. If he had, he would have driven away and claimed that he hadn't seen a thing. But the taxi driver had principles, as well as ignorance, and he wanted to do the right thing. Be a good citizen.

Alistair's job was simple. Usually. A quick word with his old school friend, Carl, in the Crown Prosecution Service tended to be enough. Witness statements would disappear, charges would be dropped, and all would be well. He had been doing 'favours' for Frankie for almost twelve months, for which he was being handsomely compensated. He split the money with Carl and the arrangement ran smoothly, giving nobody any cause for suspicion.

But Carl's wife had recently had a little girl and when Jonty O'Connor's case was being processed, Carl was on paternity leave. There was nothing Alistair could do about it. Witness statements had been disclosed, the taxi driver had confirmed he was willing to attend court and the defendant had been told that the trial was set to go ahead.

Alistair had tried to reassure Frankie that by the time it was listed, Carl would be back at work, and he would make sure that Alistair was the prosecuting barrister. Alistair promised that he would do the worst performance of his life and that a not-guilty verdict would be almost guaranteed. Frankie didn't like to take risks. Ironic, for a man who lived on the edge of the law. But Alistair had told him not to worry. He said it would be easy to discredit the witness. It had been dark. People were in the way. Everything happened so fast, and his car was on the other side of the road. The jury would believe that his testimony couldn't be relied on.

Thankfully, fortune was on Alistair's side and Carl did return to work in time and Alistair was instructed to prosecute the case.

Alistair had his questions ready for the witness. His examination was going to be polite and professional, but it would also drip drip drip elements of doubt in the minds of the jury. When the witness hadn't arrived in court yesterday, Alistair wasn't completely surprised. He assumed that he had learned who the defendant worked for, and he had lost his nerve. But the message given to him by the court usher was that the man was in hospital. Apparently, he had been robbed in his taxi and beaten up. He was lucky to have escaped with his life.

As prosecution counsel, Alistair would have been expected to ask for the trial to be adjourned. But he stood in court, holding tightly to his black gown to stop his hands from shaking, and told the judge that the reality of the situation was that he was happy for the trial to go ahead. He had advised the Crown Prosecution Service that the trial would in fact be better off without the witness, who may crumble under cross-examination. It could do the case more harm than good, he had told the young clerk. Let's just concentrate on the CCTV, he had said. He knew how to flirt and flatter, and the young CPS clerk had bowed to his better judgment, even though she knew that the CCTV wasn't any use. So, the trial had begun and was due to finish tomorrow morning.

By the time Alistair arrived home from Frankie's, Samantha had gone out. A plate of cold risotto was waiting for him in the kitchen, together with his abandoned glass of gin and tonic.

Chapter Nine
Tuesday

Sebastian held his hand to his throat as he watched the man disappear down the street. He could feel a spot of blood dripping onto the collar of his white shirt. He fumbled in the bottom of his briefcase for his phone, the search being somewhat hampered by his shaking hands. He grasped the phone and began to dial 999. But after he had pressed only two 9s, he quickly cancelled the call and put his phone into his pocket.

It was futile, he thought. The man had already gone and by the time the police arrived, he would be miles away. Sebastian knew how stretched the police were and the chances of finding the man were minimal. All Sebastian would be able to say was that he was around five feet ten inches tall, maybe six feet, and he was wearing dark clothes. The hood was covering most of his face, so he wouldn't be able to identify him, even if, by some miracle, the police managed to find him. He could tell the police that it was obvious that he was an associate of Jay Harris - friend or family - as he knew about the upcoming bail application hearing. But young people these days had hundreds of friends, so being able to narrow it down and pinpoint the culprit would be an arduous task that the police didn't have the resources for, and Sebastian didn't have the energy for. He wanted to get inside his house, see his wife and relax. He was anxious to put this day's events behind him, as quickly as possible.

"Hello, darling, I thought I heard your car, but then you didn't come inside. Have you been on the phone?" said Laila. His beautiful wife. His amazing house. His sanctuary. Sebastian felt suddenly tearful, but thankfully Laila didn't seem to notice. The last thing he wanted to do was worry her. She kissed him on his cheek and led him down the hall and into the kitchen, holding his hand tightly. "I've made your favourite," she said. "Pork and beef lasagne."

"With a little help from Mr. Marks and Mr. Spencer?" laughed Sebastian.

"Oh balls, you weren't meant to see the wrapper," said Laila, laughing. "That bin is on its way out. The lid never closes properly nowadays. My cover has been blown." She laughed again. Music to his ears.

Laila grabbed the oven gloves and opened the oven, allowing a delicious ragu and garlic aroma to fill the kitchen. Sebastian's stomach rumbled in response. She put the lasagne on top of the hob and closed the oven door. "The garlic bread will be ready in two more minutes, okay? Aren't you taking your coat off?"

As Laila turned to face him, Sebastian held out his arms and she walked into them. They stood together for a few moments; his face nestled into her hair. He breathed in the smell of her coconut shampoo. "I love you," he said, surprised to find more tears welling in his eyes. He blinked them away quickly.

"I love you, too," she said, pulling away from him. "Is everything alright? You don't seem…oh my God, Seb, what's that?" She touched the cut on his neck gently. "You're bleeding. There's blood all over your shirt collar." She backed away from him, her face a mixture of confusion and concern. "Seb, what on earth…?"

"I'm fine, I'm fine," he said. He put his hands on either side of her face and wiped her sudden empathetic tears with his thumbs, before wiping at his own, which annoyingly didn't seem to want to stop.

"Let me get you a drink," said Laila. "Sit down, here, sit down." She pulled out a dining room chair and gestured to it, as though he was about to faint at any moment and needed desperately to take the weight off his legs. He didn't argue. He was thankful for her love. "Here drink this," she said, a moment later, handing him a large glass of red wine.

"That's a very full glass," he said, forcing a smile. "You know I'm working tomorrow?" He took a long drink, emptying almost half of the glass.

Laila pulled out the chair next to him, turned it to face him and sat down. "Talk to me," she said.

Sebastian debated whether to gloss over the details of his day to save his wife from worrying about him. But they were a team. She was his rock, and he was hers. That was the way it had always been. So, he told her about his meeting with Jay Harris at Manchester Prison and then Harris's outburst in the interview room, followed by his screaming words as he was being dragged away by two prison guards. Then he told her about the man just now on the driveway, who seemed to be waiting for his arrival home and the further threat, this time at knifepoint. Sebastian touched his neck and was relieved to find that the cut had stopped bleeding.

Laila, although she was an author and a screenwriter, specialising in crime-fiction and thrillers, wasn't one for histrionics. She patiently waited for Sebastian to re-live his day, without interrupting him. She topped up his wine glass, and her own, and took the garlic bread out of the oven, cutting it into slices, as Sebastian was talking. When he had finished, she handed him a plate of lasagne and salad and two slices of garlic bread and sat down opposite him, her own meal in front of her.

"I know what you're going to say," he said, dipping a slice of garlic bread into the ragu sauce oozing out of the side of the lasagne.

Laila shook her head. "No, you don't," she said.

Sebastian frowned at her. "Call the police?" he said.

"No."

"Take a holiday?"

"Well, we can go away in a couple of weeks, so, no, it's not that."

"I give up," he said.

She nodded. "That's it," she said. "You said it. It's time to give up. Take early retirement. You know we don't need the money. You've spent your whole life defending scumbags like the one you saw today, and now you've done your bit. You deserve some time on the golf course."

"They haven't all been scumbags," Sebastian said.

She tilted her head to one side. "Really? Ninety percent of them have."

"Maybe eighty-nine percent."

"What are you smiling at?" she said.

"You," said Sebastian. He put down his fork and reached across the table to hold her hand. "I love that you can read my mind. It's been bothering me for a few weeks, maybe even longer than that, but I've been thinking that it was time to throw in the towel. I feel too old for this job now. I know I'm only fifty-eight and I always planned to work until I was sixty, at least, but I've had enough of it. I don't have the enthusiasm for it anymore."

"I think the young ones call it executive burn-out," said Laila. "Or is that just for Wall Street bankers?"

Sebastian laughed. "I don't know," he said. "This lasagne is delicious, by the way. You should make it more often."

They ate in silence for a few moments and then Laila said, "You don't think that you just want to leave because of what's happened today?" Sebastian knew that she was playing Devil's Advocate. "Because you know that nothing like this has ever happened before, and it's unlikely to ever happen again. Today was a unique day."

"I know that and no, it's not just because of today. The events of today have merely cemented my decision, that's all."

"Fine, decision made," she said brusquely. "Shall I give Verity and Peter a call and get them round for dinner, so you can talk about it?" Verity was Head of Chambers and although Sebastian didn't need her permission to retire, it was good manners to speak to her about it and agree what notice period he would need to serve. He and Laila had been friends with her and her husband for more years than he cared to remember, and he knew that she would support his decision.

"I'll talk to her tomorrow," he said. "But a dinner invitation would be good, too." Sebastian felt like a huge weight had been lifted off his shoulders. He would speak to Verity tomorrow and recommend that Robert be taken under someone else's wing. There were plenty of suitable people who would supervise the last few months of his pupillage. Then he would instruct Robert to do Harris's bail application on Friday. He was more than capable of doing that on his own, and if he made a hash of it and the bail application was refused, then justice would have been served, in his view. Sebastian was going to keep clear of Jay Harris and whether or not he was detained at His Majesty's pleasure and for how long was no longer his concern.

Chapter Ten
Tuesday

The money lender - Robert liked to call him that; loan shark was such an accusatory word - arranged for someone to meet Robert in the car park of Sainsburys. Robert was happy with the anonymity of the location. He didn't want to invite anyone into his apartment and was pleased when a public place was suggested. He waited in his car close to the entrance to the car park, watching early evening shoppers coming and going. Ordinary people, living ordinary lives.

The Golden Casino across the road cast bright orange lights onto the car park, its neon sign flashing like a lighthouse. A warning of danger to those who chose to come too near. Enter at your peril. Lives may be lost. Robert had never been in there. He told himself that he never would. The rumour was that that particular casino was run by an organised criminal gang and that they didn't take kindly to people who ran up large debts.

A silver Mercedes C-class screeched into the car park and stopped in front of Robert's car, blocking his exit. Loud rap music boomed from the open windows. Robert's heart rate increased in time to the beat.

"Robert Brierly?" A man stepped out of the passenger seat. He leaned against the car, his head on one side, both hands in the pockets of his low-slung ripped jeans.

"Yes, that's me," said Robert. He opened his car door, got out and walked towards him.

"I've got your money from Frankie." The man reached into the car and brought out a large brown envelope.

So, this isn't Frankie then, thought Robert. He should have known. All dodgy people have underlings to do their dirty work for them. Frankie himself would probably be in a fancy restaurant right now, discussing his next deal. He wouldn't be wasting his time driving around a supermarket car park with a wedge of money stuffed into the glove box. That was just asking for trouble. How would you explain that to a passing police officer? This man didn't seem concerned. If he was, he wasn't showing it. The swagger, the chin held high, neck muscles and biceps flexed told Robert that this man was afraid of nothing.

In the second before he reached out to take the envelope from him, all of Robert's instincts were telling him to change his mind, to walk away. Have nothing to do with these people. He had already been told that the interest rate was eight percent - not eight percent per year, but eight percent per week - and that it was not negotiable. Repayments had to be made weekly. Robert had agreed on the phone. Anything to get rid of his casino debt and to get the man off the phone before his mother walked into the lounge and wanted chapter and verse on who he had been speaking to and what it was about. He didn't need her motherly concern right now. But he took the envelope, throwing it quickly onto the passenger seat of his car, telling

himself that it was just a payday loan and that there was nothing to worry about. People get short-term loans all the time and pay them off quickly. He had every intention of paying the casino in full and then, when he had a bit more time tomorrow and he was thinking more clearly, he would look at sorting out his finances properly. He would pay off the loan from Frankie with a proper bank loan and would move on with his life.

He had absolutely nothing to worry about.

So, he accepted the money and shook hands with the muscleman.

As soon as the Mercedes had driven away, he got back into his car and stashed the envelope in the glovebox. He started the engine and began the short drive home. On the way, he rang Jamilla again. He was surprised when she picked up after two rings.

"Stop calling me, Robert. I don't want to hear from you right now," she said, without saying hello.

"Milla, please listen to me," he begged. "Don't put the phone down, please."

"I don't know what you can say that you haven't said before," she said. The sound of her beautiful voice made his heart ache.

"I'll do anything to make it up to you, please believe me. I know I've said it before, but this time it's different." He paused, waiting for her to speak. He thought he could hear her crying but didn't want to ask in case he was wrong. "I need you," he said.

"I don't know…"

"I'm in the car, can I come round?"

She hesitated for a second. A precious second in which Robert felt like his happiness was being held in her hands. "Samantha's here. We're having a bottle of wine and what I hoped would be a peaceful evening."

"I won't stay long, just ten minutes," he said. "I just want to make things up with you and give you a goodnight kiss."

"Yes okay," she sighed. Robert could hear the smile in her voice. "I mean yes you can have ten minutes. But this doesn't mean we're back on; you know that don't you?" she said.

Robert told her that, of course, he knew that and that he would be there in a few minutes. He knew that when she saw him, she would relent, and they would be back on track within no time. He desperately wanted to buy her some flowers, or some chocolates - she loved the ones with the hazelnut in the middle - but he had no available funds. The envelope of money held just enough to pay his casino debt. Any peace-making offer for Jamilla would have to wait.

Ten minutes later, he pulled up outside her narrow mews house. As he walked up the short path, he was surprised to see that it was Samantha, not Jamilla, who opened the door. By now, she must have heard Jamilla's side of the story. There was no hug and kiss to greet him. Just scowls and frosty stares.

"She's in the kitchen," said Samantha.

"Hello to you, too," said Robert, flashing her his best smile which he hoped would break the ice.

"Robert, please. You're lucky she's speaking to you. If you were my boyfriend, you would have been kicked into touch a long time ago."

Robert bit his tongue, stopping himself from asking how Samantha could offer relationship advice to Jamilla when she put up with a prick like Alistair day after day. But he smiled and made his way to the kitchen, as Samantha went into the living room, leaving him and Jamilla alone to talk.

Jamilla was standing with her back to the worktop, a glass of white wine clasped firmly to her chest. She didn't offer him one.

"I'm not taking any of your bullshit, I can tell you now," she said.

"And I have no bullshit on offer," said Robert. He held out his arms as though being patted down at airport security. He stuck his hands into his jacket pockets and pulled out the lining, turning it inside out. "Look, no bullshit."

"I hate you," said Jamilla, a small smile playing around her mouth.

"No, you don't," said Robert, grasping the opportunity to get close to her. He held her face in his hands and kissed her softly on the mouth. He knew that she liked that and within seconds, she was kissing him back.

"I hate the way that my body responds to you," she said, resting her head on his shoulder, her arms still tightly clutching her glass.

"That's because we're meant to be," said Robert. "It's science. You can't argue with it. Listen, I need to talk to you." He took the glass gently from her hands and put it down on the worktop. Taking her hand, he led her to the dining table and pulled out one of the slatted-back wooden dining chairs. "Sit down, please." He had practised his speech on the way over. He was good at advocacy. He had the 'gift of the gab' he had often been told at school, on the many occasions when he had been reprimanded for talking too much.

Jamilla sat down. "I'm listening," she said. She looked at the round clock on the wall. "You've got five minutes." But the way she smiled at him told Robert that if he played his cards right, he could have all night.

"You know I love you, don't you?"

"Yes, I do," she said.

"I know you want me to settle down, save some money and…"

"Of course, I do, that's what this whole argument is about, isn't it? You can't stop spending too much, going into that stupid casino and getting drunk night after night."

"Yes, yes, I know." Robert got the feeling that he was starting to lose his audience before he had even started. He knelt down in front of her, on one knee. "Jamilla, I love you so much and one day you'd make me the happiest man in the world if you would marry me."

"Robert!"

"That's not a proposal," he said quickly. "At least, it's not the proper one. I need to ask your dad first anyway, but when I've got enough money to buy you a ring and take you somewhere special, then I'll do it properly. But I just wanted to state my intention."

"State your intention?" Jamilla laughed. "Get up, you stupid man. This isn't a Jane Austen novel."

Robert stood up. "Thank God for that, wooden floors are not the easiest on the knees." He rubbed at his knee with both hands before sitting down on the chair next to her. "Seriously though, I want you to know that I will change my ways and I will be the husband that you deserve. I want to look after you and give you everything you've ever wanted. You mean the world to me. I want your dad to be proud of me too and welcome me into the family."

Jamilla nodded and smiled. Looking back, Robert blamed that smile for encouraging him to open up. He had come to the end of his rehearsed speech. He should have stopped talking there and then. He had won her over. She was smiling. From here it should be plain sailing. He should have saved himself while she had control of the lifeboat. But he was desperate for someone to talk to. Having spent the night at his parents' house had made matters worse. He thought that he might be able to open up to them, or to his mother at least, but he couldn't bring himself to shatter her illusion about him. She thought he was doing well and was on his way to a good career. She was proud of him, and he didn't want to be the bearer of bad news. He didn't want to tell her that, despite spending thousands of pounds each year on private education, he hadn't quite turned out to be the son that they had always wanted.

So, without stopping to practice another speech for another time, Robert told Jamilla almost everything. He told her that he hadn't been to work today because he got drunk again last night. He told her his finances were in a dire situation. He told her that he had wanted to bring her some flowers, but his card had been declined at the bookies yesterday and he was at the limit on his credit cards. If he had been taking notice of her shocked face, the way her hands rushed to her mouth as though it were her words that should have been suppressed, not his, then he might have taken a minute to consider his next move. But this wasn't about Jamilla. Not really. Robert was a first-class narcissist, and it was about what Robert wanted. His needs. His miserable desire to unburden himself. As long as he felt better.

So, he blundered on and told her about the debt with the casino. He told her that when he had taken out the membership, because of his job, they had given him credit, which they expected him to pay back every month, but it had mounted up.

He explained that things had got out of hand really quickly and he never expected it to be so bad. It had started out as a hobby, but it was just a really expensive one. Like golf, he had said, or sailing. He thought she might laugh when he said that. It was so middle-class. As though an expensive hobby was a necessary living expense, as vital as buying food, paying your rent or your electric bill.

But she didn't laugh. Tears welled in her eyes and rushed down her cheeks. Within minutes, she was hitting him and telling him to get off her. The noise brought Samantha running into the kitchen.

"What's going on?" she said, gathering Jamilla into her arms and turning her back to Robert, as though to protect her from any further upset.

"He's a gambling addict," said Jamilla. "He owes tens of thousands of pounds."

"I'm not an addict at all. And it's not tens of thousands," said Robert. "I'm going to pay it all off and then sort myself out. It's not as bad…"

"You need to go," said Samantha. "Just go! Now!"

There was no point in hanging around. Robert knew that he wouldn't get through to Jamilla while Samantha was acting as a barrier. He would talk to her tomorrow, make her understand.

"And don't think about talking to me tomorrow at work," shouted Jamilla, as though reading his mind. She followed him down the hall and opened the front door for him. "I don't ever want to see you again. I mean it."

She pushed him forcefully out of the house and slammed the door behind him.

Robert got into his car and drove straight to Quay Street Casino.

Chapter Eleven
Nine Days Before the Shooting - Wednesday

"All rise," said the court usher in the loud and authoritative way that brought everyone in Court One to their feet.

Alistair glanced behind him. Jonty O'Connor rose to his feet slowly in the glass dock at the back of the court. Two prison officers stood on either side of him. The judge entered the court room, her black and lilac robe flapping behind her, as she swiftly walked to her heavy wooden chair and sat down at the bench, facing the court.

"Are all parties ready for the return of the jury?" asked the judge.

"Yes, Your Honour," said Alistair and the defendant's barrister together. They remained on their feet while the twelve members of the jury filed into court and took their seats in the two rows of seats to the left of the judge. Five men and seven women had taken less than two hours to reach a decision. Given that they had retired to their room at lunchtime, and Alistair calculated that it would have taken them at least half an hour to eat their sandwiches and have a drink, it was an indication that their decision had been a pretty easy one. Alistair grasped his hands together tightly behind his back and prayed that they had reached the right decision. He didn't want to get into Frankie Byrne's bad books and risk sharing a hospital ward with the ill-fated prosecution witness.

"Please be seated," said the usher, when the jury members had settled themselves. The defendant remained standing.

"Will the foreperson of the jury please stand."

A middle-aged woman at the end of the front row stood up. She rubbed her hands down the front of her grey blouse and black skirt, and stood tall, jutting her chin forwards. Alistair could imagine her standing up in the jury room, her marker pen held aloft in front of the whiteboard, ready to jot down all the valid points made by her fellow jury members. No doubt she would have been concentrating on the prosecution evidence and she would have tried to persuade her fellow jurors to reach a guilty verdict. Women like her didn't tend to like men like Jonty O'Connor. Rough men who got themselves involved in violent altercations and drank too much beer and swore too much were generally looked upon with derision by women like her.

It had always amazed Alistair how the jury picked their foreperson. Sebastian had told him that when he was a pupil and then a young barrister, many moons ago, the juries tended to pick a man. The usher called him a 'foreman'. It was hardly ever a woman. Now, Alistair liked to take bets with himself at the start of a trial that he could correctly pick the foreperson. And more often than not, he was correct. They would usually look like a schoolteacher or someone who worked in insurance. Middle class; well-dressed; respectable and trustworthy. This particular foreperson looked like she took her responsibilities extremely seriously.

Alistair began to sweat. He quickly ran his hand under the front of his horsehair wig and wiped away the perspiration before it had the chance to run down his face.

The foreperson looked nervously around the court, at the judge, at the two barristers and at the public gallery. But she avoided looking into the dock and at the defendant. That was always a bad sign. Nobody wanted to look a condemned man in the eye. Whether he was about to embark on a long prison sentence, or just a month or so of community service, punishments were always best doled out anonymously.

"Have the members of the jury reached a decision on which you are all agreed?" asked the usher.

"We have," said the foreperson.

"Do you find the defendant, Jonty O'Connor, guilty or not guilty of wounding Peter Francis Sullivan on 20th January 2023 with the intent to cause grievous bodily harm, contrary to Section Eighteen of the Offences Against the Person Act 1861?"

Alistair closed his eyes and waited for what seemed like ages for the woman to speak. He wondered what wounds the prosecution witness had endured that had caused him to be kept in the hospital. Nowadays, hospital beds were not given out as readily as they used to be, so he must be in a bad way. Suddenly he didn't feel safe. He looked behind him to see if there were any security guards in court. He didn't see one. They were never around when you needed them.

Then he saw him. Frankie Bryne was sitting in the back row of the public gallery. His shiny bald head was reflecting the overhead spotlights in the court. The collar on his shirt was buttoned tight to his neck, causing a slight redness to his face. His dark beady eyes were focused on Alistair.

"Not guilty," said the forewoman.

"Yes!" shouted Jonty O'Connor from the dock. He punched the air with his fist, as though he had just witnessed the England football team score a penalty against Brazil.

"The defendant will please compose himself until the jury has given their decision on the second count," said the judge firmly.

"Sorry, Your Worship, Your Honour, ma'am," came a voice from the dock.

The usher continued, "In the alternative indictment, do you find the defendant, Jonty O'Connor, guilty or not guilty of causing actual bodily harm to Peter Francis on 20th January 2023, contrary to Section Forty-Seven of the Offences Against the Person Act 1861?"

"Not guilty," said the forewoman.

The judge thanked the jury for their service, while the public gallery erupted with shouts and claps. Before the judge had time for reprimands, Jonty O'Connor and his supporters left the court.

Alistair shook the hands of his opponent, the defendant's barrister, and pretended to be disappointed with the result. "You win some, you lose some," he said, with a shrug. He gathered up his papers and walked out of the court.

"Good job, Mallory," said a voice behind him. It was Frankie. Alistair kept his head down and began to walk down the corridor. He hadn't left anything in the robing room and wanted to get out of court as quickly as possible and into the safety of chambers. Frankie fell into step by his side. "Here's your payment," said Frankie. "Minus what you owe me for the stuff last night." He thrust a rolled-up bundle of notes into Alistair's shaking hand. Alistair dropped the bundle on the floor, as though he had just been handed a hot coal. He knelt down quickly and covered it with his papers, hoping that nobody had seen. As he stood up, he looked into the corner of the ceiling, where the CCTV camera was located.

"Are you mad?" he whispered to Frankie, hiding the money under his robe. "Have you any idea how many eyes are watching us right now?"

"What's your problem?" said Frankie, laughing out loud. "Just two old mates, catching up. You need to lighten up." He slapped Alistair on the back and walked off.

Alistair turned around and headed back towards Court One, towards the robing room. He suddenly needed to sit down.

Jamilla, coming out of Court Two, had seen the exchange of something between Alistair and the bald-headed man in a suit.

Chapter Twelve
Wednesday

Sebastian couldn't have asked for a better view from his desk. He was going to miss it when he retired. His second-floor office was at the front of the old building that housed Whites Chambers and the bay window gave him a view towards Deansgate to the left and a view down St. John Street to the right. On the occasions when Laila had travelled into Manchester to meet him for lunch (and then in later years to meet both him and Jamilla), she loved to peer out of the window. People-watching was one of her favourite activities. She said it was necessary, being a writer.

He stood watching the traffic for a moment. Deansgate was relatively quiet still. The afternoon rush hour hadn't yet started. It was one of those mid-spring days when the anticipation of a good summer caused people to become prematurely ebullient. It wasn't yet warm enough to discard winter coats and yet Sebastian had seen at least half a dozen people in shirt sleeves this morning. He loved that Manchester was full of optimists. All of the outside tables at the café across the road were occupied. Those customers who were shaded from the sun held tightly to their hot coffee cups, still wearing jackets and coats, yet those who were fortunate to have grabbed the sunny tables languished in its feeble warmth. Manchester was beginning to come alive. There was nowhere better to work.

Sebastian knew that he hadn't taken enough time to

appreciate this view. It had changed so much over the years. Silver and glass high-rise blocks had shot up, giving the city a Manhattan vibe. But cities are for young people. He would be quite happy to hand over his office to Jamilla when it was time for him to leave. He couldn't think of a better custodian. Robert, being his pupil, might expect it to go to him, but he still had some maturing to do and didn't deserve it.

He turned back to his desk and sat down on his old-fashioned leather chair. Jamilla would no doubt want to change it for something more modern from Ikea. The legal profession used to thrive on tradition, but it was slowly being dragged kicking and screaming into the modern day.

Why had he made the decision to have his desk facing this way, towards the door, with his back to the window? Presumably, it was so that he could greet people coming into the office. But that was a mistake, he thought. If the desk was turned ninety degrees, anyone sitting there could still see the door, but could also look out of the window. If he had his time over again, he would change that, he thought. He would change it now, in fact. He may as well spend his last few weeks in the office with a lovely view.

He got up and pushed his chair to the side. Then he moved the two vintage brown leather tub chairs which were facing his desk out of the way. It wasn't easy to move them on the thick carpet and he was sweating by the time all three of the chairs had been moved. The heavy desk wasn't going to be easy. But he was still a member of the gym, although he didn't go as often as Laila did, and he managed to move it slowly, inch by inch.

He rubbed at the flattened carpet where the table legs had been with the toe of his shoe and then sat down to admire his work. That was better. Much better. He looked around his office, smiling to himself. Yes, he would definitely miss seeing Manchester every day. Although the view from the fourth hole of the golf course was pretty good too.

A soft knock on his door tore his eyes away from the window.

"Hi, Verity, come on in. How are you?" He greeted his friend and Head of Chambers with a warm kiss on her cheek. "Come and sit down."

"I'm very well, thank you, Seb. And you?"

"Wonderful, yes. I've had a little move around."

"Yes, I can see that," said Verity. "I like the desk facing that way, you can stare out of the window when something perplexes you."

Sebastian laughed. He hadn't yet told her that he planned to retire and wasn't sure that she would take it that well. "Here, let me get you a chair." He pushed one of the tub chairs from across the room back to the desk.

"Thank you," said Verity, sitting down. "Well, what is it you'd like to talk about? You worried me when you asked for a meeting. It sounded very formal."

"Would you like a drink?" he asked. Verity shook her head. He poured himself a glass of water from the tray on the table in the corner of the room. He added a slice of lemon and sat down opposite her. "I suppose it is a formal meeting, of sorts. I wanted to tell you in private, not in a coffee shop or anywhere where walls have ears." Verity waited for him to continue. "I've decided to take early retirement. Unless you have any objection, of course. I had planned to do another couple of years, but I think the time has come for me to hang up my wig and gown." Sebastian was hoping that he would be able to leave without too much resistance. The events of yesterday had bothered him more than he wanted to admit and now he was more than ready to retire.

Verity nodded. "Are you sure?"

"Yes," he said. He frowned. "I must say, you don't seem very surprised."

"Well, Laila did mention something of the sort." Verity

smiled and Sebastian knew that Laila would have sworn Verity to secrecy.

"I thought she might."

"You don't mind, do you?" asked Verity. "You know women talk."

"No, of course, I don't mind," said Sebastian. "It's time to hand over the baton to someone younger. In all honesty, Verity, I don't have the passion for the job that I used to have."

"I know exactly what you mean."

"Do you?"

"Yes, of course I do. I've got my eye on the end game too, you know. I'm not quite there yet, there are still some jobs to do before I'd feel completely comfortable leaving chambers in someone else's hands, but within a couple of years I'd like to be joining you on that golf course."

"I'm so glad you understand, thank you," said Sebastian.

"Laila told me about that client of yours too, Jay Harris, and that someone threatened you with a knife, is that right?"

"It sounds so much worse when you say it out loud. It was nothing really." Sebastian's hand instinctively reached up to his neck, where the sharp end of the knife had cut through his skin. "He didn't hurt me."

"Did you ring the police?" said Verity.

"No, no, really it…"

"Sebastian, come on. He sounds like a dangerous man. You can't just ignore something like that."

"He didn't hurt me. It was just a warning."

"What did he say exactly?"

Sebastian closed his eyes and ran his hand over his hair. He didn't want to run through the circumstances of his ordeal again. He would rather forget the whole thing and sail comfortably into his retirement, leaving all bad memories behind. But he knew that he should have told Verity, and he also needed to warn Robert. If he is going to be representing Jay

Harris, then he should know what he's up against. "He said something about making sure that I got bail for Jay Harris on Friday." Sebastian paused and took a deep breath. "And he said that if I didn't, then I was a dead man. But really, it's nothing, an idle threat, that's all."

"Okay, well if you're not going to take his threat seriously, I am. I've got a friend in the police, she's a detective inspector, I'll get her to log the incident. I'll message you with her number and you can give her a call before you leave tonight. I haven't got my phone with me, but I'll do it when I get back to my office. Hang on…" Verity reached across to Sebastian's desk phone and pulled it towards her. She lifted the receiver and dialled the clerks' desk. "Imran, hi, it's Verity here."

"Yes, Miss, how can I help you?" Sebastian heard Imran's tinny voice inside the phone.

"Can you find the telephone number for Detective Inspector Bloomsdale at GMP Headquarters and then send it to Sebastian for me? Thank you so much. And then can you send the instructions back to Jay Harris's solicitors with a note that we are refusing representation on the grounds of his violence? He has a bail hearing on Friday apparently, so if you'd send them an email today, or give them a call, that would be helpful. We wouldn't want the poor chap languishing in his prison cell without representation, would we?" She laughed at something Imran said. "Yes, I think the papers are in Sebastian's office. Thank you, Imran."

She put the phone down and pushed back it across the desk towards Sebastian. "He's going to send James up to get the papers for Harris. I want you to call D.I. Bloomsdale before the end of the day. Imran will send you her number."

Sebastian nodded. "So, my notice period…"

"Look, I'm not going to insist that you complete another three months. What's your workload like at the moment?"

"Not too busy," said Sebastian. "I asked Imran to keep me

relatively free for the next few months so I could have a holiday. I've got some advice papers that could be transferred to other people."

"Excellent. Well, if you can sort that out, I'm happy for you to leave earlier. You can leave at the end of the week, if you like." She pushed her chair back and stood up to leave. Sebastian wondered what Laila had told her about how rattled he was by the knife attack. "After all that excitement, I need to get back to work. I'll see you later. We need to arrange drinks or dinner or something. You've left me very little time to get you an expensive retirement gift."

"Verity!" said Sebastian, as she reached the door.

"Yes?"

"Thank you," he said. "I'm going to miss you. And I'm going to miss this place."

"Oh, you daft sod. I'm going to miss you too."

Verity was almost out of the door when she stopped. "Sebastian, how did that man know where you lived?"

"I don't know."

Unbelievably, when he and Laila had been talking about his retirement, assuming that they were safe and secure in their house, their castle, once the doors had been locked and they had barricaded themselves in, it had never occurred to him to question how the man knew where he lived. Maybe he had been followed all the way from work. Although the man seemed to be already there, waiting for him.

"I'll call the police and report it," he said.

Chapter Thirteen
Wednesday

"Are you all right Robert? You look like you have the weight of the world on your shoulders. That daughter of mine giving you a hard time, is she?" asked Sebastian. They were in the kitchen at chambers, both of them waiting for the kettle to boil. Sebastian crossed his fingers behind his back, hoping that Jamilla had finally given Robert his marching orders.

"Jamilla? No," said Robert. "Well, yes, if I'm honest. Amongst other things."

"You know a trouble shared is a trouble halved, and all that. Do you want to talk about it?"

"Well…" Yes, he did want to talk about it. This burden was becoming intolerable, and he needed to put it down before the weight of it caused him to fall. Sebastian might be his father-in-law one day and it would be good to confide in him.

"Because I'll go and get Samantha if you do," Sebastian laughed. This morning's conversation with Verity had left him in a joyous mood. He had the expectation that something amazing was about to happen, like when you're queuing in the airport, about to board a flight to an exciting once-in-a-lifetime destination.

The kettle flicked itself off and he poured the boiling water into his cup and then into Robert's. Robert was standing behind him, holding the milk bottle. Sebastian turned and took it from him. "Robert, are you okay? You've gone very pale. I was only joking about wanting to talk, you know you can talk to me, if you want to…"

Robert could feel the room beginning to swim. Cold sweat rushed from every pore. "I think I might be sick," he said. He ran out of the room, almost colliding with Alistair in the doorway.

"What's wrong with him?" said Alistair. "He's just nearly knocked me flying."

"I don't know," said Sebastian. "He doesn't look well."

"You're not wrong about that. He's about to puke, I reckon. He hasn't been out on the lash again, has he?"

Sebastian frowned. "I'm sorry?"

"Drinking," explained Alistair.

"Oh, I don't know," said Sebastian. "I wouldn't have thought so. Not on a Tuesday night."

Alistair knew very well that it was more than likely that Robert had overdone it last night. It was becoming more and more frequent. But he wasn't sure how much Sebastian knew about Robert's private life, apart from the time he spent with Jamilla. He certainly didn't want to enlighten him. He could find out for himself.

Alistair poured himself a black coffee and sat down at the dining table in the centre of the room. "So, Verity's just collared me and told me your news."

"Yes," said Sebastian. "It's…"

"A bit sudden, isn't it?"

"No, not really. I've been considering it for a while," he said, nonplussed and more than a little irritated.

"Mmm." Alistair sipped at his hot coffee with a raised eyebrow, as though contemplating whether or not Sebastian was being truthful.

Sebastian had the sudden urge to swipe the cup from his hands and give him a lecture about subordination. He had tried hard to like Alistair, but there was something about him that he couldn't get along with. His arrogance and perpetual boasting about how well he was doing might have something to do with it. He certainly wasn't one to hide his light under a bushell.

He finished making the tea, wondering whether he should go and find Robert, or ask James to find him. He knew that he and James were friends. James might know a little more about what was bothering him, and Robert might be tempted to open up to him. Not that Sebastian was averse to offering a shoulder to cry on, but a more familiar, and somewhat younger one, would be better for Robert.

"What has Robert had to say about it? Have you told him yet?" said Alistair.

"I was just about to actually," said Sebastian. The accusation that Alistair was intruding on what would be a private conversation was too subtle and didn't land, but floated around in the air, unnoticed.

"Verity said that I'm the most likely candidate to be his pupil supervisor."

"Did she?" Sebastian stopped himself from saying that he had hoped it might be Samantha, particularly as she already shared an office with Robert.

"I'm the obvious choice. I mean, we've got Kathryn Taylor, I know she's got a couple of years on me, but, well, you know." He sat back in the chair and waited for Sebastian to agree with him. "Yes, well, he's a good chap, Robert. He'll need a little moulding into shape, and I've got to say that his insouciance bothers me."

"There's nothing for you to worry about. He's very bright," said Sebastian. "He'll make an excellent barrister." For a second, Sebastian wondered whether he was doing the right thing in retiring. Robert was so close to reaching the end of his pupillage. He would be letting him down if he passed him over to Alistair now. He felt like he was leaving a kitten in a bear pit.

"Ahh, here he is. All warmed up by the Grim Reaper and

returned to us." Alistair was the only one who laughed.

"Do you feel a little better?" asked Sebastian. "I've made your tea."

"Yes, thank you," said Robert. "And thank you for the tea. I'm sorry about that. I haven't been well for a couple of days really."

The last thing Robert wanted was for Sebastian to put his absence down to personal issues - a hangover shouldn't be a reason to not turn up for work, so the fact that his stress was causing sickness was, in a way, the silver lining to the ever-darkening cloud.

"If you've got one of those stomach bugs, you'd better keep it to yourself," said Alistair.

"Yes, you're right," said Sebastian, jumping on the cue. "Let's get you out of this kitchen. Come to my office, there's something I want to talk to you about. See you later, Alistair." Sebastian picked up their drinks and led Robert out of the kitchen before Alistair could suggest that he should join them. "He's a first-class prick, isn't he?" he said, when they had reached his office and closed the door.

"I couldn't agree more," said Robert. "He gives people like us a bad name."

Sebastian knew that Robert meant privately educated people; wealthy people who managed to fall quite nicely into a prosperous career, with the help of the right school or the right family name emblazoned on their C.V., which added to their privilege.

"I've never heard you call him a prick before. I thought you liked him."

"And therefore, I have done my job well," said Sebastian. "My professional persona is quite different from my private one."

Robert doubted that very much. Being pleasant to a man that he didn't particularly like in the office was admirable, but

Sebastian was Sebastian. Changing his black sharply pressed working suit for a Ralf Lauren polo shirt and jeans at the weekend didn't particularly change his personality. Sebastian was old-school. One of the good guys. Polite, amiable, ethical. Someone you could look up to and emulate.

He wasn't the type to get himself stupidly and avoidably in debt. He wasn't the type to lie to his wife and get drunk too regularly for it to be fun. He certainly wasn't the type to make ridiculously catastrophic decisions, such as borrowing money from a loan shark.

The cold sweat began to engulf Robert again when he remembered last night. He was thankful for Sebastian offering him a chair, which he needed. He drank some of his tea quickly, wishing that he had put a couple of spoonfuls of sugar in it.

He was aware of Sebastian beginning to talk to him and he tried his best to listen and smile and nod in the correct places, but he couldn't concentrate. His thoughts refused to be controlled, however much he tried to keep a tight rein; they galloped ahead of him, kicking up unwanted images of last night. This had to stop. His life was out of control, like a racehorse that had been kept in the stable too long. It was impossible for him to catch it on his own.

And now his stress levels were making him ill. He needed to do something. But what?

Should he talk to Sebastian? Should he confide in him and ask him for help? As he had said in the kitchen, a trouble shared was a trouble halved. But he had tried that last night, hadn't he? Talking to Jamilla was meant to have been the start of his journey of recovery but look how that had worked out. She had called him a gambling addict. That was out of order. He wasn't a gambling addict. It wasn't even gambling, not really, it was a recreational activity. Like he had tried to explain to her last night.

He was confident that she would calm down and they

would be okay. Hopefully, Samantha had put a good word in for him after he had left. He had more pressing issues to worry about at the moment. His problem right now was not having enough money to pay his debt to Quay Street Casino and not knowing where the money was going to come from to pay the loan shark. He had enough for the first instalment, but the second instalment would be due in another week. By then, he had hoped to be able to get enough money together to pay all the loan back and to put this terrible episode behind him. But doors were being closed in his face right, left and centre. His credit score was the worst it had ever been, and no banks or legitimate loan companies would touch him now. Before he left for work this morning, he had made a few tentative online enquiries but had given up after the fourth rejection.

He shouldn't have gone into the casino last night. That was a big mistake. He didn't know why he had done it. His car seemed to take him there of its own accord. Rather than turning up at the car park to his apartment block, he had found himself being welcomed inside and the lure of the roulette table was as irresistible to him as a Siren's voice was to a sailor. He was doomed.

And his back pocket was five thousand pounds lighter by the time he had left.

Chapter Fourteen
Wednesday

Samantha knocked on Alistair's office door gently. She knew that when the door was closed, it meant that he was concentrating. The 'open door policy' that the clerks were trying to instigate in chambers hadn't been popular.

"Come in!" She heard Alistair's muffled voice inside and she tentatively opened the door.

"It's gone half six, darling," she said. "Are you ready to leave? If not, I can get the tram home." She didn't relish that idea. The tram at this time would be jam-packed with commuters and it was too warm to be squashed against sweaty bodies, but if Alistair wanted to work late, she was happy for him to have the car.

"I'm done now," he said. He clicked off his laptop, closed the lid and placed it in the top drawer of his desk, as he did every night. He locked the drawer and put the tiny key in the top pocket of his jacket. "Let's go."

Samantha was relieved that he smiled at her. He seemed to have lost the black cloud that had been hanging over him this week. They had hardly spoken since last night. After he had stormed out of the house, she had messaged Jamilla and asked if she fancied sharing a bottle of wine and listening to her relationship woes. Jamilla had been only too glad to keep her company. But rather than it being an enjoyable girly night, Robert had turned up and confessed his gambling habit, leaving Jamilla distraught.

By the time she had got back home, it was almost eleven thirty. Alistair was in the study. When he heard her key in the door, he came out and greeted her in the kitchen.

"Where did you go off to?" she asked.

"I needed some coke."

"For Saturday?"

Alistair's coke habit was something that she didn't condone, but as long as he used it occasionally and just for recreation, then she tried to keep her views to herself. She certainly wasn't happy about it, although she had learned that moaning about it to him only resulted in arguments.

"What?" said Alistair. Then he remembered that they had arranged to see Samantha's sister and her partner on Saturday night. "No, not for Saturday. For tonight."

Samantha shook her head. "But it's Tuesday," she had said, as though the day of the week was the thing that would stop him from taking the drugs, rather than the fact that it was illegal and his career would go down the pan, along with his reputation, if anyone ever found out.

"I need to work late," he said. "I've got a closing speech to prepare."

Since when had writing a closing speech been such an arduous task? But she hadn't challenged him. She had taken herself off to bed and when sleep finally took her, she had spent a restless night alone. She had heard Alistair settling into the guest bedroom in the early hours of the morning.

This morning, Alistair was showered and dressed by the time she woke up. The sound of the morning news from the television in the kitchen had floated up the stairs as she climbed out of bed.

Twenty minutes later, dressed and ready to leave the house, she had gone downstairs to find him in the kitchen, just finishing his coffee. There was none left in the cafetiere for her, but she didn't complain. He wasn't in the habit of making their morning coffee. She usually did that for them both while he was in the shower, so she didn't complain. He wasn't being inconsiderate; he just had a head full of other things, she told herself. She wanted to ask him whether he had managed to finish his closing speech, but she didn't feel like being snarled at.

"Have you had a good day?" he asked now, as they walked down the stairs together.

"Yes, good thanks," she said. She wanted to reach for his hand and tell him that he was forgiven for last night. She wanted to tell him that she loved him. But Jamilla had warned her that she was too soft. He walks all over you, she had said last night. You need to back off. Let him come to you. So, taking her friend's advice, Samantha had left him undisturbed in his man cave until he was ready to come out. Wallowing was the word that Jamilla had used. Whatever he had been doing, Samantha had left him to it.

As they reached the bottom of the stairwell, Alistair rested his hand on the door handle before opening the door to the reception area. "Samantha," he said. "I'm sorry about last night."

"Really?"

"Yes, what do you mean really? Like I never apologise? There's no fucking pleasing you." He pulled the door open forcefully and strode through reception, ignoring Imran when he shouted goodnight.

She hadn't meant to question his apology like that. It just came out and she had ruined everything again. It was so unlike him to apologise that she was shocked, that's all.

"Alistair, wait for me." Her heels clip-clopped on the tiled floor as she rushed to keep up with him. "Goodnight, Imran," she said over her shoulder, as she left the building, following Alistair onto St. John Street.

A few metres to the left of the building was a narrow side road, leading to the back of chambers, where their car was parked. The street, only one car width, was dark and dismal; the gable end of chambers on one side and the back of an office block on Deansgate on the other side meant that sunlight had an impossible task and rarely bothered to infiltrate the street. Alistair knew that Samantha didn't like walking down the street on her own, but he didn't wait for her.

He reached the car and clicked the key in his pocket to unlock the doors. "I didn't say that you never apologise, Alistair," Samantha said as she climbed into the passenger seat. Alistair took a deep breath and squeezed the steering wheel as he settled into the driver's seat. Samantha knew that he was hovering on the edge of anger. "Look, can we move on? There's nothing to apologise for, that's what I meant. You took me by surprise, that's all."

Alistair could see Samantha's tears forming and was filled with contrition. She didn't deserve to be on the receiving end of his short temper. He shouldn't be side-lining and ignoring her the way he had been doing. He reached across the central console and pulled her towards him. "I love you and I'm sorry," he said. He kissed her cheek, which was already wet with tears. "I had a particularly stressful trial, but it's over now."

"Did you win?" she asked, sitting back in her seat and wiping her eyes.

"Yes," he said. "I mean no, he was found not guilty, but I wasn't surprised really. It was a difficult case to fight. It wasn't anything that we or the CPS did wrong." He hadn't told her about the prosecution witness being hospitalised and his decision to bamboozle the young prosecution clerk into agreeing to run the trial without him. It had been a close call. It never should have got to court in the first place. Carl, his cohort in the CPS was now back from paternity leave, so it would never happen again. In fact, he was sure that it wouldn't happen again, because he had made the decision to no longer work for Frankie.

The rolled-up bank notes were safely tucked away in the top drawer of his desk, under lock and key. But that would be the last of it. He didn't need the money. He had been greedy. They had lived well on the extra income, there was no doubt about that, and he couldn't say that he had any regrets, but he didn't want another week like this one. It had to stop. The stakes were too high. The way Frankie had handed him the money in the middle of the corridor outside Court One had proved that he couldn't be trusted. Discretion was not on his radar.

As Alistair turned on the engine and drove out of the car park, he resolved to telephone Carl as soon as he got home. He would tell him that he no longer wanted to be involved. If Carl wanted to work for Frankie, that was up to him. But he wanted nothing to do with it from now on.

"Watch out!" Samantha shouted, as they drove out of the car park and turned onto the narrow side street.

Alistair slammed his foot on the brake. Robert and another man were walking in the middle of the street.

"Robert, I nearly killed you then," shouted Alistair. He laughed and leaned out of the window. "I'll get you next time."

Robert waved and shouted his apologies. He had been too busy talking, he said. It was his fault.

"Who's that other guy?" asked Samantha, as they drove onto St. John Street.

"I don't know," said Alistair. "But they don't look like friends talking. Looks like they're having an argument."

"Does it? I can't see them now from this angle. Do you think we should stop and see if he's okay?"

"No, he's fine. Robert can handle himself. It'll be something and nothing. He's probably flirted with the bloke's girlfriend or something."

"I hope not," said Samantha. "Otherwise, Jamilla will kill him."

As soon as Alistair and Samantha's car was out of sight, the man pushed Robert up against the wall.

When Imran had phoned Robert's office and told him that a friend of his was waiting in reception, Robert had known that that was unlikely to be the case. He wasn't expecting anyone. But he had rushed down, nevertheless, hoping that one of his rugby mates would be there, waiting to take him out for a pint.

As soon as the lift doors opened, the nauseous feeling that he had been struggling to hold back all day, rushed into his stomach like a breaking damn. He swallowed the excess saliva in his mouth and took deep breaths. Frankie's right-hand man, the one who had given him the envelope packed with money last night in Sainsburys' car park, was waiting for him. His bulky frame, squinty malevolent eyes and open-legged stance oozed trouble. In whose world would Imran think for one moment that this guy was a friend? But Imran was busy on the phone, his head down, furiously writing in his notepad, so he hadn't seen the way that Robert's elbow had been tightly squeezed as the two of them left the building together.

"I've got a message from Frankie." The man said, as he held Robert against the wall with his huge arm across Robert's chest. "Just a reminder that he needs the first payment by the end of the week. A grand. I'll come here and collect it."

"No, not here," said Robert.

The sudden punch to his stomach silenced any further resistance.

The man stepped away, giving Robert the space to fall forward.

"Yes," he said. "Friday." He began to walk away. Robert breathed and leaned back against the wall, holding his stomach. "By the way." The man stopped walking and turned to face

Robert again. "If you need any more money, you just need to ask."

Robert could hear him laughing as he disappeared onto St. John Street.

Chapter Fifteen
Eight Days Before the Shooting - Thursday

Elsie pushed against the old iron gate of St Peter's churchyard. The familiar creaking of its hinges was soothing. A sound indicating the beginning of her favourite part of each day. She took care treading over the old paving slabs, making sure to step over the cracks between them. She didn't need any more bad luck and although she told herself that ancient superstitions should be left where they belong, in the dim and distant past, she wasn't one to take unnecessary chances. There was no point, was there? Whether the superstition was true or not, if she could comfortably walk without stepping in the cracks, then why not?

"Hello, my darling," she said to her husband's gravestone. "I'm a bit late this morning, I'm afraid. I've had a dreadfully busy morning. I've made some scones. You know how I love the smell of baking in the house, especially first thing in the morning. I've got them here in my bag." She held a blue cotton bag aloft with her right hand. "Not all for me, of course, although I must admit that I had a nibble of one with my tea. I keep thinking of the poor baby birds and their exhausted parents who must be getting worn out in this weather. One day it's warm, the next day it's freezing. Today is more like winter than the second week of May. The birds in the churchyard are so hungry and bedraggled. Poor pets! They'll love my homemade scones, I'm sure."

"Good morning, Elsie, are you well?" a voice shouted from the door of the church.

"Morning Lisa," shouted Elsie. "Yes, thank you. Are you?"

"Yes, thanks, but that's more than I can say for the boiler, I'm afraid," said the vicar, "It still isn't working. You're all going to have to keep your coats on on Sunday, because the plumber isn't coming until next week." As though to prove the point, Lisa, rubbed her hands together and blew on them.

"Oh dear," said Elsie. "It's typical that it's gone cold again, just as the boiler breaks down. But never mind, we're promised warmth and sunshine again from the middle of next week, I think, aren't we? I do hope so."

"God willing," said Lisa, looking up to the sky and making the sign of the cross on her chest. "Anyway, I'll leave you to chat to Stanley and I'll see you on Sunday, if not before." She waved her goodbyes and disappeared back into the church.

Elsie knelt down in front of Stanley's headstone, stroking it lovingly, just as she had stroked his face when he was alive. Today, she didn't want to cry. Since her beloved husband's death, she had cried virtually every day, but she was taking baby steps to be more positive and to 'move forward', as her friend Jean had told her to do. Jean told her that she had so much to look forward to, and although she didn't entirely agree, she was doing her best to keep optimistic. The church summer garden party and trips to the theatre with her friends were all well and good, but when you return to an empty house and your husband's chair stands empty and cold in the corner of the room, it tends to take the edge of any happiness that you can manage to build for yourself.

So, she had lowered her expectations. Happiness was out of reach. Contentment would suffice. For now. Although she did look forward to her monthly lunches in Manchester with her brother, Sebastian, and she loved spending time with Laila and

Jamilla, apart from that, joyous moments were few and far between.

"I've been thinking about the little lambs up in the hills," she said. "I hope they won't be too chilly. It must be such a shock when they're born into a cold spell. I'm going to mention them in my prayers this morning. When I was a little girl, I was always given the job of feeding the little orphan lambs on the farm, do you remember me telling you?" As she knelt and brushed away the detritus from around the grave, grass cuttings and wayward leaves, she knew that Stanley would remember her stories. He used to love hearing about her life on her parents' farm when she was young.

Stanley, a child of poor parents, had grown up in Ancoats, when it was a deprived suburb of Manchester, before someone changed its name to the Northern Quarter and filled it with trendy bars and cafés. Gentrification had still been many years away. Meat on their dinner table was restricted to once or twice a week. Elsie remembered him sitting in awe when she told him stories of her father killing an old chicken on a Sunday morning and her mother plucking it and roasting it for their dinner. Afterwards, she and Sebastian would sit around their warm fire in the huge farmhouse kitchen, their bellies full of food and their hearts full of love. They would spend the rest of the evening reading, each of them absorbed in their own stories. When they had finished their chosen book, they could swap it for another one from the huge library at the back of the house, which had shelves and shelves of books from floor to ceiling. Every now and then, their mother would take them into town for fresh supplies and they would stagger home with armfuls of new adventures.

Stanley's house hadn't had such luxuries. A box of Dominoes was the only ornament on their old mahogany sideboard. Once Stanley had taken a book from the school library and was reading it, curled up at the side of the sofa, when his father had returned home from the cotton factory where he worked. He had thrown a disdainful look in Stanley's direction and the young boy had felt the disapproval seeping from his father's pores. His mother, knowing what he was thinking, had tried to placate her husband before his anger had boiled over, telling him that the boy had to learn to read and that the book was from school. She assured him that she hadn't spent his hard-earned money on 'stupid books' and that no, the boy wasn't being idle, sitting there doing nothing, he was doing his homework.

She had turned to Stanley and winked at him and then with a nod of her head, indicated that he should run upstairs to his room out of the way. As he had climbed the steep stairs, he heard his father mumbling things about him trying to be too big for his boots and not being content with his station in life. Stanley hadn't understood what he meant entirely, but his instincts told him that he had to hide his book in the future and to look busy whenever he heard his father's footsteps approaching the house.

"I used to love feeding the little darlings," continued Elsie. "And they didn't half love the bottles of warm, sugary milk that they were given; their little tails wagging furiously, and they were always pulling the teats off the bottles. I'd have to run around the kitchen after them, do you remember? It was chaos. But we all loved them. Very few of them ever went to market because none of us could bear it, so they had long and happy lives, despite their initial bad start." She stood up, leaning on the headstone for support and dusted her knees with her gloved hands. "Look at this, still got my gloves on in May! It's never been known. Anyway, warmth and sunshine are on their way, I'm sure. You know, I always think that those wealthy people in the nineteenth century who spent the winters in the South of France or in Italy really did have the right idea! I think a nice apartment in Monte Carlo overlooking the bay with the yachts would be very nice, don't you?"

She smiled to herself and patted the headstone as she walked away down the path. She never said goodbye to him. She had told him on her first visit to the grave that she never wanted to say goodbye, so he needn't expect it. Goodbye was such a finite word, she had told him. She preferred to think of their conversations as being on pause. He knew that she would visit him again tomorrow and the day after that. There was no need for painful goodbyes.

As she walked, she scattered handfuls of scone crumbs as she went. The birds waited patiently in the old yew trees for her to pass, before they swooped down and gobbled up their welcome breakfast eagerly.

"That'll attract mice, that will."

"Good morning, Peter," said Elsie. "Mice are God's creatures too, you know." She gave the old verger the warmest smile she could muster and waved at him. Grumpy old bugger, she thought.

Chapter Sixteen
Thursday

Alistair had been running for thirty minutes on the treadmill when the gym's personal trainer approached his machine. The trainer smiled at him and tapped on the side of his ear with his index finger. Alistair ignored him. He knew what he wanted. The 'Polite Sign' on the wall in front of the row of treadmills reminded the users of the ridiculously expensive Cheshire Country Club that use of the cardio equipment was restricted to twenty minutes in busy periods. Something about fairness and equal opportunities. Fuck that, thought Alistair. He increased the speed to a fast run.

He could see the personal trainer out of the corner of his eye, dazzling white teeth and a tight black t-shirt to emphasise his tight muscles. The words 'I'm happy to help. Ask me anything' were printed on the front of his t-shirt in the company's luminous lime green font. Alistair wanted to ask him if he wouldn't mind fucking off. Would he be happy to help with that? Thank you very much.

The trainer reached over and pressed the stop button on the treadmill.

"What the fuck are you doing?" shouted Alistair, as his run was curtailed into a slow walk. "And what's all this?" He tapped his finger on his ear, mimicking the trainer.

"I wanted you to take your earphones out so I could talk to you," said the trainer. There was that smile again. Alistair wondered whether that had been part of his training. Territorial hostility wrapped up in customer service. The trainer's client stood by his side scrolling through her phone, her red-lipsticked mouth pouting at the screen. "I'm afraid you've gone over the allocated twenty minutes. Peak time between six and eight. It's a busy time." He pointed to the sign.

"Don't talk to me about being busy," Alistair screeched over the loud music.

The beat in Stormzy's 'Own It' wasn't conducive to slowing his heart rate. The cortisol his body had been producing all day had to go somewhere and if he wasn't able to get rid of it by running, then shouting would have to suffice.

"You can have mine," said the man on the treadmill next to him. "I'm done." He alighted his machine with the grace of an eighteenth-century gentleman getting off his horse in front of King George III. He almost bowed, leaving Alistair with the unsportsmanlike feeling that he was acting like a prized idiot.

Not wanting any further altercations, Alistair left the treadmill and wandered over to the punch bag in the far corner of the gym. He put on one of the boxing gloves and pulled the velcro fastening tightly across his wrist. After putting the other glove on and using his teeth to fasten it, he punched the bag as hard as he could with both hands, using the faces of the annoying personal trainer and Frankie in his imagination to assist his aim.

"You're working hard," said Samantha, walking over to him from the yoga studio, where her class had just finished. She perched on the edge of a wooden bench and sipped her water. "I feel like I should be doing tricep dips on here," she said. "But that class was enough."

Alistair smiled at her and stopped punching. The imagined trainer and Frankie had taken enough of a beating, and he hugged the punch bag to his chest to make it still.

"Do you want some water?" Samantha held out her bottle

to him.

"Thanks," he said. "I need to get rid of these first." He held out his hands and Samantha unfastened his gloves and pulled them off. She put them back in the box and handed Alistair her bottle of water.

"What was all that with Ollie?" she asked.

"Who?"

"Ollie, the personal trainer," she said.

"Oh, nothing. I'd gone over the twenty minutes on the treadmill, that's all. He was reminding me of the rules." Alistair rolled his eyes and used his fingers to make air quotation marks. He was beginning to feel calmer now. He didn't want to be angry all the time.

"You should come to my yoga class. It's much better for you than running and punching holes out of that thing." Samantha nodded towards the punch bag.

"I might do," he said. "I think half an hour of lying down in a dark room is just what I need."

"It's called shavasana, not lying down." She laughed and gently punched him on his arm.

"Whatever," he said. "Shall we have a swim? Or steam room and sauna?"

"Steam room and sauna would be lovely," said Samantha. "I'm quite hungry. I don't think I've got the energy for a swim as well."

The truth was that Alistair was usually at his most relaxed in the steam room and sauna and she was hoping that the state of relaxation would last a while. At least until they got home. Maybe all evening, if she was lucky.

Ten minutes later, as they sat side by side on the gym's white fluffy towels, folded into neat squares, in the steam room, Samantha could feel Alistair's stress evaporating into the menthol-infused steam. He leaned back against the pine clad wall and closed his eyes. Samantha laid her hand over his and when she felt his hand unfurl and grasp hers, giving it a little squeeze, she smiled to herself, closed her eyes, and rested her head against his shoulder.

Only one more working day and then it was the weekend. She much preferred spending time with him at the weekend, rather than during a stressful working week, and she was looking forward to having dinner at her sister's house on Saturday night. Beth and Sarah always went overboard with their entertaining. They were both chefs, having met at catering college, so their dining table would be groaning under the weight of delicious food and bottles of expensive wine.

"I wonder what Beth and Sarah will be cooking for us on Saturday night," she said.

"Nothing too stodgy, I hope," said Alistair, patting his flat stomach.

"They never do stodgy food," said Samantha, feeling aggrieved at the unwarranted criticism.

"I'm just saying, I'm working hard in the gym at the moment, and I don't want to ruin it."

"Well, maybe you should ease back on the cocaine. God knows what that rubbish is doing to your insides."

Alistair pulled his hand away and Samantha instantly regretted ruining the moment. They were so few and far between these days and here she was, letting this precious one float away.

"I have eased back," he snapped. "I don't need you to tell me what to do, Samantha. You're not my mother."

Samantha wasn't sure whether to laugh at his petulance or cry. She could see the recalcitrant teenager within him fighting to get out. She didn't know what he was so angry about and couldn't ask him. She didn't want to ask him. Right now, she wanted to walk away from him, go home and relax in a deep hot bath for an hour. She wanted to slide under the bubbles and stay there until every last one of them had burst and the water had gone cold. She was sick and tired of having to think about her words before she spoke. She did her best but sometimes they escaped her; the words flew from her mouth like arrows from bows, the sharp points damaging their relationship before anything could be done to stop them.

They sat in silence for a few minutes before the door was opened and they were joined by three middle-aged men, who sat down on the opposite bench and chatted about the five-a-side game they had just played. They laughed about a goal that had been let in by their keeper that should have been easily saved and about someone who had tripped up another player, which would have resulted in a red card, had anyone been bothered to stick to the rules.

Samantha enjoyed listening to them. With her eyes closed once again, she could picture them running about on the field, having the time of their lives, their friendships cemented by their weekly game.

"Shall we go?" said Alistair.

"Yes, sure," she said, getting up and following him out of the steam room.

"I'll see you in reception." As he walked off towards the men's changing rooms. Samantha saw that the sauna was empty, so she opened the door and immersed herself in the heat, alone. Alistair could wait. She was getting tired of following his schedule.

After the sauna, Samantha purposefully took her time getting showered and dressed and Alistair was waiting for her in the bar by the time she was ready.

"I had ten minutes in the sauna," she said, before he had the chance to ask what had taken her so long.

"It's fine," he said, magnanimously. "No rush."

Samantha knew that he hated waiting for her and that inside he would be seething. He was acting polite in case anyone overheard their conversation. It wouldn't do him any harm, she thought, although she couldn't help feeling guilty. She wasn't used to putting herself first, but she told herself that going into the sauna was their original plan, and he was the one who had changed his mind, so it was his own fault that he had to wait for her.

She sat opposite him in the booth. "Shall we have something to eat here, or do you want to go home?" she said.

Before he could reply, his phone pinged with an incoming text. It was the spare burner phone that he kept for communications with Frankie and Carl at the CPS. He winced and covered the phone in his pocket with his hand. It should have been on silent.

"Do you want to get that?" said Samantha.

"No, it's nobody," he said.

"Well, it clearly is somebody," said Samantha, "Because someone's just sent you a message. Who is she?"

"Come on, let's go. I don't want the bar staff listening. You know they love to gossip and now, thanks to you, we're the new Subject of the Week." He slid out of the booth and once again, Samantha followed him.

Once they were in the car, Samantha asked him whether he was going to bother reading the text or was he going to keep his girlfriend waiting.

"It's not my fucking girlfriend," Alistair bellowed. "If you must know, it's the man I get the cocaine off. He's probably just asking if I want some more for the weekend. If you think I've got the time or the inclination for an affair, Samantha, you're out of your fucking mind."

Once again, they drove in silence.

Chapter Seventeen
Thursday

Jamilla sat waiting at the bar in The Dakota Hotel. Robert had told her that he had booked a table for seven thirty in the restaurant, but he hadn't yet arrived, and she was beginning to think that he wasn't going to. She imagined him drunk in a bar somewhere, surrounded by his raucous rugby friends. It wasn't unknown for him to go for a pint after work. Just the one, he would say. But one turned into two, turned into three, turned into half a dozen. She would give him ten more minutes, then she was going. She couldn't lecture Samantha about taking shit from Alistair if she was prepared to take it herself from Robert.

But at least he was trying, she would give him that. She appreciated that he had chosen The Dakota for a reason. He could have chosen somewhere a little less fancy; something a bit more down-market. But this was the location of their first date. He knew that this held a special place in her heart. He clearly wanted her to remember that first night out; the cocktails, the giggling, their stumble up the stairs to the hastily booked room, where they couldn't wait to undress each other and jump into bed. But Jamilla didn't want to remember how good they used to be; their closeness; their good times; their laughter. She needed to stay strong. Being wistful wouldn't help her.

She looked at her watch again. It was seven thirty-one. Why did he always have to push the boundaries? Every time! She was tired and was beginning to regret coming out. Last night, after he had left and after she had dissected their relationship to pieces with Samantha, amid handfuls of sodden tissues, she hadn't slept well. The more she tossed and turned, the more she worried about him. She couldn't abandon him now. She was too far down the road to do that. They were a couple, and she was determined to help him.

She had sent him a message in the early hours of this morning and was surprised when he replied.

I'm worried about you. I want to help you x she had said.

I'm fine x he replied.

Two minutes later, another message appeared. *Shall we talk tomorrow over dinner? Dakota Hotel? X*

Yes, she had replied. *We need to talk x*

They did need to talk. Or rather, she needed to talk, and he needed to listen. She wasn't prepared to give up on him; they still had a chance to make things work, if he was prepared to listen to her.

A waitress appeared at her side. "Your table in the restaurant is ready, would you like to follow me?"

"My boyfriend isn't…oh, here he is. Yes, we're ready, thank you."

"Sorry, I'm late," said Robert, rushing over to her. "I couldn't find anywhere to park."

Jamilla stood up and allowed Robert to kiss her chastely on the cheek. She didn't want to tell him that she had paid for valet parking. It was a good sign that he hadn't. Although, if he was truly trying to save money, he could have walked. But maybe now wasn't the right time to mention that, or to tell him that driving his car a couple of miles from one side of the city centre to the other was not the most environmentally friendly journey. That was a conversation that she would rather avoid tonight. One problem at a time.

They followed the waitress into the restaurant, to the corner table that Robert told her he had specifically requested when he made the booking.

"Can I get you some drinks while you look at the menu?" she asked.

"Just some sparkling water, please," said Jamilla. "We're both driving."

"It's lovely to see you," said Robert as soon as the waitress was out of earshot. "You look beautiful, as always."

"Thank you," said Jamilla politely. She wanted to jump up and kiss him and hold him, but she was determined not to show any sign of her playful, flirtatious side. This was Serious Jamilla. This was I've-Got-A-Bone-To-Pick-With-You Jamilla.

"What do you fancy to eat?" asked Robert.

"I'm not really in the mood for food, if I'm honest. Just a Caesar salad probably."

Robert smiled and she couldn't help smiling back. She always ordered the Caesar salad. She liked to think that she was ordering something healthy, even though it probably had more calories than most things on the menu.

"And I'm paying for this," she said. "So don't go ordering a steak or an expensive fish that neither of us have ever heard of."

"I've invited you here, Milla. I'm paying. I always pay."

"Yes, but while you're skint, you need to save your money, so stop being so old-fashioned. I'm paying."

"I like this side of you. Assertive."

Robert raised his eyebrow and grinned at her lasciviously. She grinned back and whacked his arm with the menu. Then suddenly, she was serious again.

"Stop that!" she said. "This is why you're in such a mess. Life can't be one long game, Robert. You need to grow up."

"Adulting," he said.

"What?"

"It's over-rated."

"For fuck's sake, Robert. I'm wasting my time; I can see it. You drive me mad; I might as well leave." She reached behind her and took her handbag from the back of the seat where she had hung it, but the sudden appearance of the waitress at their table prevented her from standing up and storming out.

"Are you ready to order?" she said. She placed a large bottle of sparkling water in the middle of the table, together with two crystal glasses.

Jamilla clung tightly to her bag on her knee. "Two Caesar salads and a portion of truffle fries, please," she said.

She knew that Robert hated salads and she was daring him to challenge her choice. He didn't. It would do him good to have something green, she thought. The fries were her compromise.

"I guess you're staying then?" Robert asked.

Jamilla shrugged her shoulders and replaced the handbag on the back of her chair with a deep sigh. "I want to help you, but you have to be willing to let me," she said. Robert nodded. "It was a massive shock when you told me how deeply you were in debt to the casino. Ten thousand pounds! It's fucking ridiculous."

Robert couldn't argue with that. The six thousand pounds on his Barclaycard and the two thousand pound overdraft were also fucking ridiculous. He hadn't got around to telling her about those yet. And how would he tell her about the loan from Frankie, the loan shark? He couldn't bear to think about it. She would dump him on the spot when she found out about that.

"I don't know why you thought you should tell me that you wanted to marry me, when you're in such a mess," she said. "Weddings are expensive, you know, and you can't expect my father to pay for everything. In fact, they're all a complete waste of money, so I'm not even bothered if we don't have one." Robert knew that was a lie. Jamilla had wanted to be a bride since she was a little girl. "What I'm trying to say is, you know that I'm saving for a house, and I thought you were too. I thought talk of weddings would come later, when we were settled, but at this rate…"

"Milla, please," he said. "I am saving…" He tried to take hold of her hand, but she pulled it away and rested it on her lap.

"No, you're not. But that's the difference between you and me. You choose to do something different with your money. I'm saving, you're spending. How is that fair?"

"I'm sorry." Robert couldn't think of anything else to say. She was right. He was an idiot.

"Ten thousand pounds, Robert. That's halfway to a house deposit!"

"I know, Jamilla. I don't know how it got so bad, I really don't." The tears came suddenly and unexpectedly, and Robert was thankful that he was facing the wall and that there was nobody at the table next to them. "Wow, this is embarrassing," he said, dabbing at his face with the linen napkin.

"I've got two Caesar salads and a portion of truffle fries." A different waiter appeared at their table, balancing the salads on one arm and holding the fries with the other. Robert kept his head down, pretending to be busy making room for the food, rearranging his cutlery and moving the water bottle.

"Thank you," said Jamilla.

"Is there anything else I can get for you?"

"No, thank you," said Jamilla.

The waiter left them alone while they both picked at the fries and shuffled the salads around the huge bowls. Neither of them had an appetite.

"So, what I wanted to say," said Jamilla, after a few minutes of awkward silence. "Is that I want to help you. I don't think the amount of times that you gamble is normal. In fact, I know it's not normal. So, I've been looking at the Gamblers' Anonymous website and I'd like you to go to one of their meetings. You can go to one in Manchester, or you can drive out further afield, if you're worried that you might come across someone you know. Then we can start to sort out your debts. I'm not sure how we can do that, but my dad has a financial advisor who could help…"

"You're not getting Sebastian involved in this," said Robert. "Sorry, sorry." He held up his knife and fork in surrender. "A man's got his pride, that's all. I'd rather he didn't know the ins and outs of my personal financial affairs."

Jamilla nodded. "I understand that. Okay, well we'll have to Google one. There will be one somewhere."

"My friend, Lucas, does wealth management."

"Wealth management? Don't you mean absolutely skint, on your arse management?"

They both laughed and Robert had a glimpse of how it used to be. A tiny glimmer of hope, like the crack in the curtains through which the smallest amount of morning sunshine broke through.

"I'll do everything I can to get back on track," he said. "With you, with my finances. Everything."

"We're not back on track. Not by a long chalk. But I want to help you to stop gambling. But you've got to be willing to acknowledge that you have a problem in the first place. You've got to want to change it. Apparently, that's how it works. I've been reading up on addiction."

Addiction? That was a tough word to swallow. Robert chewed a chunk of chicken breast that didn't seem to want to go down. He reached for some sparkling water and forced it down. He knew what an addict looked like. They were thin and wizened. They were dirty and grubby. They hung around in groups, bent over tiny parcels of whatever respite was being offered, desperate and miserable. He wasn't at all like those people. He had a good job. A career in fact. He had his own apartment and his own car, and his life was a million miles away from the addicts he had come across in court.

But was he so different? When he thought about it, he didn't own his own place. He rented it. His car wasn't his, either. It was leased. He didn't own anything of any value, except for some expensive suits and a couple of watches. He didn't have any money in his bank, and he was massively in debt.

Suddenly, the weight of disappointment that he had been carrying with him for months, if not years, was overpowering.

"I just need a minute," he said.

He rushed to the men's bathroom and vomited into the toilet.

Chapter Eighteen
Thursday

"Cheers to retirement!" said Sebastian, as he and Laila and Verity and her husband, Peter, all clicked their Champagne flutes together.

The remains of the bottle of Bollinger was packed in ice cubes in the silver bucket at the side of their table. They were in their favourite pub, The Dog and Bone. The pub was almost halfway between where Sebastian and Laila lived in Knutsford and where Verity and Peter lived in Alderley Edge, so it had become their favourite meeting point. It was dog friendly and Verity and Peter's golden labrador, Lucy, was always particularly welcome on the grounds that she was the most beautiful dog ever seen.

"Do you have a speech prepared, darling?" asked Laila, digging Sebastian in the ribs with her elbow.

"No, I do not," he said. "Except to say that my days of long speeches are now over and I'm very thankful that the lovely ladies and gentlemen of the jury don't have to suffer them any longer."

"So, what are your plans for next week? Or is it too early to ask?" said Peter.

"No plans yet, except for a day of golf, if you can fit it in?"

"I've got surgery on Monday, Tuesday and Wednesday but I could do Thursday or Friday?" Peter had his own general practice surgery and was slowly working his way towards retirement by working part-time.

"You've arranged to have lunch with Elsie on Friday, don't forget," said Laila.

"Yes, of course. I'm having lunch with my sister on Friday, but I can do Thursday," said Sebastian.

"Thursday it is then," said Peter. "I'll look forward to it."

"Where are you taking Elsie?" asked Verity. "Has she been here yet?"

"Yes, a few years ago. But I usually meet her in Manchester. It's easy for her to get to. There's a train from where she lives, and she likes a mooch around the shops. I don't know, I'll have a think. If it's nice, we might be able to eat outside somewhere. I'll meet her at chambers as usual and take it from there."

Sebastian's lunch date with his older sister had been a longstanding arrangement, since her husband, Stanley, had died. She hadn't coped well with his loss and Sebastian had needed an excuse to drag her out of the house. He had told her that he had a particularly difficult case that he'd like to discuss with her and would she be happy to be his sounding board. Elsie, a retired solicitor, said yes, of course, and would he like to come over for dinner? Sebastian told her that he had a really busy diary for the next few weeks and would she do him the honour of taking the train into Manchester and meeting him for lunch. His treat.

The ploy had worked, and Elsie had made the trip into the city to meet him.

Sebastian had asked Imran not to book anything into his diary for the afternoon, as he wasn't sure whether he would be back. He would hate his sister to think that he was rushing to get back to work.

When Elsie arrived at chambers, Sebastian told her that he had booked them a light lunch somewhere quiet, where they could chat about his case. It was the beginning of December and Manchester was looking its best. Christmas fairy lights decorated the lampposts and twinkled in the dim afternoon light. Bars and restaurants were brimming with office workers at their Christmas parties. The pavements were overflowing with shoppers laden with gifts.

Elsie held tightly to Sebastian's arm as they walked down Deansgate and up Peter Street and when he stopped walking outside The Midland Hotel and told her that he had booked them a table for a festive afternoon tea, Elsie had burst into tears.

"Why didn't you tell me we were going somewhere posh?" she cried. "Will I do like this?"

"Yes, you'll do just fine," said Sebastian, patting her hand.

"Do you remember when mum used to ask dad that? 'Will I do?' she used to ask, whenever she was dressed up to go out, and dad would say, 'Yes, you'll do'."

"Yes, I remember," said Sebastian. "And that was all the compliment she was going to get."

"I still miss them, do you?" asked Elsie. "Even though they've been dead for nearly twenty years now."

"Yes, I do."

Sebastian hugged Elsie close to him until she composed herself and then led her up the grand steps and into the hotel foyer.

It had been a lovely afternoon. They never got round to talking about the case that Sebastian supposedly needed help with. They reminisced about their childhood, about their parents, the farm where they lived, their ridiculously strict school and the dog that they used to have, an adorable collie sheep dog called Patch.

At the end of their lunch, when they were both full to the brim with sandwiches, scones and cakes and Darjeeling tea, Elsie said that she had really enjoyed herself and thanked her brother for forcing her out of the house. Sebastian told her that he didn't force her, he had genuinely wanted to pick her legal brain, even though she had been retired for five and a half years.

They both laughed because they both knew it wasn't true, but they made a pact to have lunch together at least once a month from then on. Just the two of them, in Manchester.

"Why don't you take her to The Midland Hotel again?" asked Laila now.

"You read my mind," said Sebastian. "I think I'll do just that. I'd better tell her though, because when I took her there the first time, she was mortified that we were going somewhere posh, and she hadn't dressed up enough."

The rest of the evening flew by too quickly. A second bottle of Champagne was ordered, along with two steak and ale pies, a cheese and onion pie and a battered cod and chips and before long, it was ten thirty and their taxis had arrived.

"When you all retire, maybe we can stay out until eleven," said Sebastian, as they said goodbye outside the pub.

"By the time we all retire, we'll be too old, and we won't be venturing out after dark," laughed Verity. "Goodnight both! See you in the morning, Seb."

"Goodnight!" called Laila.

The taxi journey home didn't take long. As they settled in the back seat, Sebastian gave their address to the driver and then sent a text to Elsie (she didn't do WhatsApp), telling her to put on a nice dress next Friday, because they were going to The Midland again. Laila found the hotel's website and booked a table for them, with the special request that they were able to sit close to the window.

Before long, the taxi pulled up outside their house, they both thanked the driver and got out.

Laila saw it first.

It stopped her in her tracks, and she held tightly to her husband's arm.

Red paint had been graffitied all over their door, contaminating the tiles of their porch like blood at a crime scene.

"What on earth is that?" said Sebastian. Laila stood rooted to the ground. She tried to grab hold of his hand, to keep him close to her, but he marched up the door for a closer look.

"It's that man again, isn't it?" she said. "The one who stabbed you with the knife."

"Well, he didn't stab me as such," said Sebastian. "But it's probably him, yes."

"We need to ring the police," said Laila. "Do you think he's still here?" She looked over her shoulder in panic. "What if he's still here?"

"If he's still here, I'll kill him," said Sebastian. He stormed up to the front door and tried to open it, but was relieved to find it still locked, the way they had left it. He checked the six- feet high gate leading to the back garden. That was still closed, bolted from the other side, and there was no damage to any of the windows. Thankfully, the house seemed to be intact.

"Do you think he's gone?" asked Laila. "I'm going to ring the police." She fumbled in her handbag, with shaking hands, for her phone.

Sebastian didn't answer her. "It infuriates me when people don't use the correct grammar," he said.

'Your dead' had been spray-painted across the front door.

Chapter Nineteen
Seven Days Before the Shooting - Friday

Sebastian had planned to be at chambers early for his last day. He was never late, but by the time the police had arrived last night, it was after midnight and it was almost quarter to one when they left, so when the alarm went off this morning, Laila persuaded him to have another half an hour in bed. Neither of them had slept much.

Sebastian had given a brief statement to the police about the threat from Jay Harris and also the threat from the other man, who had been waiting for him on his driveway. The police officer had told him that Jay had a brother and they would speak to him, but without any direct evidence against him, there was nothing they could do.

"Maybe one of the neighbours saw something," said Laila hopefully.

Sebastian knew that the chances of that were slim. The couple directly across the road were elderly and their curtains were often closed by eight o'clock at the latest. The houses on either side were a different design and their living rooms were at the back of their houses, so unless the culprit had navigated his way across their back gardens and they had glimpsed him through their bi-fold doors, speaking to them wouldn't help their case. Nevertheless, the young police officer said that they would make some enquiries. Sebastian knew that his case wouldn't be a priority and he didn't hold his breath for an imminent arrest.

"Did you say that Jay Harris' bail application is tomorrow?" asked the police officer, as he was leaving.

"Yes," said Sebastian. "Although I'm not representing him any longer. His case has been passed back to his solicitors, so I don't know who his barrister will be now."

"Do you think he will get bail?" asked the police officer.

"If justice serves, then no," said Sebastian.

The police officer nodded. "That's good," he said.

"It's not good at all," said Laila. "If he doesn't get out, then Sebastian's in danger, isn't he? The warning's right here." She pointed to the sinister red words on their door, which had now dried.

Laila had burst into tears and the police officer gave some generic advice to Sebastian about staying out of dimly lit streets; making sure he wasn't alone if he went for a walk, especially after dark; locking all the doors and windows and keeping his phone charged up at all times. The same crime prevention advice that you would give to anyone. Sebastian thanked him for his time but didn't feel particularly bolstered.

As a consequence, when he arrived at chambers, it was almost nine o'clock. Having had very little sleep, he didn't have the energy to deal with the mountain of paperwork that was waiting for him on his desk. A pile that he had to wade through before he could leave. He had wondered whether he should just do another week, rather than putting himself under pressure to tie up all loose ends today.

"It won't make any difference in the long run," he had said to a bleary-eyed Laila this morning, as she poured him a cup of his tea in the kitchen. "If I do stay another week, I'll be able to take my time, help James and Imran to re-allocate my remaining cases and…"

He had stopped talking when he saw how worried his wife was. She was nodding in agreement, but he could tell that she didn't agree. Not at all. She wanted him to be at home, with her, where she could keep an eye on him. So, he told her not to worry, he would finish today and would be home as soon as possible. He asked her to order one of those fancy doorbells that has a camera attached to it and she smiled and said that she had already done it. It would be delivered tomorrow. Today, she intended to spend the day at her friend's house.

"Good morning, James," he said when he finally arrived at work. "I'm here at last."

"Good morning, sir," said James. "Can I get you a tea?"

"No thank you, but can you do a little job for me?"

"Of course, what is it?

"I've left my car in the bay outside; would you mind moving it into the car park for me? I didn't want to be any later than I already am." Sebastian passed his car keys to James, who said that he would be happy to help. James, young, fit and agile as he was, would be absolutely fine walking back from the car park, down the dark and narrow street at the side of chambers, which could, at times, be too quiet for comfort. Sebastian, older, less fit and carrying a few too many pounds - maybe not.

Sebastian pressed the button for the lift and rode up to the second floor. When the lift doors opened, Robert and Alistair were waiting to get in, to travel down.

"Ahh, morning Sebastian," said Alistair. "I'm stealing your pupil and taking him to court with me. As a sweetener, I've promised to buy him breakfast on the way. I didn't think you'd miss him on your last day, is that okay?"

"Of course," said Sebastian. "Just deliver him back safe and sound this afternoon. I'd like to pass over a couple of cases. Anything exciting going on at court?"

"A couple of sentencing hearings, that's all. We'll be back by one o'clock, shall we have lunch, the three of us?"

Sebastian couldn't think of anything worse, but he agreed and said that he would see them both later. The lift door closed, and Alistair and Robert made their way to court.

*

"Your Honour, the defendant has a long history of offending. His first offence, at the age of fourteen, was burglary. He and a friend broke into their school and stole twelve laptops from the library. They damaged property to the total value of four thousand five hundred pounds. Your Honour will see from his antecedents that he was given a youth rehabilitation order. What follows is a catalogue of offending, mainly for burglary, but also for theft and for handling stolen property. It seems that the defendant has failed to learn from any of his previous sentences and he has not heeded advice from his social worker or his rehabilitation officer." Alistair paused and waited for the judge to agree with him. The judge nodded.

"Your Honour, this particular offence, committed whilst the homeowners were away for the weekend, deserves a custodial sentence. Not only did the defendant break into someone's home and steal property, including one thousand pounds in cash, but the house was ransacked, thereby pouring salt into the wounds of the traumatised victims. The victims were targeted, as the defendant knew that the house would be unoccupied during that particular weekend. This shows a significant degree of planning and organisation on the part of the defendant. This was definitely not an opportunist crime. The only saving grace is that he pleaded guilty and has asked for other burglaries to be taken into consideration when sentencing, but he has shown no remorse whatsoever for any of them. The only viable sentence, in my view, is a custodial one and the Crown would recommend a minimum term of twelve months in custody."

Alistair sat down.

"Thank you, Mr Mallory," said the judge. "Miss Thomas, what would you like to say on behalf of your client."

Jamilla, the defendant's barrister, rose and began her mitigation statement.

Robert, sitting in the second row behind Alistair and Jamilla, listened in awe to both sides of the argument. He was excited for the time when he would be taking on more and more cases of his own. Sebastian had been a great teacher, but he liked to keep control and was wary of giving Robert anything but the simplest of tasks. Alistair, on the other hand, was a different kettle of fish and had already told him that he would be giving him lots of work to do. Delegation was his middle name.

Robert thought that he would love to be a prosecuting barrister, sending the bad guys to prison right, left and centre. Although, listening to Jamilla's mitigation argument about how her client had a difficult upbringing and didn't have an adult role model to show him the ropes, but was now trying to change his ways and had been in a secure job for the past three months and had managed to find himself somewhere new to live, far away from the area where he had grown up, had more of an effect on him than he thought it would.

Either way, prosecuting or defending, Robert was looking forward to the future. His dream was to have a caseload of his own and then go home at the end of every day and talk to Jamilla about them over dinner. Maybe one day, when he stopped acting like such a dick, he would get what he wanted.

When the judge had listened to both sides and the defendant had been sentenced - twelve months in prison, suspended for two years - and the judge and the clerk had left the courtroom, Alistair and Jamilla began to gather up their papers.

"Are you happy with that result?" asked Robert.

"Yes, absolutely," said Alistair.

Robert knew that Alistair would have said yes even if the judge had given him a ten-pound fine. He never admitted that a case of his hadn't gone to plan.

"But you're thinking that it would have been better for him to have been given a prison sentence, aren't you?" asked Jamilla. She was trying not to gloat, but she was pleased with the sentence for her client.

"He'll end up there eventually," said Alistair, failing to keep a lid on his supercilious air. "There's no way in this world that he'll keep out of trouble for the next two years. People like him…"

"Morning gentlemen, not interrupting anything, am I?" said a booming voice at the side of the prosecutor's bench. "I'm glad I bumped into you, Alistair."

Jamilla thought that she saw a flash of panic on Alistair's face, before he quickly composed himself. She didn't know who this man was, and Alistair didn't introduce him to anyone, but he looked like the man she had seen him talking to in the court corridor on Wednesday. Maybe he was a reporter or something. No doubt she would find out in due course. She excused herself and made her way over to her client, who was waiting for her outside court.

"I've got another case in ten minutes," Alistair said. "I don't really have time to talk at the moment."

"You didn't reply to my text last night," said Frankie. "So, if Mohammed won't go to the mountain…"

"Like I said…"

"Look, I've just come to give you some information, that's all. I won't keep you. I can see you're busy." He looked at Robert and flashed a gold-toothed smile, as he placed a folded-up piece of paper on the desk in front of Alistair. "Just do what you can with this."

The panic returned on Alistair's face, along with a thin line of sweat on his upper lip. "Robert, would you mind running to the drinks machine and getting me a coffee, please? You'll have time before the next case, don't worry." He glanced at the large clock on the wall. "Get yourself one too."

"Yes, no problem," said Robert, taking Alistair's debit card and leaving them to it.

"You're not supposed to be in there," hissed Alistair. "Public gallery only."

He knew as soon as the words had left his mouth that Frankie wasn't happy at being told what to do. But he had had enough of him. He picked up the folded note and, without reading it, held it out to Frankie. Frankie stepped back and shook his head.

"Read it," he said venomously. "One of my men has been arrested and you need to sort it. He's in custody at Longsight, and I want him out before he gets charged."

This was the time to tell him. Alistair needed to say no. It couldn't go on like this. Frankie was never meant to encroach into his professional life like this. Their paths shouldn't be crossing in public. Their transactions used to be private. Frankie would hand over some money when Alistair went over to his house. Alistair would drive home with a stash of fifty pounds notes and a bag or two of cocaine. Job done. Nobody got hurt. Everyone was happy with the arrangement.

But now this. Two days ago, Frankie handed him money in the corridor at court and now, here he was, standing by his side right in front of the judge's bench. This was so wrong. It had to stop. Now.

"You need to leave, Frankie. I'm working. We shouldn't be seen together," said Alistair. "Now isn't the time."

"You're right. The time was last night." Frankie pressed his two hands onto the bench and leaned towards Alistair. "Answer your fucking text and I wouldn't have to chase you around the city, like I've got nothing better to do. I'm a fucking busy man. Now read the note and get it sorted, or else."

He slammed the note onto the bench and began to walk away.

Alistair heard the door to the court open and Robert returned, carrying two coffees in paper cups.

"See you, son," said Frankie, as he walked out of court. "You too, Alistair. See you soon, yeah."

Chapter Twenty
Friday

Sebastian led Robert back to his office after their lunch with Alistair.

"So, how are you feeling?" Robert asked. "Are you happy to be retiring? I know you're going to miss seeing my pretty face every day."

Sebastian laughed. "Yes, like a hole in the head," he said. "I've got mixed feelings, to be honest. I've been looking forward to this day for so long and I thought that I couldn't wait to retire, but now I'm not so sure. It all seems such an anti-climax."

"Like waking up on Boxing Day?" said Robert. "That day you've been anticipating for months is over in a flash and then what?"

"Yes, exactly that. Come and sit down and help me to sort the last of these papers." Sebastian sat at his desk. Robert pulled up a chair on the opposite side. "This advice has been done, so it can be sent back to the instructing solicitors. And that one." Alistair handed Robert two bundles of paper, each bound together with a soft pink ribbon. "Hang on, I need to sign the back page of that last one, the Crown versus McNally."

Robert passed it back to him. Alistair unwrapped it and signed the advice page with his ancient fountain pen. He re-tied the ribbon and gave it back to Robert. "Those two can go on that pile to be sent into the post." He indicated a smaller table underneath the window on which sat a small brief. Robert got up and added the two bundles to the pile.

"Well, that was a moment that went almost unnoticed," said Robert.

"What do you mean?"

"That was probably the last brief that you'll sign and tie up. What will your fountain pen do now?"

"He will sit very nicely in the top drawer of my walnut bureau at home, and be used to sign birthday cards and Christmas cards only. He's done an excellent job over the years and he deserves to be retired too." Sebastian kissed the top of his fountain pen and placed it reverently in the top pocket of his jacket. "He might write an add note for the milkman, now and then."

Robert smiled at him. He didn't want him to leave. He liked Sebastian. Not just because he was Jamilla's father, but because he was Sebastian. He didn't want to work with Alistair for the rest of his pupillage, but at least he only had a few months left, until he was on his own.

"This is a fraud case," continued Sebastian. "I'm going to pass this to Samantha. She's good with numbers, so can you put that one over there, with a post-it note on for Samantha, please. The solicitors have confirmed they are happy for her to take it."

He handed Robert another brief. Robert wrote Samantha's name on a yellow post-it note and put the brief on the floor at the side of the desk.

"I've asked James to come and collect all these later, so if they're neatly labelled, it will save him a lot of time. Would you like to be involved in the Stella Andrews case?"

"Oh, yes, please," said Robert.

"I'm happy for you to take that one. Ask Alistair for advice though, won't you? Don't be a stubborn mule. I know you can be sometimes. But this won't be listed until after your pupillage ends, so it can be yours, if you're confident enough."

The case of Stella Andrews was one that they had been working on together for the past six months, ever since it had landed on Sebastian's desk. Stella was accused of stabbing her ex-boyfriend with a large knife. He claimed was that they had had an argument in the kitchen of her small home, and she had reached for a knife and lunged at him. His statement said that he hadn't threatened her, and the attack was completely unprovoked.

Her case was that this was a complete fabrication. She claimed that the alleged victim had been stalking her for months, ever since she had broken up with him and that he sent her menacing messages and emails almost daily and regularly turned up at the estate agent's office where she worked, harassing her and shouting at her.

On the night that she supposedly stabbed him, she was out with her friends at a hen party and hadn't been home at all. She surmised that her ex had been in a fight and had been stabbed by someone else, but he was trying to blame her for pernicious reasons known only to him. Robert was looking forward to the day when he could cross-examine him about the lack of blood in her kitchen.

Sebastian had advised the instructing solicitors to collate as many witness statements from the attendees of the hen party as possible and to gather CCTV evidence, if there was any. His hope was that the evidence would be so overwhelming, that the case against her would be dropped. If it did go to court, he was confident that Robert could win.

"I'd love that," said Robert. "Thank you. I really appreciate you trusting me with this."

"Well, you know the case as well as anyone, so don't let me down."

"Of course not."

"In fact, you can start by emailing the instructing solicitors and asking where they are at with all the witness statements."

"I'll do that this afternoon," said Robert. His grin beamed at Robert. "Does this mean that I'm likely to be kept on at the end of my pupillage?"

"You know I can't answer that, but I've written my report to Verity and recommended that you should be."

Robert jumped up and grabbed Sebastian's hand, shaking it up and down enthusiastically. "Thank you so much," he said.

"It's not a cast-iron guarantee, but I'm sure you'll be fine, if you work hard between now and then."

"Thank you so much. Jamilla will be pleased."

The ringing of Sebastian's telephone saved Robert from a conversation about their rocky relationship. Sebastian wanted to tell Robert that maybe Jamilla wasn't the girl for him, after all; they were so fundamentally different and maybe he should just concentrate on his career for a while.

"Yes, he's here," said Sebastian into the phone. "Okay, I'll tell him. Thank you, James." Sebastian replaced the phone on the receiver. "James says there's a gentleman waiting to see you in reception. A friend, he thinks."

Robert knew who it was. Frankie's right-hand man, again. He had come to collect the first instalment of the loan repayment.

"I'll be right back," he said.

"Take those bundles for the post on your way down, will you?" called Sebastian, as Robert rushed out of the door.

"Yes, of course." Robert came back, picked up the briefs and ran down the corridor to his office. He hoped Samantha wasn't in. He didn't want her to see him getting the money out of the top drawer of his desk. Thankfully, she wasn't there. He opened the drawer. He carefully counted out one thousand pounds in fifty and twenty-pound notes. He put the money into an envelope and then into his jacket pocket before running down the stairs and into reception.

"He said he'd wait for you outside," said James.

Robert gave him the bundle of briefs. "Sebastian said can you put these in the post please. I'll be right back. If I'm not back within five minutes come and find me."

James laughed. "Are you serious?" Robert nodded solemnly at his friend. "You're serious, aren't you? Who is he?"

"I've got to go. I'll explain another time."

The man was waiting for him outside the door. Robert had been expecting to have to go and find him in the narrow street, where he had been dragged the other day. But this was a different man.

He was leaning against the wall of chambers, in the space between the front door and the Georgian mullioned window of the ground floor meeting room. His right leg was bent behind him, his black shiny Brogue was resting on the wall. A cigarette was held between his teeth, like Clint Eastwood in a spaghetti western. Robert didn't doubt for one minute that he was just as dangerous as a rogue cowboy.

"Robert Brierly?" he asked.

"Yes, that's me."

"Have you got the money?"

"Yes, it's right here. A thousand, like we agreed." Robert took the envelope out of his pocket and gave it to him.

"I didn't agree nothing." The man snatched the envelope and slowly counted the cash. "Right, good," he said when he had finished. "Same time next week."

He walked away. He got into the driver's seat of the same silver Mercedes that had met Robert in Sainsburys car park. It had been left idling in one of the parking bays and Robert wondered how many times it had been used for a quick getaway. The car drove off, wheels spinning conspicuously.

Robert took a minute to catch his breath and slow his breathing before he felt able to return to work. He pushed open the door to chambers and went back inside. James was on the phone. He gave him a thumbs-up sign to indicate that all was well and jogged up the stairs back to Sebastian's office. Sebastian was standing at the window, his back to the door. Robert wondered whether he had seen the transaction between him and the cowboy. He hoped not.

"He didn't get bail," said Sebastian. "Jay Harris. He's remanded in custody again until his trial."

"How…"

"A friend of mine just called me from court."

"Oh, I don't know what to say," said Robert. "I was hoping he'd get out."

"Yes, well…"

Sebastian had told him and Alistair about the threat from Jay Harris and the other day over lunch. Alistair had told Sebastian that he should have kept the instructions and done the bail application himself and then he could have been sure of his release. Sebastian said that bail was always going to be refused. It was a no-win situation.

"Could I just take ten minutes?" asked Robert. "I need to make a phone call."

Sebastian nodded. Robert knew that Sebastian was worried about Harris and the threats. Worried more for his wife than for himself. But he didn't have the head space to think about that right now. He had enough worries of his own. Empathy was a luxury for people who had nothing else to worry about.

He went back to his office and closed the door. Samantha still wasn't back, so he had the place to himself. He got out his phone and logged on to Sports Play.

He had sent a message to his dad last night and told him that he had had some unexpected bills, and could he please help out until he was paid. His dad, as he knew he would, immediately sent him a thousand pounds with his best wishes. Robert knew that he could rely on his dad. He wished he hadn't had to. He hated lying to him and telling him that he had a bill to pay. What kind of ridiculously feeble reason was that? His dad hadn't asked him what the bill was for, which made Robert feel even worse about it. But at least he had some respite and was now able to use his debit card, without having to explain to Jamilla why he had bundles of pound notes in his wallet. When he had a chance, he should take the money into the bank. Or better still, take it over to the casino to pay off some of the debt.

In the meantime, the money from his dad could help him to recoup some losses. He hadn't had a win for a while, so maybe today was the day. He transferred five hundred pounds into his online account and pressed the button for the roulette game.

Chapter Twenty-One
Friday

Verity refused to allow Sebastian to leave without some kind of send-off, albeit a hastily arranged one. She promised him a more elegant dinner at a later date, but for now, pizza and artisan beer in the trendy Castlefield bar, Dukes 92, would suffice. Sebastian had telephoned Laila and asked her to meet him there. He didn't want her to go home on her own, after spending the day with her friend. She said she would get a taxi and would be there in half an hour.

By six o'clock, most people from chambers had logged off for the weekend, grateful for the excuse not to work late, and were gathering in the outdoor bar area overlooking the Rochdale Canal. The warm weather that had been promised earlier in the week had retreated and yet again Manchester was enveloped in a grey cloud, but nobody bothered. As long as it didn't rain, they were happy to brave the outdoors, having been couped up inside, either at court or in chambers, all day.

As soon as Laila arrived, Samantha tapped her glass with the handle of a spoon to get everyone's attention. "Quiet please, everyone! Quiet please!" She shouted above the chatter and waited for everyone to stop talking. "I'd like to say a few words on behalf of everyone at chambers. Sebastian, you have been a much-loved part of the team, and we are all really sorry to see the back of you…I mean, sorry to see you go." There was a murmur of polite laughter. "The newer members of chambers may not know, but Sebastian was my pupil master and ..."

"And that's why you lose so many of your cases," heckled Alistair. Everyone laughed again and Robert flicked his ear. Alistair pretended that he was in great pain and held a hand over his 'wounded' ear, laughing along with everyone else. But Samantha then saw his face suddenly turn serious. She watched as he glanced over at the door to the bar on his right and followed his gaze.

A tall man, early fifties, dark hair with a speckling of grey, wearing an expensive looking suit had just walked into the outside bar area and for some reason, Alistair had noticed and seemed unsettled. The man was followed by a much younger looking woman with hair the colour of a chestnut mare that fell in waves down her back, almost to her waist. Her bright red dress was at odds with the sea of gun-metal grey, navy blue and black formal suits that everyone else was wearing.

Samantha saw the man raise his arm high in the air and wave in greeting and nod towards Alistair. Who was he? Samantha had never seen him, or his wife/girlfriend before, but Alistair seemed to know him. Then it occurred to her. Was this the man who supplied cocaine to Alistair? He must be. If you were to ask anyone to paint a picture of a drug dealer, they would draw someone like him, she thought. Someone with flashy clothes and a flashy watch and an equally flashy female next to him. And if it walks like a duck and sounds like a duck, then it's a duck, isn't it?

"Anyway," she continued. "Sebastian was a wonderful mentor to me, and I know he has been equally invaluable to Robert, and we will both miss you very much, as I'm sure everyone else will, too."

As Samantha joined in with the round of applause, she looked again at Alistair, who by now had recovered his equilibrium and was looking as relaxed as ever. He'd better not buy any cocaine off that guy, she thought. Surely, he wouldn't be so stupid as to do something like that in public? Not in front of his work colleagues and the Head of Chambers.

Samantha tapped her glass again and the applause died down. "So, Sebastian, if you'd like to come over to me, please. You, too, Laila." Sebastian and Laila, holding tightly to each other's hand, made their way through the small crowd and stood next to Samantha, who was holding a pink envelope that she had taken out of her handbag. "We've had a little whip round and gathered up all the coins from under the sofas in reception and I'd like to present you with this gift, from everyone at chambers who loves you."

More applause accompanied Sebastian's and Laila's thanks as they took the envelope from Samantha and opened it. Samantha wasn't paying much attention to Sebastian's thank you speech, as she was concentrating on watching her husband. His eyes had followed the gangster-looking man, who was now sitting at a table with another couple. Although Alistair appeared to be playing it cool, she knew him well enough to know that the presence of this man was bothering him. Why? She didn't know, but she was going to find out.

As Sebastian thanked everyone for their kind wishes and said that they couldn't wait to stay at the hotel in Paris that had very generously been booked for them for two nights in July, along with the return flights and breakfast each morning, and Laila dabbed at her eyes with a tissue and received a hug and a large glass of wine from Verity, Samantha watched her husband take his phone out of his pocket, open it, read something on the screen and look over at the gangster. A look of sudden fury had overtaken the smile that was present a moment ago.

She looked across at the gangster's table. He looked directly at Alistair, grinned at him and raised his glass, in the same way that he had raised his arm a few moments ago. There was no doubt about it. They knew each other.

Alistair's fingers jabbed at his phone. He looked at Samantha as he put his phone away in his pocket. A guilty look, like a small boy who has been caught eating his sister's birthday cake before the candles had been blown out. He smiled at her, looking slightly abashed, albeit just for a second.

She looked again at the gangster, who was reading something on his phone. Were he and Alistair messaging each other? Blood rushed to the gangster's face, and it was suddenly the colour of his girlfriend's dress. He tried to stand, but his girlfriend pulled at the sleeve of his jacket and whispered something in his ear. He sat back down, swiping her hand away. He tipped his head back and emptied the contents of his glass – vodka or something similar - down his throat before bashing the glass back down onto the table.

She caught Jamilla's eyes across the crowd. She had seen it too. She was frowning and looking across at the gangster. "Who is he?" Jamilla mouthed to her.

Samantha shrugged her shoulders and made her way over to Alistair.

"Do you want to tell me what's going on?" asked Samantha, as she reached Alistair's side. "Who's that man?"

"It's Frankie, the person that you thought was a woman when he messaged me at the gym last night."

"I knew it. He looks a right dodgy character. You're not going to buy anything from him, are you?"

"Sshh, of course not. Just ignore him. I'm trying to," said Alistair, turning around so that his back was now to Frankie's table.

A sudden clap of thunder, followed by large drops of rain, forced everyone to rush indoors. Glasses and pizzas were hastily collected off the tables and taken into the bar, which thankfully wasn't too overcrowded. Samantha was whisked away by Jamilla into the toilets, ostensibly to repair any damage to their hair and make-up but in reality to get the lowdown on the man that Alistair didn't seem too pleased to keep bumping into. Twice at court, and now here, and each time Alistair wore an expression that was a mixture of fear, anxiousness and anger. Whoever this man was, Jamilla could tell that he certainly wasn't a welcome friend.

"Mens' room, now," Frankie said in Alistair's ear, as he walked next to him.

Alistair kept the smile plastered to his face in case anyone was looking. He wasn't scared. He was ready for this overdue conversation. Frankie needed to be told, in no uncertain terms, that his behaviour was out of order.

As Alistair walked towards the men's bathroom, Frankie pulled him back and pushed him into the single disabled toilet. Just the two of them. He locked the door.

"You can't fucking say no to me. Who do you think you are?" he said. He had his back to the door, blocking the exit.

"I can and I have," said Alistair. "What did you think, that this arrangement is going to carry on for the rest of my working life? It was bound to come to an end sooner or later and before either of us gets arrested would be preferable to me."

"And why would we get arrested? Have you snitched to someone?"

"Snitched?" Alistair laughed. "I'm not a fucking twelve-year-old, Frankie. I'm not going to snitch. I've got as much to lose as you have, but I've had enough."

"I'll tell you when you've had enough."

"No, you won't!" Alistair shouted suddenly. Whatever fear that had previously been present was now replaced by anger and a powerful desire for self-preservation. "I'll tell you when I've had enough." He stepped forward and was surprised when Frankie stepped back, until he could go no further, and his back was against the sink.

Alistair was expecting to be punched at any minute. To be forewarned is to be forearmed. He was slowly gathering strength. "I've spoken to my friend in the CPS, and he wants to stop too, so I'm sorry about your friend who got arrested the other day, but there's nothing we can do to help you. You're on your own."

"You don't know who you're messing with," said Frankie. "You're really fucking this up, you know that, don't you? You're going to live to regret this."

"No, I'm not Frankie. I'm not scared of you. Hit me if you want to. You look like you're going to burst a blood vessel unless you take your frustration out on someone. But listen to this." Alistair leaned in close to Frankie's face. "I can hit back too. You're not the only man around here. Now, leave me the fuck alone." He unlocked the door and walked back into the bar.

Two hours later, Alistair and Samantha left the bar, leaving their good wishes with Sebastian and Laila and promising to keep in touch with him. Sebastian told them that he was meeting his sister at chambers next Friday and taking her for lunch, and said that he would say hello, if they were around.

"Is everything okay?" asked Samantha as soon as they left the bar. "I didn't want to ask you about Frankie while we were still in there, but he didn't look happy. You don't owe him money, or anything, do you?"

"No, of course not. Don't worry," said Alistair. "I won't be having any more dealings with him."

"Really? That's good news. I don't like the look of him. I'm sure all drug dealers are the same..."

"How do you know he's a drug dealer?"

"Because you buy cocaine from him, don't you? So, he's a drug dealer."

"Oh, I didn't class him as a dealer, but I know what you mean." Frankie was the most successful drug dealer that Alistair had ever come across. The mansion he lived in; the holidays he went on; the cars he drove; the nightclubs he owned and the dozens of men who worked for him were all signs of a successful man. But Alistair didn't want Samantha to think that he knew more about him than he did.

"Alistair," she said. "I don't want to tell you what to do, but I've got to say this. I don't want you to buy cocaine anymore. Not from him. Not from anyone. I don't want you to engage with people like him. He looks dangerous."

"I told him I didn't want any more stuff and he was absolutely fine. End of." Alistair could feel his temper rising. First Frankie and now Samantha telling him what to do. Why couldn't they both leave him alone?

"Okay, that's good."

"So, let's change the subject," said Alistair, anxious to talk about anything else except Frankie Byrne. "Have you got much on next week?"

"Just a couple of things," said Samantha. "I've got a conference with Olivia Stevenson on Tuesday."

"The murder charge? And are you going to tell her to plead guilty like I told you to?"

"No, absolutely not," said Samantha.

"Fucking unreal. The CPS will chew you up and spit you out. You're making a big mistake."

"Alistair, I can make my own decisions about my own cases, you know. I've discussed it with Jamilla, and we have both…"

"Of course, if you want to take Jamilla's advice instead of mine, fine. Don't bother asking me about it again."

"Alistair! Okay fine, I won't." Samantha wished that they were at home. She had a sudden urge to throw something at Alistair or, at the very least, slam a door or two. But they were in public. The car park was overseen by the bar, so she restrained herself. But when Alistair mumbled that she was a fucking idiot, that was the last straw. She slammed the car door as hard as she could when she got in. She knew he'd hate his prize possession to be treated so roughly.

As they drove home, she told herself not to cry. She didn't want him to know that he had upset her again. She told herself that it was his frustration about Frankie that he was taking out on her. He didn't mean it.

Their third car journey in a week was spent in frosty silence.

Chapter Twenty-Two
Five Days Before the Shooting - Sunday

Samantha opened her eyes.

She didn't know where she was. The room was dark. Tiny shafts of daylight shone between the crack in the curtains. Where the fuck was she? Her head felt groggy, as though she was waking up with a terrible hangover after only a couple of hours sleep. She had no recollection of last night. She hadn't planned to have any alcohol, but she must have changed her mind.

Was this Laura's house? Yes, it must be Laura's. She had recently moved house and she hadn't invited anyone over yet. She was waiting for a new dining table to be delivered and had promised to have a huge party as soon as it arrived. Laura loved a party and moving house was as good an excuse as any.

Samantha turned over in bed and lifted herself up onto her elbows. Alistair wasn't by her side, but then again, he wouldn't be. She looked over at the chest of drawers in the far corner of the room for her phone, but it wasn't there. She must have left her handbag downstairs.

Fuck! Her sister would kill her for not turning up last night. And she couldn't begin to contemplate what Alistair would say when he realised how drunk she had been. Why couldn't she remember anything? Someone must have spiked her drink. That was the only explanation for the temporary (or she hoped it was temporary) memory loss. She would give Alistair a call as soon as she found her phone downstairs. If she smothered him with apologies, he would be fine. He hadn't wanted to go to her sister's for dinner anyway. No doubt he had had a relaxing night in with his PlayStation, takeaway food and beer.

Oh God, poor Beth. All that food that she would have prepared. She'd have to go round on her way home and explain what happened. Thankfully, Beth was more understanding than Alistair and would probably laugh. It was so unlike Samantha to get so drunk. She had never done anything like that, ever. Not even on her hen party. Beth would think it was hilarious.

She lay back on the pillow as she tried to recall the details of her afternoon shopping trip and late lunch in Manchester with her old friends. "Are you staying for one more drink?" Chloe had asked her, catching her surreptitiously looking at her watch. "Laura and I are up for one. Please, just one more?" Chloe had waved the cocktail menu towards her. "They do espresso martinis. I know you can't resist them."

"No, I've got to go," she had said. "I haven't seen Beth and Sarah for ages, and I don't want to be late. We'll do this again soon though."

She remembered kissing her two friends and telling them to have a good time. She remembered walking the short distance from Castlefield down Deansgate to her car. She had parked it in the car park behind chambers. She had felt perfectly fine at that point. Completely sober. She had only had one alcoholic drink, because she was driving. So, what had happened? Surely, she wouldn't have changed her mind and gone back to her friends and the promise of an espresso martini? She couldn't remember doing that.

She closed her eyes as she tried to re-trace her steps in her mind. Had she left the bar when she said goodbye, or did she stay for a cocktail after all? Fragmented memories came to her slowly, fighting their way through the haze in her brain. She was sure that she hadn't stayed for another drink. She could remember walking into St. John Street, down the narrow street at the side of chambers and into the car park. Both of her hands had been full of shopping bags, so when she felt drizzly rain on her face halfway down Deansgate, she had put her bags down on the floor, fastened her Burberry jacket up to her neck, fighting with the breeze as she did so, picked up her bags and quickened her pace.

Yes, she had definitely left the bar and walked away. She remembered putting her head down and walking quickly, cursing the rain as she did so. She had spent ages straightening her hair yesterday morning and she had been worried that the rain would frizz it up again in no time.

Then the funny thing was, try as she might, she couldn't remember reaching her car. Her mind was completely blank from the moment that it had started to rain.

She tried to quell the panic that was rising in her chest. Wherever she was, it was clear that Alistair wasn't here, and he would no doubt be worried about her. She needed to find her phone and let him know that she would be home as soon as possible. She also needed to send an apologetic message to Beth and tell her she would come over for a much-needed coffee later.

She pushed back the quilt and climbed out of bed. She was dressed in her bra and knickers. Her t-shirt and jeans that she had been wearing yesterday afternoon were neatly folded on the floor. One of her friends - presumably Laura, if that's whose house she was in - must have put her to bed.

She got dressed quickly, went over to the window and pulled back the curtains. It was just beginning to get light, so she calculated it was around six a.m. She couldn't hear a sound from anywhere in the house. Everyone else must still be asleep. She stared out of the window, trying to guess where Laura's new house was. She hadn't told her that she had such a gorgeous rural view. Lucky her! There was no sign of a road, just a long garden and beyond that, a huge field with a small herd of cows, who were already awake and grazing. To the left, she could see an old church and a churchyard sprinkled with ancient trees.

She tip-toed softly to the door and pulled on the handle. It didn't open. She didn't want to wake anyone, but she was bursting for the toilet, so she tried again, rattling the handle loudly and with more force. It still didn't open.

She put her ear to the door. There was no sound. Nobody seemed to have heard her.

She knocked on the door. She had no choice. She needed to get out. "Hello! Laura! Are you there?" She waited for a moment, then shouted again, "Laura! Chloe! Is anyone there?" She put her ear to the door and was relieved to hear footsteps and the rattling of the door handle. "Oh, thank God, I thought….Oh, hello. Who are you?"

The door was opened by a man, who stood with the key to the door in his hand. He didn't reply. Samantha's brain fog was still clouding her thoughts and it took a few seconds for her to work out what was going on. She looked at the man's hand, then at the door and noticed, for the first time, that it had a lock.

"Have I been locked in?" she asked. She smiled, nervously at the stranger, presuming that the door had been locked accidentally. "I'm Samantha, Laura's friend." It was always awkward meeting your friend's new boyfriend for the first time, especially if the friend in question wasn't around to help with the flow of the conversation. This guy was going to be hard work, Samantha could tell instantly. Laura hadn't said that he was the strong silent type. She hoped that Laura would be getting up soon.

The man was still blocking her way. And still not smiling. This is awkward, she thought.

"If I could…could you point me in the direction of the bathroom please?" asked Samantha.

The man looked worried. Panicked. A little manic. Not at all calm and not at all friendly. Samantha noticed that his forehead was glistening with sweat, and he had large sweat marks under both arms of his short-sleeved pale blue shirt. Maybe he was still drunk. Or high. His right arm was covered in a sleeve tattoo. A black zig-zag pattern emerged from his shirt sleeve and ended at his wrist. There was a smaller tattoo on his left forearm Samantha thought she could make out the word 'Emma', amongst the pattern, but she wasn't sure. That will be embarrassing for Laura, if this guy sticks around, she thought. Having an ex-girlfriend's name shoved in your face day after day wasn't the ideal situation. If Laura was called Gemma, it wouldn't be too bad, he could simply add a G to the tattoo. But even the most talented tattoo artist couldn't make 'Emma' into 'Laura'.

"The bathroom's there," he said, pointing to a closed door across the landing.

"Thank you," she said.

Samantha flicked on the bathroom light. She closed and locked the door behind her. After she had used the toilet, she stared at her reflection in the bathroom mirror, as she washed her hands. She hadn't worn much makeup yesterday afternoon, but there were some traces of mascara around her eyes. She wiped at them with a wet finger and then dabbed her face with toilet roll. There were no towels anywhere.

When she opened the bathroom door, the man was still there. Waiting for her with his arms crossed. She smiled at him, unsure of what to say. Should she offer to make him some coffee, or would he make his own when he came down? Maybe she should just have some water and then ring for a taxi.

"Oh sorry, I didn't know you were waiting, sorry," she said, stepping to one side so that he could go into the bathroom.

"Stop fucking talking, woman!"

"What?"

"Get back in there!" The man grabbed her arm and pulled her towards the bedroom.

"What are you doing? Get off me!" She pulled at his fingers which were gripping her upper arm tightly. She knew that his fingertips would leave a bruise. Her skin was as delicate as a peach. Who was this guy and who the hell did he think he was talking to? Alistair would kill him when she told him about this. "Get off my arm! Laura! Laura! Where are you?" Samantha shouted for her friend, but there was no answer.

At the threshold of the bedroom, he pushed her in roughly. She stumbled onto her knees. The door closed behind her, and she heard the key turned in the lock. She jumped up and ran to the door.

"Let me out!" she screamed, as she rattled the door handle. She hammered on the door with both fists.

"Stop that!"

She stopped and stepped back. She stared at the closed door, trying to process what was going on.

"Why have you locked me in? Where's Laura?" she asked. Then, "Who are you?" she screamed. She wasn't sure that she wanted the answer to the last question.

Her mind was racing at a hundred miles an hour. Last week she had watched a horror film, where a group of crazy people ran around a small town in America and kidnapped all the young women, with the intention of keeping them captive and breeding from them. Samantha's logical mind told her that that type of thing only happened in films. "Laura!" she shouted again. "If this is a joke, it isn't funny. I need to get home. Alistair will be worried about me. Let me out!" She banged on the door again.

"Shut up!" He shouted suddenly, through the door. "If you know what's good for you, you'll shut the fuck up!

Samantha shrank back against the wall. She sank to the floor and hugged her knees to her chest with her arms, taking deep breaths in an attempt to slow her racing heart. "Who are you?" she whispered to herself.

She couldn't hear any receding footsteps and assumed that he was still on the other side of the door. Her heart was pounding out of her chest and cold sweat seeped from every pore. Was this the man who had spiked her drink? But even if that had happened, she would have been with her friends, wouldn't she? Why hadn't they looked after her? How she had got into this house, she had no idea, but she needed to get out. Now. It was clear that this wasn't where Laura lived. She jumped up and ran to the door.

"Let me out!" she shouted. "I'll scream."

She could hear the lock turn again in the door.

She took a deep breath.

Suddenly he was in front of her, his large hand covering her mouth. He squeezed his fingers into her cheeks. She could tell he had recently had garlic. And beer. She blinked and tears flowed down her face.

"Don't even think about it," he said, his wide, wild eyes staring into hers. Then he released her and turned back to the door. "You know what," he said, suddenly turning to her again, "Do it! Scream if you want to! Nobody will hear you. There are no neighbours for miles."

She didn't know whether to believe him or not. He could be bluffing. But what did she have to lose? She needed to try something. Someone had to help her. She took a deep breath and screamed as loud as she could.

Then she waited.

He stood watching her.

Nobody came.

He walked out of the room and closed the door behind him. Samantha heard the door lock, again. She climbed onto the bed and cried into the pillow.

Chapter Twenty-Three
Sunday

Samantha had hammered on the door until her hands were sore. She had screamed until her throat was sore. But it had made no difference. She couldn't see how to get out of this room. She contemplated smashing the glass in the window and jumping out, but what would she smash it with? There was no furniture except for the bed and an old pine chest of drawers, neither of which she would be able to pick up and throw, not in a month of Sundays. And if she did jump out, she would probably kill herself in the fall.

Now, as she lay on the bed, she could hear the man moving about downstairs and the muffled sound of the TV. Where the fuck was she? And who was the psycho-kidnapper? Was this his house? Did he live here? And if so, who with? Was it Emma, the woman whose name was permanently inked into his arm? It didn't seem as though a woman's touch had been sprinkled around the place - the lack of towels in the bathroom and the horrible brown velour curtains hanging across the window were evidence of that. No woman in her right mind would choose those, unless she was stuck in a nineteen seventies time warp. But the bedding was clean, she was grateful for that much.

In the film she had watched last week, the victims were held in a dark and cockroach-infested cellar drug den. This house didn't look to be a typical drug den, not that she had ever been in one, but she had seen them in films. This seemed to be a normal family house. Although she was pretty certain that the family weren't here now. If they were, nobody had rushed to investigate when she had screamed.

The bedroom walls were covered in woodchip wallpaper, painted a horrible dark mustard yellow colour. It hadn't been decorated for a very long time. But the bathroom looked like it had been freshly painted. She wondered whether the man downstairs had painted it. He looked like the DIY sort. Practical. Big Muscles and callused hands. Maybe he and his paintbrush would make their way around the house, one room at a time.

She thought of her own bedroom at home and the hours she had spent flicking through Pinterest and the Farrow and Ball website before finally settling on neutral tones – 'Skimming Stone' on three walls and 'Elephant's Breath' on the wall behind their huge, buttoned headboard. The skirting boards, door and window frames were 'Strong White'. When the decorator had finished and she had finally been able to take up the dust covers and put the new White Company cotton bedding on the bed, she had led Alistair into the room by his hand. "Isn't it beautiful?" she had said, holding her arm aloft and moving it in an arc across the room, as though she was a stage director and the walls, the bedding and the plethora of mixed-sized cushions on the bed were the actors, waiting to take their final bow to an appreciative audience.

"The cat will ruin that," he said, pointing to the soft grey cashmere throw at the bottom of the bed.

"Well, we'll have to make sure we keep the bedroom door closed, won't we?" she had said, trying not to let him ruin her mood.

Tears came again at the thought of her home, her husband and her beloved cat. Yes, Alistair was sometimes acerbic and very often thoughtless, but she loved him. She wondered whether he would remember to feed the cat this morning. Would he be up by now? Yes, of course he would. He would be frantic, wouldn't he? He didn't know where she was. He would have called the police by now and reported her missing when she hadn't answered the dozens of calls he would surely have made to her phone.

She needed to get out of this room and find her bag, then she could call him herself. Let him know that she was alive, if not entirely safe and well.

Maybe the next time the man came to the room, she could run out. She could dodge under his grip and race down the stairs to freedom. How hard could it be? He might be big and muscly, but she was lithe and quick. He had power, but she had speed.

But she knew that the reality was that it wouldn't be that easy. She had no idea where the front door was and whether it would be locked. And if she did escape, what then? He would run after her, surely.

But there had to be something she could do. She couldn't just lie in this room. She couldn't give up.

She tried to think clearly, but her thoughts were a jumbled mess. As the minutes slowly plodded by, she waivered between being incensed one minute and then being beyond scared the next. She assumed that if the man planned to kill her, he would have done so by now. That gave her hope. Had she been kidnapped? Well, that seemed pretty obvious. He must have known that she had money. If he had followed her to the car park at the back of chambers, he would have known that she was a barrister. Only people who worked there could use the car park. Plus, her car was an obvious status symbol.

Why hadn't he just taken the car? It was worth tens of thousands. She would have given him the keys and he could have sold it on the black market. This must be money-driven. Most crimes were. If he wanted to claim ransom money, then he wouldn't harm her, would he? She would need to be delivered back to Alistair safe and sound. Wasn't that usually the deal?

She tried to remember how many police dramas she had seen on TV. She couldn't remember a kidnap one in particular, but she told herself that it would end well. She would be okay. She would just need to be patient and calm and wait it out until Alistair paid the ransom money.

She tried to relax and for a moment, she felt slightly more optimistic, imagining Alistair discussing the best rescue method with the police. They would be able to trace the whereabouts of her phone, wouldn't they? She didn't have one of those location apps, but nevertheless, they could find her approximate area and come and find her. Sniffer dogs would be sent out, after sniffing one of her unwashed jumpers. She wondered which one Alistair would choose to give them. Not her new one from Reiss, she hoped. She didn't want it covered in dog hairs.

The kidnappers had probably told him not to contact the police. But he would do. He wouldn't take any notice of them. He wouldn't deal with this alone. Any minute now, the police would be here, and she would be safe.

For now, she needed to stay calm and simply wait.

*

After what felt like hours, Samantha could wait no longer. She needed a drink and some food.

"Hello!" She screamed at the locked door. "Is anyone there? I need a drink."

She banged three times on the wooden door.

She heard footsteps coming up the stairs. The door opened. There he was, standing in the doorway. His wild eyes flicked around the room, from left to right. Samantha wondered whether he had taken some kind of drug. Was he evil, or was he just insane? He must be both, because normal people didn't kidnap women and lock them in a bedroom, did they?

"Did you take my clothes off me?" she asked. It suddenly occurred to her that he must have done. It wasn't Laura who had lovingly taken care of her and laid her gently down on the bed. She wasn't in Laura's new house. She was trapped with this stranger, who must have drugged her or spiked her drink or something. "You fucking pervert. You undressed me! You filthy bastard!"

She slammed one fist into his chest as hard as she could. The other one reached up to his face, intending to punch him in the eye socket. She imagined that he would cry out in pain and hold his hands to his face. Later, he would be blessed with a bruise the size of Cornwall, the cause of which he would struggle to explain to Emma, whoever she was.

But it didn't work like that.

He grabbed her hand and twisted it. "Don't push it," he said. "I have been nice to you so far, but don't scream at me."

"Are you joking? This is being nice to me? Locking me in a room…" Samantha was silenced by the punch to the side of her head. Her fall to the floor was prevented by the fact that he still had hold of her wrist.

"I said don't push it. If you behave, I won't hurt you."

Samantha closed her mouth. He released her and she scrambled to the edge of the bed. She sat down, tears streaming down her face. She wanted to ask him why she was there, what his intentions were and whether someone had contacted Alistair, but fear prevented the words from forming. She wanted to kick him, spit at him and scream until her throat hurt. But for the moment, she kept silent.

"I'll get you a drink," he said. "Just be quiet and you won't get hurt." He looked towards the window. "And you can't escape, so don't think about it. The window doesn't open. It's locked."

"Have you got my phone?" she managed to ask as he was leaving, fresh tears appearing.

"Yes, it's downstairs."

"Have you phoned my husband?"

"Stop with the fucking questions," he barked at her. "When you need to know something, you'll be told. Until then keep it shut." He ran his thumb and forefinger across his mouth, as though zipping it shut and left the room.

Chapter Twenty-Four
Sunday

After the church service, the vicar opened the huge wooden doors of St. Peter's Church and allowed the children of the congregation to spill out into the churchyard. They burst into the open air with the power of fighter jets and raced across the grass to the trees, spilling past the graves at the back of the church. Elsie followed them, her cup of tea in her hand and made her way over to Stanley's grave.

"Oh Stanley," she said, "Those poor choir members were shivering. It's freezing cold in there. I don't know why they insisted on building churches with their main windows facing east. Facing south to catch the sun would have been a much better idea. Jesus wouldn't have minded, would he? He wouldn't want our old bones to get cold. Anyway, I've done my bit for today. I made the tea for those who wanted it at the end. Everyone's perished, so I don't think anyone said no today. The pianist came over rubbing his hands together, they were so cold. I don't think he's taken a sip of his tea; he's just using it as a hand warmer." She laughed at the thought of their old pianist, Trevor, using his cup like a hot water bottle, clutching it for dear life. "I felt thoroughly ashamed of the lack of heating, I've got to say, Stanley. It's not a very warm welcome for our new family, is it? A very cold welcome in fact. And there I was last week, saying what a good thing it was that the boiler has become defunct at the beginning of the warm weather, rather than in the middle of winter. How wrong could I be?"

"Who're you talking to?" Elsie turned around and saw a little girl, about four or five, staring at her quizzically.

"My husband, Stanley," said Elsie.

"Where's Stanley?" asked the little girl.

"Daisy, there you are. I've been looking for you everywhere. You shouldn't run off like that." Her young mother, looking harassed, visibly sighed in relief when she spotted her daughter. She walked over and grabbed hold of her hand.

"It's Emma, isn't it?" asked Elsie. "Lisa, the vicar, told me that you've just moved here?"

"Yes, last month. Hello." Emma shook hands with Elsie and then rested her hand on her daughter's head. "And this is Daisy. I still haven't found my other one. I turned my back, and they were gone."

"Don't worry, don't worry," said Elsie, waving her arm around to indicate the churchyard. "It's perfectly safe here. There's an extremely high wall around the whole of the garden. They won't come to any harm. The first thing all the children do at the end of the service is escape outside. I wish we were allowed to run from the sermons sometimes, but being grown up doesn't give us such a privilege, does it?" She held her hand to her mouth as though ashamed of her supposed blasphemy.

"No, I don't suppose it does," said Emma.

"Mummy, can I go and play?" asked Daisy.

"Yes, okay. Not for long though. Go and find Michael, will you?"

"Shall we have a sit-down?" asked Elsie, pointing over to a bench under a large oak tree. "We can watch the children from there." She could see that Emma wouldn't properly relax if she couldn't see her brood. She knew that their village was as safe as houses, but Emma, being new to the area, still had her suburban anxieties, wearing her down.

As they sipped their tea, Elsie explained that Stanley had died suddenly of a heart attack a year ago and that was his grave over there, which she liked to visit and chat to at least once a day. Keeping contact with him was keeping her sane, she explained, so that she didn't miss him quite so much. Emma told her that her husband was called Jake. He was lucky to be alive right now, having been involved in a road accident just a few days after they moved house. Not knowing the country roads very well, he had taken a corner too fast and had careered into a tree. He walked away with bruises, nothing more than that, and a quite painful whiplash, but their old car hadn't survived.

Elsie said that she had heard about the accident. Nothing in their village went unnoticed, usually. "I've seen the state of the tree," she said. "He really was lucky, wasn't he?"

"Well, that's what the doctors said, yes," said Emma. "Of course, being lucky would be arriving home having not been in an accident at all, or having fully comprehensive insurance, which we don't have."

"Oh dear," said Elsie. "Yes, that's a bit of bad luck, isn't it?"

Emma nodded, raising her eyebrows and rolling her eyes at the same time, which Elsie took to mean that the husband had arranged the car insurance and tried to save a few pennies by not insuring it properly. If she was reading the situation correctly, this had probably caused a few harsh words between the young couple.

"So, for now, we're walking everywhere. Good job the summer's on its way, eh?" She smiled but Elsie could see her eyes glistening with the start of tears. She didn't want to ask why they hadn't bought another car yet, as it was obvious that they didn't have the money for one. Elsie reached into her handbag for a tissue and passed it to Emma, who took it and silently dabbed at her eyes.

"Well, you're going to love it round here," she said, anxious to change the subject. "The countryside really is the best place for children. I'm sure they'll love watching all the wildlife and the farm animals."

"Yes, they will, they love animals," said Emma, beginning to cheer.

"Well, you can tell them that if they sit quietly in the churchyard, they might see our local sparrow hawk. Last night it had a bit of an adventure. It attacked a pigeon on the top of the church roof. There was a flutter of wings for at least a minute, but then the pigeon escaped and flew onto the top of the vicarage and the hawk flew off in the other direction! I have never known a hawk to not kill its prey, once it had hold of it, so I can only assume that it was a young one and didn't quite know what to do. It was weird how much noise the pigeon made with its wings when it flew off and the hawk was absolutely silent."

"Wow, the children would have loved to see that."

"Well, there you go, there's always something beautiful in each day, isn't there?"

Emma smiled and nodded, although any beauty around her was often rendered invisible by the cloud of their worsening finances. All she could see was the dark tunnel of debt that they were heading for.

Moving from Manchester to the Lancashire countryside was meant to be their new start. A smaller house meant a smaller mortgage and smaller heating bills, but so far, they hadn't seen any improvement in their bank account. Moving house was so expensive and now, without a car, her life was extremely difficult. The nearest big supermarket was over six miles away and the corner shop in the village, lovely as it was, had a limited stock and what they had was twice the price of anywhere else.

But as she gathered her children and wrapped them in their coats, ready for the walk home, she told herself that at least her husband was alive and well. For that, she felt lucky.

Last night he had told her that he had a new job. Just something temporary. A cash-in-hand kind of job. The downside was that he had to stay overnight for a few nights. But it was worth it, he had said, because it paid well. He said that a stack of money would be in his hand before the end of next week. She didn't entirely trust that everything was above board. He hadn't mentioned that the job had come via his cousin, Frankie, but it probably had. She knew not to ask too many questions. This was precisely what they were trying to escape from. Dodgy deals, late-night jobs and the police knocking on her door were meant to be something of the past. But what choice did they have? As he left for work yesterday, telling her that he would be home in a few days, she had buried her head in the sand and wished him luck with his new job.

Chapter Twenty-Five
Sunday

Samantha slept fitfully for an hour or so. When she woke, for a fraction of a second, she forgot where she was and was confused when she wasn't in her own bedroom, with Alistair by her side in their king-sized bed. Then, she sobbed and screamed into the pillow.

She longed for her whisper-soft Egyptian cotton quilt cover and her feather pillows. She longed for the Jo Malone candle that she lit every night for half an hour before they went to sleep. Its familiar lime, basil and mandarin scent soothed her soul and helped her to drift off to sleep. But more than anything, she longed for Alistair. She wanted to curl her body against his back; the little spoon to his big spoon. She wanted to feel his warm body.

Why wasn't he coming to rescue her? They must have told him where she was by now. Someone must know where she was.

She didn't want to keep crying, but she couldn't stop the tears. She didn't have any tissues, so she wiped her face on the shoulder of her t-shirt, hoping that the stain would wash out. It was one of her favourite t-shirts, from Pink in Victoria's Secret. It was a comforting one. One that she wore when she wanted to be relaxed and casual. It seemed really important to her right now that she would be able to wash away the evidence of this terrible ordeal. Surely, she wouldn't be here much longer.

She focused on her washing machine in their narrow utility room at home. As soon as she got home, she would put the t-shirt inside the machine, maybe with a couple of towels from the bathroom and the hand towel from the downstairs loo. She would throw one of the liquid pods into the drum, close the door and switch the machine to a forty-degree cycle. She would wait until she heard the click of the door and the first rush of the water before she walked away, as she always does, into the kitchen to make herself a coffee.

If she could manifest it, she could live it. That's how it worked, right?

But the more she thought about home, the more she panicked. The life that she loved, seemed so far away. She couldn't quite believe that only yesterday she had been at home, safe. Would she ever get out of here? Would she ever live that life again? Her precious life.

She would never take anything for granted again. She would never be bored by domestic tasks again. Her thoughts flitted back to Alistair. Her darling husband. Her bad-tempered, cantankerous and often stubborn husband. She loved him and she missed him.

What was he doing right now? Had he thought about his shirts? They would need to be washed ready for work on Monday. Was that tomorrow? She wasn't sure what day it was.

How was he managing without her? She could see him in the utility room, pressing his face into her clothes and breathing in her scent, before he threw them into the machine. No! That wouldn't happen. He didn't know one end of the washing machine from the other. He wouldn't be able to manage without her.

What about her parents? Her sister? How would they manage? Her poor mum would miss her dreadfully. They all would. Her dad would be strong and stoical, being the strength that her mum needed. But she knew that he would be crying inside.

Fear and dread rushed through her veins with every breath and every thought. She told herself that she wasn't going to die. She needn't worry about how everyone was going to cope without her, because they wouldn't have to. She would be home soon.

This would be over before she knew it.

Her memory had started to return, slowly. Flashes of yesterday, of strong arms grabbing her, her mouth being covered by a cloth and a smell that reminded her of the dentist's chair and someone forcing her into the boot of a strange car, increased her fear as she relived every terrifying moment. Her car was left abandoned in the car park at chambers. Nobody would see it until tomorrow morning. She wondered whether the man had touched the car and whether he would have left any fingerprints. But, even if he had, that wouldn't help to find her, would it?

She was lost. She might not ever be found.

She began to pray, asking God to help her. She promised to go to church and live a Christian life, if He would just get her out of this nightmare. She asked him to strike down the lunatic stranger downstairs and send him straight to Hell. Give him a heart attack or bring a storm with fatal blows of lightning to end his life. Anything would do. However, first, she would need to find a way to get herself out of here. As she closed her eyes to pray again, hoping that God would forgive her for her lifetime non-attendance at church, she heard footsteps coming up the stairs.

He was outside the room.

He unlocked the door and pushed it open. He was holding a large mug of coffee, which he put down on the chest of drawers. "I'll get you a ham sandwich," he said, as though she was a guest in his house.

"Don't bother," she said. She immediately regretted opening her mouth and didn't know why she had been so stupid. Fear was making her bold. Her boldness would make him angry. The side of her head was still smarting from the punch he had given to her earlier. She anticipated another one, but he surprised her by remaining calm.

"You one of those vegans?" he asked. "I bet you are. You don't look like the type to eat ham."

"How do you know what I eat and don't eat?" she said. "You don't know anything about me."

As soon as she said it, she knew that wouldn't be true. Of course, he must know something about her. Women didn't get abducted off the street for no reason, unless they had been targeted. He must know that she and Alistair are well off.

The stranger laughed. An ugly laugh. Not a beautiful one that brightens someone's face and makes other people around them smile. This man had an ugly laugh. An ugly soul.

"You really think I'm stupid?" he asked her.

Was this a rhetorical question or was he expecting an answer? The answer isn't no, is it? He obviously is stupid. Only a stupid person would kidnap a woman in broad daylight, from her work's car park where her car would be found, abandoned, on Monday morning. People of average intelligence don't tend to do stupid things like that. The chances are that she will be rescued, and he will spend the rest of his days getting used to being confined to a cell and eating cold porridge.

She kept quiet.

He didn't wait for her to reply. "I know who you are, and I know exactly who your husband is, and I know what he does."

"Clever you for being able to do research."

Why had she said that? She needed to get him on her side, didn't she? Wasn't that what you were supposed to do? If you made a friend of your captor and made them realise that you were a real person, a human being with thoughts and feelings and emotions, your chances of getting away were greatly increased. Apparently. She shouldn't be winding him up, she was certain of that.

He laughed again, but she detected a glimmer of panic in his face. She hadn't met any kidnappers before, but she had met many criminals and the usual bravado and confidence seemed to be missing from this man.

She stared at him while she processed what he had just said.

"My husband will pay, you know that, don't you?" she said. "If it's money you want, you can have it." He didn't answer. He stood in front of her, towering over her, staring at her. His impassive face wasn't giving anything away.

"Have you asked him for money? I presume you have. I mean, it might take him an hour or so to get it together, but this could all be over by the end of the day. Neither of us will contact the police. I just want to go home, and I'm sure you do too." She was waffling. She couldn't help the words from tumbling out. "You know bank transfers can happen really quickly these days, instantly in fact, so you can have the money and then let me go. I promise I won't go to the police. You can cover my face when you take me home, so I won't know where I've been held. I mean, I don't know you, do I …"

"Shut the fuck up woman!"

She stopped talking.

"You have no idea who you're dealing with," he said.

What could she say? No, she didn't have a clue who she was dealing with. He probably wasn't working alone.

"Well, do you?" he screamed at her, leaning down, his face only inches away from hers.

His rancid breath made her suddenly angry.

"No! I don't fucking know!" she screamed back at him. "And I don't care!" That clearly wasn't the answer he wanted or expected. The back of his hand sliced across her cheek. Pain shot through her skull, and she instantly felt blood begin to drip down the left-hand side of her face. "You are not going to scare me," she said slowly, in an attempt to convince herself, as well as him.

He turned away from her. He ran his hand through his hair as he walked towards the door. He gripped the door handle, his knuckles white and the muscles in his forearm twitching. His obvious stress was worrying Samantha. Stressed people do unpredictable things, she told herself. But then again, the fact that he seemed uncomfortable cemented the fact that he was working for someone else. Maybe the kidnap wasn't even his idea. He was probably just following orders. Whatever the situation, he didn't seem to be in control. And if that was the case, could she talk him into letting her go?

She could try again and appeal to his better nature. Everyone had a good guy deep inside. She knew that from her years of interviewing criminals. Despite their evil deeds, very few of them were actually evil.

"Believe it or not, it was never my intention to scare you," he told her suddenly. He took a couple of deep breaths. "Stop annoying me and things will be better. I don't want to have to hurt you."

Samantha didn't know what to say. Should she say thank you? Who knew the etiquette in kidnap situations? "My husband will pay you," she said quickly. "Ring him and he will have the money in your account in the next hour. His number is zero seven seven three…"

"It doesn't work like that. You are going to be here for a few more days, at least," he said. "So, you better get used to it."

He walked out of the room, locking the door behind him.

For a moment, Samantha didn't know what to do or what to think. How could she stay in this room for a few more days? She'd go out of her mind.

She climbed off the bed and walked over to the chest of drawers. She picked up the mug of coffee and sipped at the hot liquid.

She imagined her kitchen at home. Her pale blue Smeg kettle and her beautiful white china cups. The tea bags were kept in the cupboard above the kettle. She imagined herself reaching up for the tea bags and closing the cupboard door. She imagined the kettle slowly heating up the water until it reached boiling point. She would be home soon, making herself a drink. She really really hoped, more than anything in the world, that what everyone said about manifesting was true.

Chapter Twenty-Six
Four Days Before the Shooting - Monday

Robert's Monday morning started extremely well, and his good mood continued all the way into work. He sang to himself as he poured himself a coffee in the kitchen at chambers.

Jamilla had been asleep beside him in the bed when his alarm had gone off at seven o'clock. She had stayed at his apartment all weekend and he was over the moon. Last night they had snuggled on the sofa, watched an old film and ordered Thai take-away food and, for now at least, all was perfect.

On Friday afternoon, he had gambled five hundred pounds on an online roulette game using the money that his dad had sent him and amazingly, had won. He had been terrified of pushing his luck, but also equally terrified of missing out on the winning streak that had been eluding him for so long. But luckily for him, his good luck had continued and after two or three games, he had gained almost a thousand pounds.

After Sebastian's party, he was about to gamble the whole lot, but the late-night phone call from Jamilla had stopped him. She was a little tipsy and was missing him. She told him how much she loved him.

Although the words were sweet music to his ears, Robert told himself not to get too giddy. Alcohol was talking. Not the real Jamilla. When she woke up in the morning with a hangover and had taken her beer goggles off, she would very soon bring him straight back down to earth, off his pedestal with a crash.

But he was wrong. She had messaged him first thing Saturday morning and asked if he wanted to do something. Of course, he did, he'd replied. He jumped out of bed, got showered and dressed and went to collect her. They drove to Tatton Park in Cheshire in his Porsche, where they had a walk around the park, holding hands the whole time. Afterwards, they ordered lunch from the café in the stable yard and the rain had abated long enough for them to sit outside on a wooden bench, tucking into their sandwiches and coffee.

On the way home, he asked whether she wanted him to take her home and she said no. Robert had winked at her and said that it was okay, she could admit that he was irresistible. She had laughed and said that the only reason she didn't want to go home yet was because she didn't have any food in the house, and also, she got bored in the house by herself and his company was as good as any.

As Robert was making breakfast on Sunday morning, he realised that he hadn't had the urge to do any gambling all weekend. He had been so happy with Jamilla that he had forgotten all about it.

On Sunday evening, they had walked down Deansgate, towards Quay Street Casino and he had paid five thousand pounds off the debt he owed. It felt good to do it with Jamilla by his side. A tiny step towards complete transparency. The lady at the casino had been helpful and had talked Robert into signing a direct debit agreement, to pay the rest of his debt off at five hundred pounds a month.

As he signed the paper, he couldn't help wishing that he had gone to speak to them in the first place, just like Samantha had advised. He could have been paying the whole amount off by direct debit, rather than being lured in by the loan shark. But you live and learn. He still had enough money for this week's instalment to Frankie and by next week, he would have sorted something else out. All would be well.

"What are you so happy about?" said Alistair now, as he walked into the kitchen. "You're usually still drunk on a Monday morning, aren't you?"

"Not me," said Robert. "That's someone else you're mixing me up with. Do you want coffee? There's still plenty in the pot." He was feeling magnanimous and more than able to deal with Alistair's banter.

"Yes, please. Had a good weekend?" asked Alistair.

"Excellent," said Robert. He poured filter coffee into a mug and handed it to Alistair. "I'm not sure whether you have milk or not."

"No, black is fine, thank you."

"Is Samantha with you? I can pour her one too."

"No, she won't be in today," said Alistair. He sipped his coffee.

Robert couldn't fathom the expression on Alistair's face and waited for him to explain. He could sense that something was wrong. What was it?

"Morning gentlemen," said Jamilla, as she entered the kitchen. She put her bag down on the table and pulled out a plastic box filled with chicken salad, to be put into the fridge. "Is everything alright?" she said. "I feel as though I've walked into a situation here."

"No, not at all," said Robert. "I was just asking where Samantha was, and Alistair said she won't be in today."

"Really?" said Jamilla. "She hasn't said anything to me. I messaged her yesterday and she didn't reply, but I assumed she was busy. Is she ill?"

"No. The truth is, I don't actually know where she is," said Alistair.

"What do you mean, you don't know where she is? Is she missing?" Jamilla was alarmed that something terrible had happened to her.

"No, no, nothing like that." Alistair pulled out a chair and sat down at the dining table. He wrapped his hands around his coffee mug. "She went out with some friends on Saturday afternoon, shopping and lunch and whatnot and then she didn't come home. We were meant to go to her sister's house on Saturday night, but she sent me a cryptic text message saying that she was fed up of us arguing and she needed some time out."

"Time out? What the bloody hell does that mean?" asked Robert.

Jamilla smiled to herself. She was secretly pleased that Samantha was finally standing up to Alistair, whilst at the same time being a tiny bit pissed off that she hadn't confided in her that she was planning to leave Alistair. She would have enjoyed nothing better than discussing her escape route.

"I don't know." Alistair shrugged his shoulders. "She couldn't have gone far because her car is still in the car park. I just don't know."

"I reckon she's booked herself into one of the hotels in town and is right now sitting in the jacuzzi or having a swim, or something," said Jamilla. "Is her swimming costume missing? Have you checked?"

"No, I haven't," said Alistair.

Of course, you haven't, thought Jamilla. She wanted to ask him what exactly he had done to make Samantha feel loved. Had he called all the hotels, trying to trace the one she was in, so that he could beg for to come home? Had he spoken to her sister, to ask whether she knew anything? How many times had he left Samantha a voicemail, telling her that he loved her and missed her? But the look on Alistair's face stopped her from going in too hard. He looked devastated. Defeated. A different man.

"The thing is," he said. "It's so unlike her. And I've never ever heard her use the phrase time-out. I don't know where she's got that from."

"One of her friends probably," said Robert. "They could have talked her into it after a skinful of cocktails."

"A skinful of cocktails?" asked Jamilla.

"Oh, I don't know, whatever women drink when they get together." Robert laughed.

Alistair took a sip of his coffee. "So, yeah, that's it. She's having time out apparently."

"Like you said, that's so unlike her," said Jamilla. "You must have pushed her to her limit. Sorry, Alistair, I didn't mean to sound harsh, but you know that she and I talk, and I know you've been arguing."

Alistair waved his hand, batting away the comment that was meant to wound him. "No, you're right," he said. "We have been arguing a lot lately and I can understand that she's upset with me. I just wish she'd call me and let me know where she is and then we can talk about it."

"Haven't you heard from her at all, apart from the text?" asked Jamilla.

"No, her phone's switched off. I've called a few times, but it goes straight to voicemail."

"She'll be coming to work though, won't she?"

"Probably not today. There's nothing in her diary. She's got a conference with someone tomorrow though, so she'll have to come back to collect the car and the brief."

"You'd better get the flowers ordered then," said Robert. "I'd suggest putting them on her desk, front and centre, so she can see them when she gets in. Dozens of red roses."

"Excellent idea. Can you sort that out for me? Here's my card." Alistair took his debit card out of his wallet and passed it to Robert.

"Sure, I'll do it now."

"She'll love that," said Jamilla. "I'm sure she'll be fine when she gets back, refreshed and rejuvenated from her spa break."

As Robert walked out of the kitchen towards his office, he wondered which of them was the bigger prick. Was it Alistair, who asked someone else to order his wife's flowers for him? Or was it himself, who constantly fucked up and who couldn't afford to buy flowers? For a second, he wondered whether Alistair would notice if he ordered two bunches from the same card. Of course, he would. What was he thinking?

He sat down at his desk and logged onto his laptop. Within minutes, he had ordered the most expensive bunch of roses that he had ever seen, to be delivered to chambers this afternoon. He wanted to make sure that they would be the first thing Samantha saw when she walked in tomorrow, however early that might be. Alistair hadn't told him what to write in the message card, so he simply wrote "I love you and I'm sorry, Alistair x." That would do.

Then he sent a message to Samantha. *I hope you're okay. Alistair said you are having some time out. Jamilla and I are here if you want to talk x*

Chapter Twenty-Seven
Monday

Sebastian had been scrubbing at the graffiti on the front door for half an hour before the last of it was finally washed away. He opened the door and shouted for Laila to come and inspect his handiwork.

"Who knew there was such a thing as graffiti remover, eh? I'm a retired barrister of thirty-five years and yet I'm still learning." Sebastian tried to keep his tone light. He didn't want Laila to realise how shaken he had been, and was still, by the events of the previous week. An idle threat from someone like Jay Harris was one thing - by the time he gets out of prison after a lengthy sentence, the threat will be long forgotten - but having someone come to your house and hold a knife to your throat while calling you a 'dead man' was a completely different ball game.

He hadn't been out of the house all weekend. Not even to buy the graffiti remover, which he had ordered from Amazon Prime. He told himself that it was because the weather took a nosedive and it was too cold and wet to do anything. But now the sun had reappeared, he had no excuse.

"It looks good," said Laila. "You've managed to get it all off. Well done." They both looked down at the puddle of blood-coloured paint that was spreading from the porch tiles onto the path.

"It looks like there's been a massacre, doesn't it?" said Sebastian.

"No, of course not," said Laila, although she thought that it looked exactly like that. "I'll get a bucket of warm soapy water to get rid of it."

"Just clean water will do. Washing up liquid is harmful to plants. I don't want my garden ruined, as well as the front door."

"Is it really harmful to plants? I didn't know that," said Laila.

"Yes, there's two things we didn't know a few days ago. I'd heard about it somewhere, so I googled it just to be sure." He stroked the wood panels of the door, which he had carefully and painstakingly painted sage green last summer. It was a beautiful colour. Calming. But now it was ruined. He could cry. But he wouldn't. Not in front of Laila. He swallowed the tears back down. Man-up, you old fool, he told himself. "It's not perfect, but I've done my best. There are some marks left by the wire wool, I'm afraid. Look, you can see them if you get up close."

Laila peered at the door, at the hundreds of tiny scratches, concentric circles all over the door. They were everywhere. "You can't see them from the street though, can you?"

"Well, no, but…"

"Or even from here." She stepped back from the door and peered at it, her head on one side. Then she nodded and allowed the tears to fall down her cheeks.

"You can see them, can't you?" said Sebastian.

"Yes."

Sebastian threw the wire wool brush onto the floor and rushed over to Laila, pulling her into a hug. "I'm sorry, my love, I'm so sorry."

"It isn't your fault."

"I should have told Harris what he wanted to hear. I should have appeased him somehow and then this wouldn't have happened." He pulled Laila towards him even more, wrapping his arms tightly around her shoulders.

"Appeasing him wouldn't have got him bail, though, would it?"

"I could have tried my hardest to persuade the judge."

"It wouldn't have happened, and you know it. Now stop being silly. The victim is never to blame, you know that."

Sebastian did know that. He had always believed it. He knew that crime prevention would help, and was important, but if someone wanted to leave their front door unlocked, or their car unlocked, or a woman wanted to walk down a dark alleyway in the dead of night, or a man wanted to walk past a group of youths with his expensive new phone in his hand, then they should be able to do that without becoming a victim of a crime.

Nevertheless, he couldn't help thinking that he should have dealt with Jay Harris in a different way.

Now that Harris had been remanded into custody, would his brother - if the man who attacked him last week was his brother - continue to blame him? Would he carry out his threat? Was Sebastian's life really in danger? Would the man blame him when Harris got a custodial sentence at the end of the trial? Because that was highly likely.

Laila pulled away. "Come on, let's get this cleared up and then shall we go out for lunch somewhere? There's a new deli café in the high street that's getting good reviews. I saw it on Facebook the other day."

"Are you sure you want to go out?" Sebastian followed Laila into the house. He closed and bolted the front door, even though he would be going back outside within minutes, with a bucket of water.

"Yes, I'm sure," she said. "I refuse to be a prisoner inside my own home. You don't think he's stalking us, do you? Is that what you're worried about?"

"No, not at all."

"I don't believe you. I know exactly what you're thinking." Laila began to run the tap, holding her hand under the water until it became warm before filling a bucket that Sebastian had pulled out from under the sink. "But even if he is watching the house, waiting for a chance to strike and kill us both dead, isn't it better for us to go out? Surely, he wouldn't be so audacious as to kill us in the street, not in broad daylight anyway."

Sebastian wasn't sure what he was thinking. His thoughts had been so jumbled and out of control since Friday night when he had arrived home from his retirement party to the warning daubed on his front door.

"If I were him," continued Laila. "And I was peeved at a lawyer who hadn't acted in the best interest of my psychopathic brother, assuming I'm as much of a psychopath as he is, I'd lie in wait for the said lawyer and shoot him dead in the street. Not outside the house. In somewhere like Knutsford, with its tiny high street and lots of alleyways, where I could be away in a shot - pardon the pun - out of sight and miles away before the old, fat Country Bobby got there, wooden truncheon in hand, magnifying glass in his back pocket, looking for clues."

"You're pulling my leg, aren't you?" It took Sebastian a few minutes to work it out. As Laila was talking, he pictured them both walking down the high street, on the way to the new deli café for a delicious lunch, oblivious to the danger they were about to face. "You got me there, I've got to say."

"Until I mentioned the wooden truncheon?"

"And the magnifying glass. No wonder you're a crime writer with that imagination."

"Here, take this and wash away the evidence."

She gave him the bucket, now full to the top with hot water. Sebastian took it from her. He placed it by the side of the front door, unlocked it again and peered outside. When he saw that there was nobody about, nobody that he could see, at least, he picked up the bucket, took it outside and threw the water onto the porch. Laila followed him outside with a brush and began brushing the pink liquid down the path and into the grid, where it disappeared.

They worked together quietly for fifteen minutes, bucket after bucket until every trace of the red paint had been eliminated.

"It looks as good as new," said Laila. "In fact, the door hasn't been that clean since it was new." The words caught in her throat, but she didn't want to cry again. She didn't want Sebastian to feel guilty for upsetting her.

"We need a new door," said Sebastian.

The beautiful bespoke oak door, their very expensive door, made by an extremely talented local carpenter, with a square stained glass window that cast dancing sunbeams of green and blue into their hall first thing in the morning, was now ruined.

"Yes, we do," said Laila.

Chapter Twenty-Eight
Monday

Samantha was thankful for the comfortable double bed, the soft pillows and the warm quilt. The room definitely wasn't south facing and after the morning sun had moved to the other side of the house, it was bleak and cold for the remainder of the day. The cold radiator tempted her with a false promise of warmth.

She wrapped herself in the quilt and sat up, resting her back against the pillows. The cover was white with little yellow and black bees dotted all over it. She had seen one just like it in the Wayfair app. This one was a supermarket cheap copy. She wondered what kind of person had picked it off the shelf and nestled it amongst their bread and tins of beans in the trolley. Had they known that at some point in the future, it would be used to keep a captive warm? Had they bought it knowing that it would be wrapped around the shoulders of a woman who had been taken away from her family and kept prisoner?

She had spent most of yesterday staring out of the window, trying to locate any known landmarks; trying to figure out where she was. She watched the birds outside, going about their ordinary business, oblivious to her plight. A male blackbird hopped around underneath one of the trees, pecking at the grass before flying across the field and disappearing from view, twigs and dried grass cuttings bursting from his beak.

As the sun began to set and it began to rain again, Samantha had taken the quilt off the bed and had sat on the deep windowsill watching the raindrops fall down the glass. She wondered why some of them rolled down the glass, picking up more drops as they went, but some stayed stuck to the glass and didn't move. She wished she knew more about physics, but she had never cared about it in school. Her sister was the one who was clever at science.

Today, she had spent an hour or so planning her next holiday in the minutest of detail. She imagined the hotel foyer, polished marble and glass tables, and the immaculately made-up receptionist who would welcome her and Alistair and hand over the keys to their room. They would travel up to the top floor in the glass elevator. In the room, the warm outside air would rush in through the open patio doors, bringing with it a beautiful smell of sun cream, swimming pools and barbequed chicken. The unpacking would wait. She would leave a bikini at the top of the suitcase, so that she could quickly get changed. By the pool, she would lie there, with a book in her hand and a cocktail on the table next to the sunbed, catching the last of the sunshine before it disappeared behind the edge of the sea, leaving a golden glow across the sea. Then she and Alistair would shower and change and walk hand-in-hand to one of the nearby restaurants, one with a view out across the beach.

When she closed her eyes, she could hear Spanish guitars, cicadas and the gentle splashing of cold wine in a glass. She wanted to keep them closed, so she could pretend that they were inches away from her. When she eventually opened her eyes, she released the tears that she had been holding back.

She tried to stay calm. She'd be rescued soon. She had to be. Her phone would be able to tell the police where she was, wouldn't it? Did that work if it wasn't turned on? She had no idea.

She wondered what the man downstairs would normally be doing on a Monday. Did he have a job, or did he live a life of crime? And what about Emma, the love of his life indelibly marked on his arm, did she work? Was she a respectable person, or a criminal, like him? Did she know what kind of man she was involved with? Did he have any children, and if he did, where were they? Was this his house? It didn't seem likely that he would bring a victim of a kidnap back to his own house, but someone must live here.

To pass the time, she imagined that he lived here with his wife. She imagined their two children, a boy and a girl. Or maybe two boys; identical twins. Their mother was a tall, elegant woman with long blonde hair that shone in the sun. Right now, they were skiing in Italy. The boys won't be at school yet, because they are only four. They are having private lessons on the baby ski slope, while their beautiful mother sips herbal tea with her girlfriends in the chalet bar. The boys will come back after their lesson tired and grumpy but will be cheered by hot chocolate with whipped cream and marshmallows. She imagined that they would fly home later today, or maybe tomorrow, and the beautiful woman would find her locked in this bedroom. She'd be appalled at what her husband had done, and she would rescue her. The police would come and arrest her husband.

Samantha prayed that that was true, even though she knew deep down in her heart that it wasn't.

Right now, she could hear muffled voices from the television downstairs. What kind of sick weirdo sits and watches TV while there's a kidnapped woman upstairs? She didn't want to understand his twisted mind. He seemed to have a plan and she trusted that he was going to contact Alistair, like he said he would. Then she could go home. Very soon, she would be back to work. Her life could be normal again. Presumably, the kidnapper wanted that, too.

Apart from a couple of hours yesterday afternoon, the man had never left the house, as far as she was aware. The car was parked at the back of the house, in front of what she presumed was the kitchen door. She had watched him drive away and then return with a couple of carrier bags from the supermarket. Shortly after, he had brought her food and a drink – the promised ham sandwich, a supermarket pre-packed one that was probably made three days ago – and a large bottle of water.

Suddenly, she heard him on the other side of the door. The door unlocked. He pushed it open and placed another supermarket sandwich, a packet of crisps and a mug of tea on the chest of drawers. He picked up the cup of cold coffee and the plate of untouched toast that he had left earlier this morning.

"Wait," she said, as he began to walk away.

"What do you want?"

She noticed that he hadn't shaved, and his chin was covered in dark stubble. It had gone beyond the length that was trendy. He looked weary and tired.

"Can I please have a shower?" she said. "My clothes stink and I need to clean my teeth."

He seemed shocked at the question, as though this was something he had never considered.

"Is there anything else I could wear?"

"Like what?" he asked, as though she knew the contents of each of the wardrobes in the house.

"I don't know," she said. "I don't really care. Pyjamas, anything that's clean. And please can I have a shower?" she asked again.

"Fine," he said. "I will get you some shower gel and a towel."

He closed the door behind him, and Samantha could hear it being locked. A few minutes later, he returned and led her to the bathroom. He warned her that he would be waiting outside.

She tried not to think about that, as she stepped into the hot shower and rubbed herself with the cheap, but extremely welcome, shower gel.

She felt better after her wash. He didn't have a toothbrush for her, but she scrubbed at her teeth with her finger and some toothpaste. He gave her a long t-shirt and a pair of underpants to wear. He said he would wash and tumble-dry her clothes.

The clothes were clearly his, but she couldn't give that too much thought. She was just glad to be clean again.

As he walked her back to her room, his fingernails digging into her elbow as a reminder that it wasn't safe to try and run, she noticed a bookcase in the bedroom next door to hers. The door to this room had previously been closed.

"Please could I read something?" she asked him.

"Nice try," he said. "You want me to let go of you and get a book and then you leg it down the stairs? I don't think so."

He pushed her back into her prison. The door was locked behind her.

Samantha was filled with a sudden rage and hammered on the door with her clenched fists.

"Let me out!" she screamed.

She continued hammering and screaming until she could stand it no more. She fell to the ground and with her back to the door, hugged her knees tightly and sobbed.

Chapter Twenty-Nine
Monday

Elsie pulled up the weeds from around Stanley's grave and threw them into the hedge at the side of the churchyard.

"Hello, my love, how are you?" she said, stroking the top of the gravestone. "I've been out to lunch with Jean today. I'm ever so stuffed. We had fish and chips in the pub, and I treated myself to a glass of wine. It wasn't that nice red that you used to like. I don't think red goes with fish somehow, but it was nice all the same. Anyway…Oh, what's that? It sounded like the clatter of a bin lid coming from the house at the back there. You know, the empty one behind the big wall? It sold for over a million pounds apparently. Who on earth has got that kind of money around here? I don't know anyone that rich, do you? Not even Sebastian."

Elsie stood up straight, chuckling to herself. She rested a hand on the top of the gravestone and listened.

"There it is again. I thought I heard it right. It definitely sounds like a bin lid crashing down. I wonder if someone is moving in there. Or maybe they're renting it out as a holiday let or something. I'm going to have a little look. I know you'd tell me not to, but I'm just being a careful neighbour. If it was being broken into and nobody reported it, well, that would be very remiss, wouldn't it? Although, I don't think there's been a crime since 1987 when that packet of sweets was stolen from the shop." She laughed again. "I think that glass of wine has gone to my head. I do wish you were here with me, Stanley. You loved a glass of red, didn't you? You know how much I miss you. But don't worry, I'm being strong and I'm getting stronger every day. Anyway, I'm going to go and see what's going on at that house."

Elsie kissed her fingertips and then placed them gently on Stanley's engraved name before making her way across the churchyard, down the path, and out through the front gate. She closed the gate carefully behind her. She stood still and listened, but the only thing she could hear now was birdsong and the wind gently whistling through the trees. The road was quiet, as it usually was at this time of the day. The children were still in school, and people hadn't yet arrived home from work. Elsie loved the village in the afternoon, especially when she felt as though she had the whole place to herself.

She turned left at the bottom of the path, passed the corner shop, navigating the wooden boxes full of fresh vegetables and salad that spilled out across the pavement, and stood at the entrance to the empty house.

Two solid wooden gates, which were firmly closed and at least six feet high, blocked her view of the house and garden and the surrounding wall was also too high for her to see over, but she had seen the house on the internet when it was for sale. The whole village had been talking about it. The extortionate selling price and the secrecy surrounding the sale fuelled the village gossip for months.

The house had been occupied for twenty-five years by Ted and Alice Jones. Both of them ran the G.P. practice and were well-known and loved in the village. Shortly after they retired, Ted was diagnosed with dementia and spent the last three years of his life in a nursing home. When Alice died, a few years ago, the house was inherited by their son, who lived in Canada. The last time Elsie had seen him was when he had flown over for his mother's funeral, which had been held in the church. He didn't stay long. Just long enough to visit the estate agent in Lancaster and make arrangements for the house to be sold before he flew back to his life overseas.

It had taken six months before the 'For Sale' sign was taken down and during that time, Elsie and Jean had spent many a happy hour perusing the estate agent's website, peering into all the rooms and giving a critique of the decor and the remaining furniture, which was all being sold along with the house itself.

"I'd keep that kitchen," Elsie had said. "You can tell it's real wood, look at those cabinets. Beautiful, aren't they?"

"Ooh yes, they had a few bob, didn't they, the doctor and his wife?" Jean, as old-fashioned as though she was living in the nineteenth century, always referred to them as the doctor and his wife, even though Alice was a doctor too.

"Yes, they certainly did," said Elsie. "Look at those sofas. I can't imagine how much they paid for those. If the son was selling the furniture individually, I'd buy one."

"He's got more money than sense," said Jean. "I've never liked him."

As far as Elsie knew, Jean had met him only twice - once at Ted's funeral and then again at Alice's funeral, but she didn't argue with her. "They've got a gorgeous view out the back, haven't they?" she said.

There were half a dozen photographs of the view from the back of the house, taken, it seemed, from the upstairs windows. The garden was a hundred metres long, according to the estate agent's website, and beyond that were fields, as far as the eye could see. In the winter, some of the fields were used for grazing sheep, which had spent the spring and summer months up in the hills in the Forest of Bowland and some were occupied by a small herd of cows.

Right now, the far field was empty and silent; the sheep and their new lambs had been taken back to the hills weeks ago.

As Elsie was about to turn around and make her way back home, the huge gates began to slowly open. Creaking and groaning, they opened inwards, revealing the front elevation of the house, situated at the end of a long driveway. For a moment, Elsie wasn't sure what to do. Should she pretend that she was out on a walk and just carry on? Or should she turn away, and pretend she was visiting the corner shop? Before she could make up her mind, she saw a large midnight blue BMW inching its way towards the gates, like a greyhound waiting for the traps to open, so it could race out.

She waved at the driver. Everyone in the village waved at each other and said hello, whether they had previously met or not. That's what she loved about the village. If you were ever lonely or just fancied a chat, all you had to do was step outside and someone would talk to you, sooner or later.

The young man in the car looked shocked to see her, and didn't wave. She must have startled him, thought Elsie. The wheels of the car spun on the gravel and he shot off.

Elsie, feeling slightly embarrassed at being caught snooping, walked back to the graveyard to tell Stanley.

"You'll never guess what has just happened," she said. "I've just seen a car coming out of Ted and Alice's old place. Do you remember me telling you that we think it sold a while ago, but none of us have seen anyone moving in? Well, I knew I was right about hearing a sound coming from the garden. It was definitely someone putting something in the bin, you know that plastic on plastic clatter when you close the lid? Well, I walked round there and then the gates opened and this big car drove out and sped away. I don't know what kind it was, but it looked new and expensive. The driver looked really shocked when he saw me." Elsie laughed to herself. "I think I frightened him. But you know what? I seem to know his face from somewhere. I can't think where from, but you know me, I never forget a face."

She pottered around the graveyard, dead-heading flowers and pulling up any weeds before they got too big. Then it suddenly occurred to her who the man was. She had seen him walking to the park with the two children that she met yesterday. Emma's children.

So the man must be Jake. Emma's husband.

Chapter Thirty
Three Days Before the Shooting - Tuesday

The first thing Alistair did when he arrived at work on Tuesday morning was check his phone. Still no word from Samantha. He had checked it at half past one and quarter to three this morning, too, just in case she had woken up in the night contrite about leaving him so suddenly. He had checked it again as soon as his alarm went off and then again when he got out of the shower.

This whole situation was bothering him. Something wasn't quite right, but he couldn't put his finger on it. For a start, Samantha didn't usually send a text; it would be a WhatsApp message. And 'time out' was an odd phrase for her to use. But he didn't know what that meant. He kept telling himself not to worry, but it wasn't working.

He had phoned his mum last night and told her that Samantha had temporarily left him. He didn't know how else to word it. He said that it was so unlike her, but his mum said she wasn't surprised. She said that the way that they bickered drove her crazy. Alistair had said that he wasn't aware of it and his mum said that was the problem. It was too ingrained into their everyday life that it had become normal. Arguments should never be classed as normal.

She said that she and Alistair's dad hadn't had an argument for years. She couldn't remember the last time. It was so pointless. They had both sat down one day and questioned why they argued with each other, when they didn't argue with anyone else on earth. There was no reason for it. So, they stopped.

Alistair had said that he wished she had given him this advice on his wedding day. His mum said she had; it was the greatest advice she could offer, but he had been too drunk or too pig-headed to listen. Alistair had wanted to scream at her then and ask her why she didn't tell him again. Why didn't she badger him and badger him until he had listened? He had ended the call then. He couldn't bear for his mum to think that their marriage was on the rocks and that it was his fault because he hadn't listened.

But she was right. This was all his fault. His beautiful, gentle, thoughtful, kind-hearted wife had been driven away because of the way he had been speaking to her recently. The sad part was that Frankie should have received the sharp end of his tongue, not Samantha. She didn't deserve to be spoken to the way he had done recently. She never did. He had been taking his frustrations out on the wrong person.

Hopefully, right now, she would be getting dressed in her hotel room, The Hilton or The Lowry, having calmed down and she would walk into chambers as though nothing had happened.

He knew that she had a conference today with the woman who had been charged with murdering her boyfriend. He loved that she was passionate about helping this woman. He wished that he had supported her more and listened to her argument. What made him think that he knew best? They had both qualified as barristers at the same time; they had both come away from university with a First. So why did he have to belittle her all the time? He didn't deserve her and today, he would tell her.

He went immediately to Samantha and Robert's office. The flowers had arrived from the florist on Deansgate yesterday afternoon. Two dozen red roses were waiting in the middle of Samantha's desk. Alistair couldn't wait for her to see them.

"Is she here yet?" he asked Robert, hoping that she had popped out to the sandwich shop for some breakfast or was in the kitchen and would be back any moment.

"I haven't seen her yet, no," said Robert. "Have you heard from her overnight?"

Alistair shook his head. "No. This is so unlike her."

"Did you have a particularly bad argument or something?" asked Robert. "I hope you don't mind me asking, but at Sebastian's party, you looked like a normal couple. You didn't look like you were fighting."

"We did have a few words on the way home," admitted Alistair.

"What about? Sorry! I shouldn't be asking, but I'm worried about her, too."

"No, it's fine. I don't mind you asking. It's nothing personal and I'm sure she would have told Jamilla anyway. It was about a client of hers actually. We had a disagreement about whether Sam was giving her the correct advice about her plea."

"Olivia Stevenson?"

"Yes, that's the one. The woman who murdered her boyfriend," said Alistair.

"Yes, she feels pretty strongly about that one, doesn't she?"

"Yes, she does, and I should have been more supportive. I don't know why I had to go blundering in with my huge feet, telling her what to do. I hardly know the case and I certainly don't know it like she does."

"Well, the good news is that the brief is on her bookcase," said Robert. "So, she'll have to come up to the office to pick it up before she goes to the conference."

"And that's when she'll see the flowers," said Alistair. "I hope they'll do the trick."

"I'm sure they will," said Robert. "Is the defendant in Styal Prison?"

"Yes, she is, so she will need her car. And hopefully, by the time I get home, she'll be at home too and we can put this behind us. I'll take her to her favourite Italian restaurant for dinner. Anyway, let's get to work. I'll be leaving for court in fifteen minutes, okay?"

"Yes, I'll be ready," said Robert.

Alistair went to his office and had another look through his brief. Today was day two of a three-day trial of a man who had been accused of stealing twelve thousand pounds from his employer. In the police interview, he said that the money had been paid to him as a bonus. He couldn't explain why there was no tax record and put it down to an admin error. He claimed that the young woman in the H.R. department was new and had made a mistake. Alistair couldn't wait to cross-examine him today. Apart from anything, the trial would keep him busy all day and take his mind off Samantha.

*

As soon as the trial had adjourned for the day and the judge and the jury had left the courtroom, Alistair said a hastily goodnight to his opposition barrister and he and Robert walked back to chambers as quickly as possible. He wanted to see whether Samantha had taken the flowers off her desk. Even if she was still mad at him, he knew that she wouldn't be able to resist red roses.

On the way back, he took his phone out of his pocket and turned it off silent. There were three missed calls from a number he didn't recognise, plus a text message from the same number.

Hi Alistair, it's Jamilla here. I'm in chambers. James told me Samantha hasn't turned up for the conference and I can't get through to her phone. It goes straight to voicemail. Please can you call me when you get this message?

"I've had a message from Jamilla," he said, showing the phone to Robert.

Robert quickly read the message. "Call her back," he said.

Alistair returned the call and waited for Jamilla to pick up, which she did after two rings.

"Jamilla, it's Alistair, I've been in court all day and just got your message."

"Alistair, I'm out of my mind with worry. Samantha hasn't returned any of my messages and then James told me that she didn't turn up for the conference." Jamilla burst into tears. "Even if she's mad at you, she wouldn't ignore me, would she?"

"No, I wouldn't have thought so," said Alistair with a sigh. You two have been as thick as thieves ever since you met, he wanted to add, wondering how many of his personal foibles Samantha had discussed with Jamilla.

"So, what are we going to do?" said Jamilla, between her sobs. "We need to ring the police."

"Do we? I mean, I've got a text from her saying that she needs time out. What are the police going to do with that?"

Jamilla sighed heavily. "Right, okay," she said.

Alistair stopped walking. He wanted to concentrate on what Jamilla was saying and they were approaching The Ivy and The Alchemist at Spinningfields, which were always busy and noisy.

"What do you mean, right okay?" he said. "I don't really like that tone, Jamilla. I've got enough on my plate…"

"You've got enough on your plate?" shouted Jamilla. "I might have known that it would be all about you. What about what Samantha's going through?"

"What the fuck do you mean by that?" said Alistair. "She's taking a break, that's all. I'd be grateful if you could mind your own fucking business. She'll come home when she wants to come home."

"Don't talk to me like that, Alistair. I'm not Samantha, I don't have to put up with it."

"Talk to you like what?" said Alistair, aware that he was raising his voice and that people walking past were beginning to stare, but he didn't care. "I can do whatever I like. So don't give me any attitude. Do you know where she is, or not? I bet you do."

"I wouldn't have called you if I knew where she was, would I?"

Alistair knew that it was a stupid question. But this woman was irritating him beyond belief. He knew that she didn't like him, but he had enough to deal with right now and dealing with a self-righteous, know-it-all little bitch wasn't on his agenda.

Robert took the phone out of Alistair's hand. "Jamilla, hi, it's me," he said. "Are you okay? Yes, I know you're worried. Listen, you and Alistair arguing isn't going to solve this issue of where Samantha is. We're all worried about her. Did she say anything to you about having planned some time out, or wanting to have time out? No? Okay, well if you hear anything from her, will you ring me immediately? Okay. We'll be back in chambers in a few minutes. I'll come and see you. Bye."

Robert handed the phone back to Alistair, who was running his hand backwards and forwards through his hair.

"She's a bitch," he said.

And you can be a prick sometimes, he thought. "You and her just don't see eye to eye, that's all," he said. "But she is my girlfriend, so I'd appreciate it if you didn't talk about her like that."

"Sorry, yes. I didn't think," said Alistair, shocked at Robert's assertiveness.

"Do you think you should ring round her other friends? The ones that she went out with on Saturday? One of them will have heard from her, surely?"

"Yes, I should do, but I don't have their numbers."

"Do you think her sister will have them?" asked Robert.

"I honestly don't know. Maybe," said Alistair. "I think I'll go straight home. I'll ring Beth when I get home. I don't need to go back into chambers for anything. Would you mind dropping the papers on my desk for me?"

"Sure, no problem."

The truth was that Alistair couldn't bear to see the roses in Samantha's room, waiting for her to return. He just wanted to get home as quickly as possible. He would ring her mum and her sister from the car. One of them must know something. Samantha told them everything.

He said goodbye to Robert at the door of chambers and continued walking to the car park round the back. Samantha's car was still there, where she had parked it on Saturday afternoon, in the middle bay. She liked to park it there. She said it was the easiest one to manoeuvre out of.

He had parked his own car next to hers this morning, wanting to be close to her.

He clicked his key fob to unlock the door and was about to climb into the driver's seat when he noticed something shining on the floor, close to the front nearside wheel of Samantha's car, half hidden by an empty crisp packet. He bent down to look, swiping the crisp packet away.

It was Samantha's car key.

Chapter Thirty-One
Tuesday

Sebastian had to go out. He didn't want to, but they were in desperate need of a supermarket shop. Laila was busy editing her latest book, so he would have to go alone. He wasn't sure what he was the most worried about, going out or leaving Laila at home alone.

He took a coffee and a plate of biscuits up to her study and silently put them on the side of her desk. She had her reading glasses perched on the end of her nose and a look of intense concentration on her face.

"How's the editing?" he asked.

"Arduous," she said. "But I'm nearly done now. We can go shopping together, if you want to wait an hour or so."

"No, don't be silly. I'll be fine. You can relax when you've finished. Have a nice bath or something. You deserve it. I won't be long." He tiptoed out of the room, but then hesitated at the door.

"What's wrong?" she said.

"Well, I don't want to disturb your work, but I'd feel happier if you'd follow me downstairs and put the bolt across the door."

"But then you won't be able to get back in."

"I'll ring you when I get home and you can let me in," he said.

"Yes, okay." Laila was happy with the extra layer of security and followed her husband downstairs to the hall. As soon as he was out of the door, she closed it, bolted it and returned to her study.

The supermarket was relatively quiet, and Sebastian had finished the shopping within twenty minutes. He couldn't remember a time when he had come shopping and gone home without having a custard slice and a pot of tea in the café. But not today. He was desperate to get back to Laila. He lifted the last of the bags into the trolley and made his way outside, back to the car.

It was as he was returning the shopping trolley to the bay in the middle of the car park that he saw him. The man who had threatened him. The thug who had held a knife to his throat last week. Probably the same man who had ruined their front door. He was sitting in an old, faded blue Ford Focus, smoking a cigarette, less than two hundred metres away. The window was wound down, his right elbow resting on the door frame. As Sebastian watched him, he blew a plume of smoke into the air. There was no doubt about it, he was watching him. Had he followed him here? Or was this a coincidence? Did he live around here?

From where he was standing, Sebastian couldn't quite make out the registration number of the car. He walked closer so that he could see. The man watched him the whole time.

"You alright there, Mr Thomas?" he said, shouting across the car park. "Not working today?"

Sebastian's heart began to race with anger. The man didn't look as though he had done a day's honest work in his life and here he was, questioning him about not working. The criticism in the man's voice was clear.

Sebastian took his phone out of his trouser pocket and pressed the number for the police station. The kind police officer who had attended their house on Thursday night had left them the direct number and told them to call if there was anything else to report. Unless it was an emergency, in which case he should ring 999. Sebastian had stored the number in his phone straight away and had asked Laila to do the same. He had debated for a second whether this would be classed as an emergency, but then decided that it wasn't. Not really. Although it felt like one.

"Ringing the police, are you?" the man shouted from his car. "Fucking waste of space. Wankers, the lot of them." He laughed and continued to watch Sebastian, not at all worried about the imminent presence of police cars, screaming into the car park with blues and twos wailing, ready to drag him out of his car and into handcuffs.

"Hello, Knutsford Police Station, how can I help?"

"Hello, my name is Sebastian Thomas, number four, Oakfield Drive. I reported a knife assault last week and some vandalism to our house and right now, the man who assaulted me is in Waitrose car park, right in front of me."

"Is he threatening you right now?" asked the operator.

"No, but…"

"Could I please ask you to report the incident using the number 111, or you can do it online…"

"No, the officer who came to the house on Thursday night, PC Simms, PC Tyrique Simms, gave me this number and told me to report any sighting."

Sebastian heard the clicking of a keyboard. "PC Simms isn't on duty today."

"It doesn't matter, I just want someone to attend Waitrose car park and arrest this man. Preferably before the end of the day."

"Please try and stay calm, sir. I can ask a patrol car to get to you as soon as possible."

"Can you make a note of the registration number? It's PN05 AVR. It's a light blue Ford Focus. It's driving off. Is there anyone who can chase him?"

"I'll put the call through…"

"Forget it," said Sebastian. "He'll be gone by the time you get here." He ended the call.

The man drove past him, his arm waving high in the air through the open window as he did so. "See you, Mr Thomas," he shouted. "You take care now. You never know who might be following you. Don't want you getting hurt or nothing." He laughed and disappeared out of the car park, turning quickly onto the main road.

Sebastian took a photograph of the man's receding car with his phone and then ran back to his car. The man had turned left. The way to his house. Is that where he's going? He will know now that Laila is likely to be at home alone. Panic coursed through Sebastian's body like a river breaking through a dam.

As he got to the car, he rang Laila's number, but she didn't answer. He left a hurried voicemail, knowing that she probably wouldn't listen to it. "Laila, I'm on my way home. Don't open the door to anyone but me."

He remembered seeing her phone on the kitchen table and cursed himself for not making sure she had it with her in the study. Ordinarily, she didn't like to take her phone into the study. She said it was distracting. She was tempted to scroll through Facebook and Instagram too often when she was meant to be working. But right now, they were living through extraordinary times, and she should have her phone. Always.

Sebastian reached home in less than ten minutes and was relieved to find that the Ford Focus wasn't parked outside the house. He wasn't sure what he had been expecting. Some vandalism. More graffiti. A broken window or two. A masked man running out of his house. A bloodbath.

Leaving the shopping in the car, he ran to the front door and rang the bell. He lifted the letterbox cover and shouted through it. "It's only me. Let me in." He tried to keep the panic from his voice, but he wasn't doing a very good job, he knew it.

"I'm coming!" He heard Laila's voice down the hall and then watched through the letterbox as her feet made their way to the door. She pulled back the bolt, turned the key and opened the door. "That didn't take long," she said.

"Is everything all right?" he said, kissing her on the cheek, whilst simultaneously looking over her shoulder, as though the man would be right behind her, wielding a knife above her head.

"Yes, fine," she said. "I'm still in one piece. You really need to stop worrying. I think this storm in a teacup has blown over."

Sebastian wasn't so sure. "Okay, well you might as well put the kettle on while I get the shopping bags," he said. "Don't stand around doing nothing."

"Cheeky bugger," she said, laughing. She walked off to the kitchen, shouting over her shoulder, "They'll be trouble if you haven't brought me any digestives."

Sebastian walked back to the car and unlocked the boot. He collected the three shopping bags, putting two of them over one arm and one over the other. He didn't want to have to make two trips back to the car. He struggled back up the garden path, dumped the heavy bags in the hall and locked and bolted the front door once again.

Chapter Thirty-Two
Tuesday

Samantha's evening meal was delivered later than yesterday's. She had no idea what time it was, but it was almost dark when she heard footsteps on the landing. She lay on the bed and didn't look at her captor as he left her meal on the chest of drawers and silently left the room. She didn't want to eat it. She wanted to protest and throw it against the door. But she was hungry, and she had to admit that it smelt good. He had made her fish fingers and oven chips. The fish fingers were burnt and some of the oven chips were hard, but she knew that she needed to eat. It was also the first hot meal she had had since Saturday lunchtime.

Five minutes later, he returned carrying four books, which he left on the floor, together with her clothes, which were clean, although not ironed. He turned to leave.

"Have you spoken to Alistair yet?" she asked.

"None of your business," he said.

Samantha took a deep breath and tried to stay calm, but she couldn't stop the tears. "It's been three days now," she said, trying to keep the hysteria out of her voice.

He didn't reply, but the way he was looking at her was different, softer somehow.

"I don't judge you, you know," she said. "I understand that you are doing this for money, and I told you that Alistair will pay you. So, the sooner you tell him where I am, the sooner you can have your money and we can both go home."

He was starting to leave the room. He had his hand on the door handle, but Samantha didn't want him to leave. She wanted to talk to him, to get him to see that she was a human being, not just a commodity to be traded.

"You know what husbands are like. He dotes on me. He will do anything for me, as you would for your wife, if you had one, that is. Do you have a wife? If you do, you would get it…"

"Shut up! Just shut up! Stop talking! You don't know anything about my wife."

He pulled open the door, stormed out and slammed it shut behind him. He then locked it.

Samantha sat on the bed, stunned and shocked by what he had just said. So, he must have a wife. He clearly didn't mean to tell her any personal information about himself, it had slipped out. His incompetence was shining through more and more. Maybe he would slip up, forget to lock the door or something. Every day since Sunday morning, she had lain on the bed, thinking of ways she could escape. But he never forgot. Every day, she heard the same sound and resigned herself to staying where she was a little longer.

She thought about fighting, but she knew that she couldn't possibly overpower him. She knew that it wouldn't do her any good to even try. He was much stronger than her, so it wouldn't get her anywhere.

Each time he entered the room, to deliver her food or allow her to use the bathroom, she used all the willpower she had not to scream and shout at him and lunge for him and scratch his eyes out. He would hit her again, that was a certainty. She couldn't risk being tied up or, even worse, transported into a cellar with no windows. At least in this room, she could look out of the window, even if there was nothing to look at, except the birds and the cows in the field.

She needed to be patient and wait it out. Alistair and the police would be doing everything possible to rescue her.

She clambered off the bed and undressed, taking the t-shirt and underpants that didn't belong to her off as quickly as possible. When she was dressed in her own clothes she felt better, although the smell of them made her cry again. Her t-shirt didn't have its usual smell of Spring Freshness fabric conditioner and the denim of her jeans was stiff and hard.

She folded up the clothes she had taken off and put them in the top drawer of the chest of drawers. She wanted them out of sight.

After taking a bite of one of the fish fingers, she crouched down to have a look at the books he had left her. There was one written by an author that she hadn't heard of, with a front cover showing a woman from the 1940s; an Inspector Morse book by Colin Dexter; Misery by Stephen King and Jane Austen's Pride and Prejudice. She dismissed Misery immediately, putting it away in the drawer with his clothes. The last thing she wanted to read about was someone being held captive in a room by a mad woman.

She picked up Pride and Prejudice, a book that she hadn't read since she was in year nine at school, and took it over to the windowsill, along with her plate of fish fingers and chips. She sat on the sill with her back to one of the walls and began to eat. He hadn't remembered cutlery, but she wasn't bothered. At least she now had books.

She opened the book but was distracted by movement outside. The man was pacing up and down on the patio at the back of the house, next to where he had parked the car. He was holding a mobile phone to his ear. She could hear his voice but couldn't make out the words. Whoever was on the other end of the line was clearly making him angry.

He looked up at the window and she shrank back against the wall. He had seen her, that was obvious.

As she heard his feet thundering up the stairs, she stayed where she was, frozen on the windowsill, as still as a statue, fear making her immobile. She told herself that he had seen her sitting there before and he hadn't bothered, but maybe this time he thought she had overheard his conversation. She shouldn't have been looking out of the window.

The door was unlocked and thrown open.

"I need you to text your husband," he said. Samantha could see that he was holding her mobile phone. "Give me your finger!"

"What? No!" Samantha had a vision of him cutting off her finger. She sat on her hands, shaking with fear. The plate of fish fingers and chips fell to the floor.

"I need your finger to open the phone," he explained.

"Oh," said Samantha, still not moving.

"I'm not going to cut it off," he said, reading her mind. "Just hold it onto the phone and unlock it."

As he walked over to the window, she thought desperately how she could get the phone from him. She had seconds - one or two at the most. If she could snatch it, she could run, dialling 999 as she went. But she was on the other side of the room to the door, the bed was in the way, and he was blocking her exit.

"Don't fuck about now," he said. "Just hold out your finger."

"Which one?"

"Your right one. The one you use to open the phone, you stupid bitch."

"Sorry, I -"

"It's fine, just give me your finger," he said in a more conciliatory manner.

She held out her right index finger and he grabbed it, holding it tight. He pressed it to the button on the bottom of her phone. The phone lit up. The wallpaper photograph of her and Alistair on their wedding day made her gasp and instantly cry.

"Stop!" she said, as he began to leave the room. "Can I send it? What are you going to say?"

"No, I'll send it." He paused. "He just needs to know that you're all right, so he doesn't report you missing, that's all."

"Report me missing? Why would he do that?"

The man let out a big sigh. "Because he doesn't know that you're here," he said. "Look, I've said too much. Just…" He paused again and Samantha held her breath. "He thinks you're having some time out on your own. For now, at any rate."

"But why?" Samantha struggled to speak through her sudden heartbreaking sobs. "Why haven't you told him that I've been taken? Then he would pay you to return me."

"It's not my decision, okay. Don't ask me any more questions." The man spoke softly and for the first time in four days, he seemed to look at her properly. Then he turned to leave.

"Please let me send it," she said. She would beg if she had to. She needed some contact with Alistair, however small. "You can watch me, stand over me. Anything. You can dictate it to me. Just let me have some contact with him, please." She wiped at the tears dripping down her cheeks. "It might be better if I do it. If you send it, he'll know it wasn't from me. It won't be the same style as mine."

He nodded. "Okay, but if you press the send button before I've authorised it, you're in deep trouble."

"I know, thank you."

"I'll hold the phone, you type. Tell him you are okay, but you need some time to yourself."

He held the phone out to her. The text messages between her and Alistair had been opened. She could see the message that had been sent to Alistair on Saturday afternoon.

Am ok but I need some time out. Don't try and find me. Am fed up with the arguments.

She couldn't believe what she was reading. Did Alistair really think that text had been from her? Before that, they hadn't communicated by text for months. She tended to use WhatsApp. She wondered what he had thought when he had read it. That would certainly explain why she hadn't been rescued yet. He clearly thought she was having time out, whatever that meant. Surely, he wouldn't have been taken in by that text, would he? He must know that she would never leave him voluntarily. Yes, they had been arguing recently, but she would never leave him.

How did the kidnapper know they had been arguing? Had they been followed on Friday night when they had left Sebastian's party? Or was it just a good guess? All couples argue, presumably.

She wondered how closely Alistair had really looked at the message. Had he scrutinised it? He must know it wasn't from her. It didn't sound like her. She always ended their messages with a kiss, even when she was angry with him.

Apart from that, hadn't he wondered why she hadn't contacted her sister, or her mum? She never went more than a couple of days without speaking to them. And what about work? Alistair wasn't stupid. In fact, he was an extremely intelligent man with an analytical brain, so he must be suspicious, especially when she hadn't turned up for the conference with Olivia Stevenson.

That was it.

She had to send him a clue.

She had one chance.

"Shall I tell him I'm with a friend, someone he doesn't know?" she asked. The man hesitated. "You said that you don't want him to report me missing, so…"

"Yes, fine," he said quickly, shrugging his shoulders.

Samantha began typing, slowly with one finger. She wanted to ask the man to let her hold the phone, but she knew that he wouldn't, and she couldn't let this chance slip through her fingers, literally.

I am okay but I am still having time out with a friend, Olivia Stevenson. You don't know her

"That's enough," said the man, pulling the phone away before she could finish. He stared at the phone, studying the text.

"I needed to mention the friend's name, to make it sound authentic," she said quickly. "I don't have any friends called Olivia Stephenson. You can check in my contacts."

The man scowled at her and then opened her contacts and scrolled through them. He nodded when it seemed as though she was telling the truth. There was no telephone number listed for Olivia Stevenson.

"Fine, I've sent it," he said.

"What happens now?" she asked.

"You mind your own fucking business, that's what," he said, as he left the room, locking her inside.

Chapter Thirty-Three
Tuesday

Alistair arrived home and was putting the key in the front door when his phone vibrated in his pocket. He fumbled with the lock, anxious to get inside so that he could check who the message was from. He felt like he had called Samantha's phone dozens of times over the past few days. Maybe this was her, finally getting back to him.

He opened the door, rushed over to the alarm keypad and switched it off, before getting out his phone. Samantha's name was on the screen. He opened the message quickly, his heart jackhammering in his chest.

I am okay but I am still having time out with a friend, Olivia Stevenson. You don't know her

What the fuck? He sat down on the bottom stair in the hallway and read the text again. Olivia Stevenson?

"Alistair? Are you okay?" It was Jamilla. In his rush to turn off the alarm, and read the message, he had left his front door wide open. She had followed him all the way back from chambers, driving Samantha's car home for him, after he had found the car keys on the floor of the car park. "You look a bit pale. What is it? Have you heard from her? Oh my God, what is it?"

Alistair silently held his phone out and Jamilla read the text out loud. "I'm still having time out with a friend, Olivia Stevenson?" She paused and frowned at Alistair. "Olivia

Stevenson?" she repeated. "It doesn't make sense. What does it mean?"

"I don't know," said Alistair.

Although he did know. Or at least he thought he knew. He knew now that something wasn't right. In fact, it was terribly wrong. Everything was adding up to Samantha being in trouble.

"I don't know what to say. I'm completely confused," said Jamilla.

"I know," said Alistair. "I don't know what to think either."

Jamilla closed the front door behind her and slowly took off her jacket. She hung it over Samantha's on the newell post at the bottom of the stairs. Alistair was still staring at his phone. Was he avoiding meeting her gaze?

"This isn't right," she said eventually. "I know for a fact that she wouldn't have left you, whether she wanted time out or not. If she did want some time on her own, which was highly unlikely, she would have told me where she was going. She would never disappear without letting me know where she was. Even if she had booked herself into a hotel, there was no way in a million years that she would have missed her conference with Olivia Stevenson this morning. Her missing car keys wouldn't have stopped her. She would have taken a taxi, a bus, or crawled the whole way on her hands and knees."

Alistair knew that Jamilla was right. Samantha would never have sneaked off suddenly, leaving her work and her friends. She would have booked a weekend away at Champneys or something if she wanted 'time out'. She had been there once before with a group of female friends, one of them had turned thirty, or got engaged or had a baby or something, he couldn't remember, but she had kept in contact with him the whole time. When she had walked through the door late on the Sunday evening, it had felt as though she hadn't been away, they had talked and messaged each other that much throughout the weekend.

The discarded car keys in the car park had sounded an alarm bell which he should have heeded. When he first spotted them, he had tried to tell himself that it meant nothing, that she had clearly dropped them on her way to the hotel and probably hadn't even realised that they were missing. But as soon as that thought had begun to form in his mind, he knew it was rubbish. The bell that he had quietened was now ringing loud and clear.

The conversations with his mum and Samantha's sister, hadn't settled his mind, either. His mum was right, they did argue a lot, but she didn't know Samantha as well as he did. She wouldn't have left him. Simple.

He had phoned Beth, reluctantly on the drive home. When he first spoke to her on Saturday, to tell her that they wouldn't be going over for dinner, he knew that she would take Samantha's side and he was prepared for a verbal battering. He knew that he didn't need to tell her about the arguments they had been having recently. She would have already been armed with the facts. Her arsenal would be well and truly stocked up, facts given to her by Samantha over the years would be used to beat him with. But he had been pleasantly surprised that the conversation hadn't turned into the battle he had been expecting. She just asked him to let her know when he heard from her.

Today, he wasn't sure whether to tell her about Samantha's car keys being found. She was bound to be worried about Samantha, and he didn't want to make it worse. But he had needed to speak to someone who loved Samantha as much as he did. Beth had agreed with him that it was out of character for Samantha to take herself off like that. Very much so. He could hear the catch in her voice as she tried to stop herself from crying and he had ended up consoling her, offering her hope that she could cling to. By the end of the call, during which both of them had agreed that Samantha would have her feet up in one of the most expensive luxury suites in the most prestigious hotel in town, neither of them were convinced that was the case.

And now this. This cryptic message saying that she was with Olivia Stevenson, the defendant accused of murdering her boyfriend.

"She's not with Olivia Stevenson, is she? Because she didn't go to see her today." Jamilla stood in front of him with her hands on her hips.

"I know," said Alistair. He didn't need someone stating the bleeding obvious. "I need a drink," he said, getting up from the stairs. "Have you got Samantha's car keys?"

"Yes, here you are."

Jamilla held out the keys and Alistair took them, walked down the hall into the kitchen and put them in the bowl on the worktop, alongside his own.

"Do you want a drink?" he shouted to Jamilla, who was still in the hall.

"Yes, sorry. Yes, please. Whatever you're having," she said, following Alistair into the kitchen. "You need to ring the police."

"Yes, maybe," said Alistair.

"You need to, Alistair. Otherwise, I will," she said.

Alistair poured two large measures of whiskey into two crystal tumblers and handed one to Jamilla. "Ice?"

She shook her head and took the glass. They both drank.

"I knew immediately that she wasn't the one who sent that text on Saturday," said Alistair.

"What do you mean?"

"I fucking knew it, but my mum and Beth convinced me that everything was fine. She would never send a text without punctuation at the end of it. She's probably the only person in the world who still uses semi-colons in messages. I can't believe I've been so fucking stupid." He hurled the glass into the ceramic Belfast sink. It smashed into a hundred tiny pieces.

"Alistair! What do you mean, she wasn't the one who sent the text? You're scaring me now."

"I don't know," shouted Alistair. "I just don't know."

Jamilla wiped her tears. She took another drink. "I did think it was weird that she didn't reply to me, but I thought she was just pissed off and had turned her phone off."

If only it were that simple, thought Alistair.

Jamilla put her drink on the table and walked over to the sink. Smashed glass was everywhere. She picked up a couple of the biggest pieces.

"Leave it, leave it!" said Alistair. "I'll sort it out later."

Jamilla put them back in the sink. "Alistair. Please ring the police. I'm worried about her."

Alistair wanted to. More than anything in the world, he wanted his wife back. More than anything in the world, he wanted to be able to confide in someone. He wanted to tell Jamilla that he had an idea where Samantha was, or at least who had her. He wanted to tell her what he had been doing for Frankie over the past twelve months. He wanted to tell her about their argument on Friday night in the bar and how he had told Frankie that he wasn't prepared to work for him anymore. It didn't take a genius to figure out who was behind Samantha's disappearance. But he didn't know Jamilla well enough. She was Samantha's friend, not his. And if he didn't know her, he couldn't trust her.

"Not right now," he said. "Listen, I'm worried too. I don't want to admit it, but I think someone has taken her. This text is a clue, isn't it? I don't know how she's been able to send it, but I know it's a clue that she's not safe."

"Oh my God, Alistair, I can't believe this is happening. It feels so unreal." Jamilla pulled a sheet of paper towel from the roll next to the sink and held it to her eyes while she sobbed. When she looked up, Alistair was staring at the floor, his back resting on the kitchen cupboards. He looked so defeated. "Have you had any other communication from whoever has taken her?" she asked.

Alistair shook his head. He pulled out a dining room chair and sat down, resting his arms on the wooden dining table.

Jamilla had to treat him gently. She could see that he was about to snap. Although her instincts were telling her that there was more to this than met the eye, that Alistair's reluctance to call the police when his wife was clearly in danger was not normal, she decided to bide her time and wait for him to speak. He looked like a man who needed to get something off his chest, and she would be here when that happened.

She opened a couple of cupboard doors until she found the one that stored the glasses. She took out a fresh glass and poured another whiskey.

"Here, drink this," she said, handing the glass to Alistair.

He held the glass tightly with two hands but didn't take a drink. He needed to keep a clear head. He had a feeling who was behind this and the only way to get Samantha back was for him to go and see Frankie. He needed to talk to him, face to face.

He looked at Jamilla, wondering how much, if anything, he could tell her. This was too much for him to bear on his own. But Jamilla was so young, so naive. What did she know about organised criminal gangs and threats? She had never dealt with them personally and had only been a barrister for a couple of years, so Alistair doubted that she had dealt with them professionally. Frankie had a knack of avoiding court appearances.

"I'm not ringing the police," said Alistair. "Not yet anyway. But I think I know who's behind this. Can you trust me?"

"Yes," said Jamilla. No, she wanted to shout. Her instincts were telling her that Samantha's disappearance had something to do with the man she had seen Alistair talking to in court last week. The same man that he seemed anxious about bumping into at her dad's leaving party. Samantha had told her that that man looked like a gangster, and she was right, he did. Apparently, Alistair bought some cocaine from him every now and then, Samantha had said. But from what she had witnessed, there was more to their relationship than an occasional transaction. She had a feeling that Alistair was up to something, and she was determined to find out what it was.

*

Twenty minutes later, Alistair arrived at Frankie's house. Unusually, the huge iron gates were open, so he drove in and parked at the front of the house. He had told Jamilla that he would explain everything to her as soon as he could, and she had promised to give him some time. He had thanked her for driving Samantha's car home and had given her fifty pounds for an Uber. Ironically, one of the fifty-pound notes that Frankie had given him for his services.

He rang the doorbell and knocked hard on the door. "Frankie," he bent down and shouted through the letterbox. "We need to talk."

The door was opened within seconds.

"Come in," said Frankie, with a huge smile. "The wife's on her way out. Pilates tonight, is it, darling?"

Alistair had never met Frankie's wife, but the tall, elegant brunette in the hallway, dressed from head to toe in Lululemon, wasn't the same woman that Frankie had taken to the bar on Friday night. She gave Alistair a quick smile, kissed her husband on the cheek and left them alone, closing the front door behind her.

Alistair, ordinarily, wouldn't have wanted to be alone with Frankie, especially if an altercation was about to ensue. But right now, any fear or trepidation that he may have had in the past had been replaced by blind fury.

"What the fuck have you done with my wife?" he said.

"Whoa, steady on now," said Frankie, holding his hands up, palms facing out. "You can't go throwing accusations around like that, you know. Slander can get you into the courts. And you know how expensive lawyers are."

"This is not a fucking laughing matter, Frankie. Where is she?"

"I've told you before not to tell me what to do," said Frankie, his smile instantly disappearing. "I don't know what you think you're doing here. What's your plan? Go on! Tell me! You wanted to get me by the throat, and push me up against the wall and beat the truth out of me, is that it?" That was exactly it, thought Alistair. "Grow up, man."

Frankie turned his back and walked into the living room, forcing Alistair to follow him. He picked up the remote control from a smoked-glass coffee table in the middle of the room, pointed it towards a giant TV mounted on the wall. He sat down in the middle of one of a pair of leather sofas. "Are you still here?" he said, shooting a disparaging look to Alistair who was hovering in the doorway. Frankie flicked through half a dozen channels until he came to a football match. He turned the volume up high, and the baritone voices of thousands of men filled the room.

"Where is she?" Alistair rushed over to Frankie and knocked the remote control out of his hand. It flew across the wooden floor and came to rest underneath the window.

"Careful now," said Frankie, jumping up to face him. Alistair raised his right fist and punched him as hard as he could in the face. Frankie fell back onto the sofa, holding his bloodied nose in his hand. "You're going to regret that," he said, his voice muffled through his fingers.

"No," said Alistair, standing over him and bending down so that their faces were just inches apart, "You're the one who's going to have regrets. If you don't tell me where Samantha is, I swear to God, I'll kill you."

Frankie laughed. "Finally, you get a pair of balls. But I'm sorry to say, I don't know what you're talking about."

"I don't believe you," said Alistair.

"Believe what the fuck you want. I don't know what you're talking about. Now, I'll give you ten seconds to get out of my house. If you value your life, you'd get going."

"Fuck off, Frankie. I don't know who you think you are. This isn't Chicago and you're not a mafia boss. You live in a poxy house in Manchester…"

"Ten, nine, eight…" Frankie's gun was hidden down the side of the sofa, where he could get his hands on it quickly. He pulled it out and pointed it towards Alistair.

Alistair left the house as Frankie continued his countdown to zero.

Chapter Thirty-Four
Two Days Before the Shooting - Wednesday

Jamilla was one of the first in chambers on Wednesday morning. She knew that Robert would be going with Alistair to court for the last day of his three-day trial, but she desperately needed to speak to him before he left. She needed a second opinion on what she saw last night. Questions were running around her head, frantically searching for answers. She was exhausted. As she was walking back to her office from the kitchen, a steaming coffee in her hand, she saw Robert getting out of the lift.

"Robert," she called. He seemed distracted but his face lit up when he saw her. "I called you last night, but you didn't answer," she said. She tried to keep the accusatory tone out of her voice, but fuck it! He wasn't there when she needed him. "Where were you?"

"Just watching the football with the lads. We had a few beers, that's all. Nothing much."

"I can smell it on you. You can't go to court smelling like that, Alistair will go mental."

Robert fumbled in his pocket for some mints and shovelled a couple into his mouth quickly. He leaned forwards to kiss Jamilla but she turned her face to the side. His kiss landed on her cheek. What was she mad at him now for? Okay, he had had some beers, but not too many. Three or four at the most. He certainly hadn't gone overboard. Admittedly, there was a bit of a gamble on the game, but that was instigated by Harry and Josh. It wasn't his idea. He had to join in. That's what they did, the boys, when they watched football. They always had a bit of a gamble. Just for fun. He had thrown a fifty-pound note onto the sticky table in the pub and, with raucous laughter and pints raised in cheers, encouraged his friends to match his bet. His ego had assured him that his recent winning streak could continue, making it impossible for him to change his mind. Not that he had wanted to. The thrill of the possibility of a win had rushed through his veins. The high lasted until the end of the game. When his team lost, his fifty-pound note was snatched up by Josh, along with the other pound notes, and pushed into his pocket. Robert had forced himself to laugh and Harry had patted him on the back, saying that there was plenty more where that came from, no doubt.

It had been a great night, but this morning when he had checked the pile of cash that Frankie's gorilla-man had given him last week, there was less than four hundred pounds left. Where the fuck had it all gone? Five thousand had gone to the casino, as part payment of his debt. That's why he borrowed the money in first place, so he couldn't worry too much about that. But the rest of it? He didn't want to think. He didn't want to remember. Winning and losing, that's what his life was about these days. And lying.

As he followed Jamilla down the corridor to her office, he told himself that this couldn't go on. He needed to change. What was more important, he wanted to change. As soon as he came out of court this afternoon, he would find a Gamblers' Anonymous meeting. He would tell Jamilla that's what he was doing. Maybe that would calm her down, because her anger and frustration was surrounding her like a smog right now and he found it difficult to breath.

"Come in, hurry up," said Jamilla. "I need to close the door."

"Milla, before you start, I've already decided to find a GA meeting. I'm going to search for one as soon as we come out of court."

"A what?"

"A Gamblers' Anonymous meeting," said Robert.

"Oh right, yes, great," she said.

Robert frowned. As long as he lived, he wouldn't understand women. "I thought you'd be pleased," he said.

Jamilla closed the door behind him and ushered him to the other side of the room, next to the window.

"Listen," she said quietly. "I don't know where Alistair is, but I don't want him to overhear anything. I'm really worried…" The tears that she had been holding in suddenly appeared and she dabbed at them gently with a tissue. She took a few deep breaths.

"About Samantha? Have you still not heard from her?"

"No, I haven't," she said. "That's what I wanted to tell you last night. I think Alistair knows where she is."

"Oh, that's okay then. As long as she's safe…"

"She's not fucking safe, Robert," said Jamilla in a hissed stage whisper. "I mean, he knows who's responsible for her going missing."

"What do you mean? She's not in a hotel?"

"No. On Friday night, this bloke appeared at Dukes Bar, I don't know if you noticed him - expensive suit, beautiful woman on his arm, sycophantic friends. He looked like a gangster, you know, it was obvious. He had an aura about him. You know the type?"

"Go on," said Robert, nodding.

"Well, Alistair clearly knew this guy. The man waved at him when he walked in and then they appeared to be texting each other."

"How do you know that?"

"I was watching Samantha, and she was watching Alistair. So, I looked across at him and I could tell that something was going on. Samantha was clearly worried about something; you could see it in her eyes. Anyway, Alistair and this guy were having a text conversation. At least, that's what it looked like. They both kept looking down at their phones and they both looked furious."

"A coincidence?" asked Robert.

Jamilla shook her head. "When the rain started, Samantha and I ran into the toilets, and I asked her what was going on. She wasn't sure at that time but we both agreed that the man looked like a nasty piece of work."

Robert nodded again. He had met a few men like that throughout his short career, and in the past few days, he had met a couple more. "Alistair has probably prosecuted him for something, has he?" asked Robert.

"No," said Jamilla. "He buys cocaine from him." She emphasised the word cocaine with a raise of her eyebrows.

"Alistair's a cokehead? Wow. I didn't know that."

"Well, I wouldn't call him a cokehead. Samantha says he takes it occasionally, but that man was the dealer that he gets it from. He lives in Chorlton somewhere. Frankie he's called."

"Frankie?"

"Yes, why? Do you know him?"

"No, no," said Robert quickly. "I just didn't hear you properly." He tried to keep his face neutral. He tried to prevent the flush that he could feel rushing up his neck from reaching his cheeks. But Jamilla wasn't stupid, and Robert could tell by the way she was examining his face that she wanted to ask him more questions. "So, what has this got to do with Samantha?" he said.

Jamilla couldn't stop the tears from falling now. She grabbed hold of Robert's hand. "I followed Alistair last night and he went to Frankie's house."

"What do you mean you followed him? And how do you know it was Frankie's house?"

"The man who opened the door was the same guy that I saw in the bar on Friday, the one that Samantha told me was called Frankie. Whatever his name is, it was him. He answered the door and Alistair went inside. I followed him because I don't trust him, Robert."

"And where were you?"

"I was in an Uber. Alistair had given me some money to get home, so I gave the driver an extra fifty quid and asked him to follow Alistair's car. At a distance of course."

Robert sat down on one of the chairs facing Jamilla's desk. He had gone suddenly pale. "Robert? Talk to me. What do you think's going on?"

"I don't know," he said. He pulled Jamilla onto his knee and gave her a huge hug, while she cried onto his shoulder. He took deep breaths to slow his racing heart and prayed that there were two Frankies in Manchester and that, for whatever reason, Alistair wasn't involved in the same one that he was.

"I need to speak to Alistair," said Jamilla eventually, lifting her head. "He asked me to trust him, and he said that he thought he knew who was behind all this, but if he's done something to upset this guy and Samantha has been taken to punish him, well…." Jamilla sobbed and clung onto Robert's neck, while he stroked her back. "I couldn't bear it."

"Jamilla, you know I love you, but do you think that you might have got the wrong end of the stick?" said Robert. "I mean, from Alistair buying cocaine occasionally, to this man kidnapping his wife is a huge leap. Is that what you think happened?"

"Yes, yes, I do," said Jamilla. "What I haven't told you is that Alistair got a text from Samantha's phone last night. It said that she was having some time out with Olivia Stephenson."

"What? Samantha's client?"

"Yes!"

"The one on remand for murder?"

"Yes, exactly. She obviously isn't with her, is she? But she was trying to tell us something."

"Wow," said Robert. "I don't like the sound of that at all."

"Have you seen him yet this morning?" asked Jamilla.

"No, I haven't," said Robert. "Come on, let's go and find him."

"Okay, let me just nip to the ladies' and blow my nose. I need another tissue. Wait here for me, I'll be two minutes."

After she left the room, Robert sent a text to Frankie's number. *I can only repay £500 this week. Please can you add the rest to the balance and I can pay it next week?*

Whatever had happened between Frankie and Alistair, whether or not it involved Samantha, Robert guessed that Frankie had bigger fish to fry than him. The repayment of a few hundred pounds would be way down on his list of priorities. He felt dreadful taking advantage of his friend's dire situation but needs must.

Chapter Thirty-Five
Wednesday

Samantha was asleep when the man unlocked the bedroom door. She was vaguely aware of him putting a cup of coffee on the bedside table. She opened her eyes and saw his great bulk looming over her. She was no longer frightened of him. She was beginning to accept her fate. She told herself that she would be free eventually, and, in the meantime, whatever will be, will be. She had done all she could by sending Olivia Stephenson's name to Alistair. She hoped that he had picked up on the clue that all was not well and that the police would have launched a massive hunt for her. She didn't need to be here much longer.

"Do you want your shower now or later?" he asked her.

"Now please," she said, sitting up in bed. "I need the toilet." So far, she had managed to avoid using the bucket in the corner of the room. She waited for the man to leave the room. She was wearing her t-shirt in bed, but not her jeans and she didn't want to give him the satisfaction of seeing her other than fully dressed. Not again. "Can you wait outside please?" she said. He stared at her as though he didn't understand the question. "I need to get my jeans on."

He nodded as the penny dropped. He left the room and closed the door. She got up and quickly put her jeans on. When she opened the door, he was waiting on the landing. He followed her to the bathroom, as was their daily routine.

As she walked across the landing, she could feel a soft cool breeze whirling around her body, causing goosebumps on her arms. She hadn't felt it before. The doors and windows were usually tightly locked, and the house was always too hot. She hadn't felt any fresh air since she got here. She had lost count of how many days ago that was. She wondered which window he had left open and whether she would be able to fit through it. As soon as the thought formed, she dismissed it as a foolish idea. If she managed to locate the window and climb through it (if indeed he had been stupid enough to leave one open), he would be right behind her and would grab her leg. She imagined herself kicking him in the face, but he would hold on for dear life and would pull her back in.

She went into the bathroom. The man's phone rang, and he closed the bathroom door behind her, before he answered it. Samantha locked herself in, as she usually did.

"Yeah," she could hear him say, as he answered the call. That irritated her. Who answered a phone like that? Why couldn't he say hello, like normal people? After a brief pause, she heard him say, "That's not what we agreed. You're not doing this. I won't allow it." Then he said, "No. You can't do it. I've been here long enough now. You said three days."

She didn't know who he was talking to, but whoever was on the phone was making him angry. She listened with her ear to the door. It appeared that the moron on the other side of the door wasn't master of his own destiny after all. There were clearly other people involved. How dare he say that he had been here long enough! What about her? At least he had the chance to go out. Just this morning, she had seen him in the garden, wandering around the huge lawn with his phone pressed to his ear.

She wasn't sure whether she should be comforted by the fact that he wasn't working alone, or not. An organised kidnapping rarely ended well, if you could believe what happened in films. But then again, it was encouraging to know that she hadn't been kidnapped by a lone maniac. An incompetent maniac at that. Wasn't it better that he was carrying out orders from someone with a modicum of intelligence?

As she strained to hear the one-sided conversation, she realised, unbelievably, that the man was walking away from the bathroom door. She could hear his footsteps on the landing and his voice was fading. Then she heard his voice coming through the adjoining wall. It was faint, but it was there. He had moved into the other bedroom. The one at the front of the house.

Without another thought, she quietly opened the door, just an inch. She couldn't see him.

This was her only chance.

She had to take it.

She turned the water on in the shower. She quickly tiptoed out of the room. She closed the door behind her. As long as the shower was running, he would assume she was still in there.

As long as he was on the phone, he was occupied.

She took her first tentative step onto the stairs, praying that she didn't step on a creaky floorboard. She could still hear the man's voice coming from the front bedroom so, as carefully as she could, she made her way down the stairs. As she stepped into the hallway at the bottom of the stairs, she could feel a definite breeze coming from somewhere.

Next to the open kitchen door was another internal door. It was open just a crack and she could smell the fresh spring air beyond it. This was where the draught was coming from.

She gently pushed the door open and found herself in a small room, no more than ten metres long. In the middle of the wall straight ahead of her, a decorative stained glass window shone a kaleidoscope of colours onto the stone floor. A wooden bench ran down the length of one side. A row of iron hooks had been nailed into the wall above the bench. It appeared to be a boot room. She imagined whoever lived here coming back from an afternoon of grouse shooting with friends. Labradors of various colours would accompany them. They would congregate here, chatting and laughing, taking off their muddy boots and towelling their dogs before retiring into the living room for hot toddy in front of the fire.

Another time, under different circumstances, Samantha would have thought that the house was beautiful. It would make a great party house.

To her left was a wooden external door with a round metal handle. She could feel that the draught was coming from around the door, which hadn't been closed properly. The oak, weathered and old, didn't quite fit the doorframe and probably needed a shoulder to push it into place.

She could still hear the man upstairs, his muffled shouting into his phone told her that his conversation wasn't yet finished. Nevertheless, she didn't have time to spare. She twisted the door handle gently and opened the door, inch by inch. Thankfully, whoever owned this house had maintained it well. The hinges didn't need oiling and the door opened without a sound.

She couldn't believe that he had been so reckless as to leave a door unlocked.

As soon as her bare feet landed on the concrete path outside, she began to run. At first her legs were stiff, after days of lying around with no exercise. Her lungs struggled to take in enough air, but she kept going, down the path and across a cobbled yard, which was enclosed by a tall brick wall. This was probably a stable yard, in the old days.

She could see that the gate at the other end of the yard was open and ran towards it. This must be the side of the house, as she didn't recognise where she was. Her prison bedroom was at the back.

As she ran, she registered the fact that she didn't know whether the gate opened into the back garden or the front. She didn't know whether freedom was within reach, or not. But she had no choice but to keep running. This was her only chance to escape.

In another hundred metres, she would be there.

But he was quicker than her.

He was taller.

His legs were longer.

He was upon her before she reached the open gate.

She felt him tug at her t-shirt from behind. It slowed her down, but her legs carried on running, as she tried to shrug him off.

But he was too strong for her.

As he grabbed her arm and she tried to pull it back from him, she lost her footing.

She fell.

Her head hit the cold, wet cobble stones with a force that knocked her out instantly.

Chapter Thirty-Six
Wednesday

Alistair wasn't in his office, but Jamilla and Robert tracked him down in the kitchen. He was staring out of the window, watching the activity on St. John Street, holding tightly onto a large mug of coffee.

"There you are," said Jamilla, striding up to him. She had her phone in her left hand, her right index finger poised over the call button. "Tell me you've called the police, or I'll do it. Right now." She glared at him, waiting for him to challenge her.

Alistair turned around. The dark circles underneath his red-rimmed eyes were shocking. Jamilla had never seen him looking anything less than perfect. He was clean-shaven, but his shirt was un-ironed, and he wasn't wearing a tie. Jamilla's anger immediately dissipated. She put her phone onto the worktop and held out her arms to him. She never thought in a million years that Alistair would welcome a hug from her. She never thought in a million years that she would want to go anywhere near him. When he stepped into her arms, she embraced him warmly and told him that they would find Samantha. Everything was going to be fine. Samantha was going to be fine.

Alistair pulled away and sat down at the table. Jamilla sat down next to him. Robert poured himself and Jamilla two coffees and topped up Alistair's half-empty mug.

"I thought I knew where she was," Alistair said.

"With Frankie?" asked Jamilla.

"Yes, how…?"

"I saw him at my dad's leaving party and Samantha told me that you buy cocaine from him sometimes." Alistair nodded and shrugged, as though buying cocaine wasn't a big deal.

"Did you think he was involved?" asked Robert.

Alistair nodded again.

"Why, because you owe him money or something?" asked Jamilla.

"No, no, I don't owe him anything," said Alistair. He drank some more coffee and stared into the cup, swirling the hot liquid around and around. How could he tell Jamilla and Robert what he had been doing? How could he tell anyone? He would be instantly arrested, and the subsequent trial would result in a very long prison sentence. Perverting the course of justice was seen as an extremely serious offence. The courts gave out prison sentences to act as a deterrent. To make people think twice before they lied on oath. If a barrister was caught doing it, using his position as prosecuting counsel to sway juries one way or the other, or to prevent a case from even getting to court for its due process, it would be a million times worse. The book would well and truly be thrown at him. The prison door would be locked, bolted and the key thrown away.

"What then?" persisted Jamilla. "Why did you go to his house last night?"

"How did you know that? Did you follow me?"

"Yes," said Jamilla. "Of course, I did. You said that you might know something. She's one of my closest friends and I'm worried about her." Jamilla wiped at her tears.

Alistair didn't have the mental strength to be angry with her for following him. If he were in her position, he probably would have done the same. It must seem strange to her that he hadn't contacted the police, but he had felt sure that Frankie was behind this, and he thought he would be able to sort it out. Frankie was the type of man to pull a stunt like this, just as a show of power. When he had denied it, Alistair was gutted. He felt as though he had reached a dead-end and didn't know which way to go now.

On the way to Frankie's house, he had expected to have some kind of fracas with him. That was inevitable. He had been ready for it. He imagined that he would hear Samantha's stifled cries from another room. He would walk into the living room and there she would be, tied to a chair with a rag in her mouth. He would run over, yank the rag out of her mouth and carry her out to safety. Like Richard Gere in An Officer and a Gentleman.

The ping of an incoming text interrupted the silence. All three of them looked at their phones, but the message was to Robert. *You're a fucking joker. The last person whose payment was late paid by losing their little finger. Your choice.*

"Who was that?" asked Jamilla.

"No-one," said Robert. He put the phone and the threat from Frankie into his jacket pocket. "Just my mum," he added quickly. Jamilla wasn't one to settle for the 'no-one' answer. He pulled out a chair and sat across the table from Alistair. There was a sudden wobble in his legs. What a fucking mess!

Alistair got up from the table and began to rinse his mug under the tap. He opened the dishwasher and put it, upside down, on the top shelf. "We need to leave for court very soon," he said to Robert.

"Alistair?" said Jamilla. "You haven't answered my question. Why would you think Frankie had anything do with where Samantha is?"

She's like a dog with a fucking bone, thought Alistair. On another day, another time, he would have snapped back at her and told her to mind her own business. He would have marched out of the room with his head held high, demanding that Robert follow him. He would have played his role as leader of the pack very nicely. It was what he was used to.

But today he was tired. He had hardly slept. One moment he was satisfied that ringing the police was the right thing to do, and the next, he had changed his mind. He wasn't convinced that Frankie was telling the truth. Maybe he should make another visit to his house?

As last night wore on and sleep seemed so far away, his despair grew and grew. He didn't know what to do and who he could trust. Eventually, when the singing birds had told him that dawn was around the corner, he had gone downstairs and made himself a black coffee. He opened the patio doors and stepped into the garden. As he drank his coffee, sitting on the uncomfortable iron bistro chair that Samantha had bought from the garden centre just last week - a definite case of style over comfort - he watched the sky change from inky blue to white-blue as the sun began to rise. When his alarm went off, he went back inside and reluctantly began to get ready for work. He wished he didn't have to work today, otherwise he would go to Frankie's right now. Kick his door down and drag him out of bed.

"I've known Frankie for a long time," said Alistair. "He's not a man to be messed with and last week, we had a few cross words. It was nothing, but to him, it was a stab at his masculinity. His ego is so big, he doesn't know how to control it sometimes."

"You think kidnapping your wife would be recompense for an argument? Over nothing?" Jamilla's tears were now being replaced by anger, backed up by incredulity.

"I don't know, Jamilla. Men like him are unpredictable. They don't think like we do," he said. "Look, don't worry, I'm going to go and see him again tonight. I'll get to the bottom of this, and I'll get Samantha back home. I don't believe that he doesn't know where she is. There's no other explanation."

Jamilla said nothing.

"Robert," said Alistair. "Come on, time's getting on."

As he and Robert walked out of the room, Jamilla called the police. She couldn't wait for Alistair any longer and she was taking matters into her own hands.

Chapter Thirty-Seven
Wednesday

"Thank goodness the sun is out today, Stanley," said Elsie. She bent down and pulled up a couple of weeds from the soil around his gravestone. "So, I'm going out for lunch with Sebastian on Friday, do you remember me telling you? Guess where we're going." She paused, as though waiting for her husband to have a think and give her a considered response. "He's taking me to The Midland Hotel for an afternoon tea. Isn't that lovely? I'm having my hair washed and blow-dried in the morning. Jenny was very good and managed to squeeze me in. You know how busy it can be at the hairdressers. Oh look, there's Emma." Elsie waved at the young woman who was passing the churchyard. "I'll go and have a quick word."

She walked down the path and met Emma at the churchyard gate.

"Hello, Emma? How are you? Lovely today, isn't it?"

"Yes, lovely," said Emma. "I'm good thanks, well…" The sudden sob forced an end to her sentence.

"Oh dear, whatever is the matter? Here let me get you a tissue. I've got one somewhere." Elsie searched in her handbag and brought out a fresh tissue, which she handed to Emma.

"Thank you," said Emma, taking the tissue and wiping her eyes.

"Do you want to talk about it?" asked Elsie. "I don't want to pry, if it's something private, but talking sometimes helps. I find it does anyway."

Emma looked at Elsie tearfully. She could feel in her heart that she was a good person. Honest and law-abiding. She had probably been blessed with the good fortune of always having enough money, which had kept her safely on the right side of the law. Emma and Jake hadn't been so fortunate. No, she couldn't tell her. Elsie had empathy in bucket loads, but if Emma told her what she was upset about, she wouldn't understand. Not one tiny bit.

"Oh, you know how it is when you're worried about something, and you think you're coping, but then you see a friendly face and it brings the tears out."

Elsie laughed. "I know that feeling," she said. "There's many a time that I think I'm alright and then I see a friend and I start blubbering about my Stanley."

Emma nodded. "I'm just worried about Jake, that's all," she said. "It's nothing. He'll be fine. But thank you for the tissue."

"Okay, love. Well, if you need anything, just let me know. I'm always here for a chat and a brew. It must be quiet in your house now that Jake's working again. And he's got a lovely new car, I see."

"Yes, yes," said Emma. She wondered how Elsie knew about Jake's job. Then she realised that she had probably seen him driving off early Saturday morning in the car that Frankie had lent him and assumed that he was going to work. "Oh yes. He's borrowed the car from his cousin. But it's good that he's working though. Bringing in a bit of money, you know. That's always welcome, with two kids around."

"And it's nice that he's local, too," said Elsie. "I saw him coming out of the driveway of that big house the other day. Is he doing some work on it?"

Shit! Elsie had seen him! Emma tried to stay composed. "Yes, bits and bobs. Anyway, I've got to dash. I'll see you later, and again, thanks for the tissues."

She dashed away before Elsie could ask any more questions.

*

Emma was desperate to speak to Jake. She needed to make sure that he didn't make any mistakes. He wasn't the best at cleaning up, but she could help him with that, when the time came. Leaving evidence for the police forensic team to find would result in him being in prison for the rest of his life. She didn't want to be a prison widow. She wanted her husband to be at home with her, where he belonged. She needed to remind him to wear gloves at all times. Not to leave any fingerprints in the house.

When they had spoken last night, he had finally confessed what he was doing. She had always known that his new job wasn't legal. She would have preferred not to have been made aware of the details, but he had never been away from home for this long before. She was worried about him. She needed to know what he was doing, so she had asked him. The truth was, Jake was desperate to tell her.

But Emma hadn't been prepared for what he was about to say. She had expected a tale of stolen goods, maybe some drugs. But nothing like this. When he admitted that Frankie had given him the job of kidnapping a woman and keeping guard over her for a few days, she had shouted and screamed at him and told him what a pathetic excuse of a husband he was. She knew his work wasn't above board, but this was something else. He was a fucking idiot! She had cried and wailed down the phone and told him that she never wanted to see him ever again. Then she hung up.

He called her straight back. He apologised and begged her to listen to him. He said that he knew he had been stupid to get involved with Frankie again. But he couldn't turn it down. Frankie had promised him that, if he worked for him on a regular basis, he needn't have any money worries ever again. But he would just do this one job and then that would be it. He said he would go legit after that. He promised. He begged her not to give up on him. He was doing this for them. For their family. He could work at Tesco or work for the council picking up litter in the park, he wouldn't be bothered, as long as he had enough to pay their bills and keep the police off his back. The money from this job would be enough to ensure that they could have a holiday this year.

Eventually, Emma calmed down and began to listen to him. Maybe he was right. Accepting this job would be good for them, as a family, she had said. The children had never been abroad. She wanted to take them to Spain. Jake laughed and promised her that they could go in August. The kids would love it. All inclusive. Kids clubs. The lot.

She looked around the house as they talked and asked him whether they would be able to afford new carpets. The house was lovely, but it had been owned by someone who had a taste for the nineteen seventies. Jake laughed and said that their carpets were the height of fashion. Mid-century, that's what they called it on those antique shows on the telly. Never mind that, Emma had protested. Just something grey, neutrals, that's all she wanted. Jake promised she could have the earth on a plate, and he would serve it to her. As soon as this job was over.

Then he told her where he was. She couldn't believe that all this time he was only a few hundred metres away, in the big house near to the churchyard. They had laughed and he had told her how beautiful the house was. She made him give her a virtual guided tour. He told her that Frankie had bought the house as an investment, but at the moment, he wasn't using it. And then it had come in handy as a place to hold this woman.

She told him that she loved him and told him to be careful. She knew that he didn't want to do Frankie's dirty work, but he was doing what he thought was best for his family. And for that, she was proud of him.

After the phone call, as she was putting the children to bed, she wondered where the woman was sleeping and who she was. She hadn't asked whether the house was furnished. She hoped it was and that the poor woman wasn't lying on the floor. Frankie wasn't known for his kindness and consideration. She kissed both children, told them to sleep tight and made her way downstairs.

As she waited for the kettle to boil, she had told herself that not knowing was best. But when her imagination began to run riot, she needed to know more. She had phoned Jake back and told him to assure her that the woman wasn't being hurt. Jake told her that she was clean, well-fed and he had even given her some books to read. That was kind, Emma had told him. But who was she? Jake said she was the wife of someone who was giving Frankie grief, that's all he knew. He told her not to worry, said goodnight and told her that he would see her soon.

When she woke up this morning, Emma had tried not to think about the woman, whoever she was. She tried not to think about how the woman's husband would be missing her and whether she had children. She hoped that she didn't. Her own children, she knew, would be distraught if she wasn't there every day to take them to school, feed them their tea, and tuck them into bed at night. Michael told her that she was the only one who could tie his shoelaces properly. He said that daddy did them the wrong way round. It should be right over left, not left over right.

At the school gate, she couldn't stop looking at all the other mums dropping off their children and wondering if one of them was missing. She didn't know them well enough to know if one of them wasn't there, but by the time she had said goodbye to the children and began her walk home, she was on the edge of tears. Seeing Elsie in the churchyard had brought the tears to the surface.

As soon as she reached home, she rang Jake's phone. He answered after two rings.

"Emma!" said Jake, as he answered the phone. "Emma! Oh my God, it's all such a fucking mess!" He sounded as though he was crying.

"Jake, what's wrong?" she asked.

"The fucking stupid woman tried to escape and now she's on the floor of the yard and I can't wake her up."

"What? Is she dead?"

"I don't know, I don't know."

"What have you done to her?"

"I didn't do anything. I just pulled her back and she fell, and she must have banged her head or something."

"Check whether she's breathing."

"How do I do that?"

"Bend down close to her face and see if you can feel any breath."

"Right, wait there."

Emma could hear the phone being put down onto the floor. She waited and waited.

"Yes, I think she's breathing," said Jake, eventually.

"Okay, well can you carry her?"

"Yes, I think so. Shall I pick her up and take her inside then?"

"No, don't take her inside. She'll have concussion, Jake. She needs to go to hospital."

"I can't take her to hospital. Fucking hell, Emma, I might as well hand myself in, if I'm going to do that."

"But you can't let her die. You can't go to prison for murder. For fuck's sake, Jake."

"I don't know what to do." Emma could tell he was on the verge of hysteria.

"Listen," she said. "Put her in the car and drop her off outside the hospital and then drive off. Or take her to the park or something and leave her there, but then ring an ambulance. No, no, that's a stupid idea, I know. Oh my God, Jake, what the fuck have you got into?"

Chapter Thirty-Eight
Wednesday

The longer Alistair waited for the jury's decision, the more frustrated he became. Usually, being able to sit in the court café drinking coffee and chatting with other barristers and solicitors was fun. Waiting for a jury to make its decision was exciting. The culmination of weeks of hard work, grafting over witness statements and evidence files. But today the wheels of justice were turning far too slowly, in Alistair's view. This was a cut-and-dried case. He couldn't believe that the defendant had the audacity to plead not guilty. His defence that twelve thousand pounds of his employer's money had made its way into his bank account by legitimate means was completely unbelievable. He couldn't understand why the jury hadn't returned with an immediate guilty verdict. What was there to talk about?

On Monday, the young woman from the H.R. department of the company where the defendant had worked had given evidence saying that she had no idea about the money in the defendant's bank account. If it was a bonus, she hadn't been told about it. Alistair had asked her whether any other members of the team had been paid a bonus and she had given him a categorical no. In cross-examination, the defendant's barrister had asked her to agree that the lack of a paper trail was an error. She was young, yes, the witness had said, and had only been working at the company for three months, but she had previous experience, and she was sure that she hadn't made a mistake. Alistair couldn't have asked for a better witness.

Her evidence was followed by the defendant's manager. He also denied that he had agreed to pay the defendant a bonus. He said that the defendant's evidence that there had been a conversation between the two of them, outside of working hours on a Friday night in The Royal Oak, was untrue. The defendant's barrister had asked him how sure he was and asked him whether the conversation could have taken place but he had forgotten about it. Half a dozen pints of lager had been consumed, according to the defendant, and that would have an adverse effect on his memory, wouldn't it? The manager was adamant that he hadn't forgotten, and that the defendant was telling lies. But isn't it true that they were at the company's summer party? the defendant's barrister asked. A time for drinking and eating to excess. Nobody expected him to remember every conversation.

Alistair had sighed to himself and looked over at his opponent. Surely, he couldn't believe the bullshit that he was spouting. The judge should have brought an end to the trial there and then. He wanted to jump to his feet and shout 'Objection!' He wished that English courts were more like the ones he saw in American films. He was waiting for the day when he could get over-exuberant and shout, "I want the truth!". But he wasn't Tom Cruise and the man in the witness box wasn't Jack Nicholson. All he could do was keep quiet and wait for the ridiculous and pointless questioning to end.

In other circumstances, Alistair would have enjoyed ripping into the defendant in the witness stand. The manager had provided Excel spreadsheets to show the sales figures of every member in the company. The defendant's sales were mediocre at best and the manager could prove that nobody else had been paid a bonus, due to the unhealthy state of the company's finances last year. But Alistair's mind was elsewhere. If it hadn't been for the prompts and hastily written notes from Robert - thank goodness he was there - Alistair's performance would have been embarrassingly poor. The evidence weighed so heavily against the defendant that this case should have been a walk in the park for him.

He looked at the clock on the café wall. The jury had been out for almost an hour.

"What the fuck have they got to talk about?" he said. "He's a guilty man. Absolutely no question."

"Yes, I agree," said Robert. "But it is nearly twelve, so I presume they're having sandwiches and…"

"It's not a fucking jolly. They're here to do a job. Give us the verdict and then we can all fuck off home."

A middle-aged solicitor on the next table tutted and raised her eyebrows disapprovingly.

"What?" he asked her. He was in the mood for a fight, verbal or otherwise. He had met that particular solicitor before. She was a snooty cow.

The solicitor stood, gathered up her papers and walked out, mumbling to herself. Robert kept quiet.

"Honestly, what's the world coming to when a man can't even swear in a courthouse café? We're surrounded by people who use expletives constantly. Don't tell me she's not used to hearing them?"

Robert wanted to tell Alistair that it probably wasn't the use of bad language that she objected to, but more likely the aggressive volume. But now wasn't the time to lecture him on professional etiquette.

Now also wasn't the time to tell him that Jamilla had called the police this morning. On the way to court, Alistair had told him that he would rather keep the police out of the picture for now, just because Frankie was so unpredictable and violent. Robert knew exactly what he meant. Jamilla had texted Robert earlier this morning, just as they had arrived at court. The police were taking Samantha's disappearance extremely seriously and were on their way to chambers. They had promised to be there before lunchtime. Jamilla said that James was going to ring her when they arrived. Robert had texted her back, telling her she had done the right thing. The truth was, despite Frankie's reputation, Alistair should have done it on Monday, or maybe even Sunday. He could understand that the text from Samantha telling him she was having time out would have thrown Alistair. But it now meant that Samantha had been missing for nearly forty-eight hours, and if Frankie really was behind it, then God help her. He didn't want to think about it.

"Can all parties in the case of The Crown versus Jackson return to Court Two, please," said a voice over the tannoy.

"That's us, let's go," said Alistair, jumping up. His plastic chair scraped on the tiled floor. He was still wearing his wig and gown, anxious not to be delayed by a single minute.

Robert collected all the papers, put his wig on and followed Alistair out of the café and down the corridor, putting his arms into his gown as they walked.

By the time they arrived at Court Two, the defendant's barrister was already in his place and the defendant was in the dock. The judge returned and promptly ordered the return of the jury. Alistair had no enthusiasm for his usual game of guessing who the foreperson was. He kept his head down and waited for the verdict, thinking about his wife and praying that she was safe. Even the guilty verdict, when it came, gave him no pleasure. When the court had emptied, the case having been adjourned for sentencing at a later date, he went through the motions of shaking hands with his opponent and left as quickly as he could.

Robert trailed Alistair back to chambers, wondering whether he should tell him about the police's imminent arrival or should he leave that job to Jamilla? As they marched up Byron Street and into St. John Street, he still hadn't decided what the best course of action should be. Alistair's phone ringing saved him the job of making a decision.

"It's a withheld number," said Alistair, staring at the screen. He pressed the answer button and put the phone to his ear. "Are you fucking with me?" he said, after a beat. Alistair's face drained of colour. Alistair thrust the phone back into his pocket and sprinted down St. John Street at a speed that Mo Farah would be proud of.

"Alistair! Wait for me!" shouted Robert, running after him.

Alistair ran straight past the front door of chambers, towards the street at the side of the building. As Robert reached the top of the street, he caught sight of Alistair disappearing around the back of the building and into the car park. His legs felt like jelly and his lungs were hurting, but he pushed himself to sprint as fast as he could.

As he turned the corner into the car park, he could see Alistair on the floor, on his hands and knees. He was crouching over a body. Bare feet and grubby jeans were sprawled on the cold stone. Alistair's body was covering the top half of the body, but it was clear who it was.

"Samantha! Samantha!" Alistair shouted. He cradled her head in his arms. Her dark curls were matted with dried blood. Purple bruises covered one side of her face. "Call an ambulance!" he screamed.

Chapter Thirty-Nine
The Day Before the Shooting - Thursday

Jamilla liked to stay at her parents' house. On Christmas Eve or after a summer barbeque or on her mum's birthday in September. On those special occasions, it was a treat to sleep in their guestroom. She liked to take a long bath in their Victorian roll top bath and then stretch out in the king-sized bed. Her mum usually put a tiny vase of flowers from the garden on the bedside table and a pile of freshly laundered towels on the end of bed. Last Christmas it had been a tiny pink and white orchid in a pale pink vase that she had picked up from Waitrose, along with the mince pies and shortbread biscuits.

Jamilla knew that both her parents loved having her over to stay as much as she loved to be there. Her visits brought laughter, joy and happiness. But last night when she unexpectedly arrived on the doorstep, she brought with her tears, misery and distress.

She had made the telephone call from the car, giving them twenty minutes notice, just as her parents were going to bed. Between hiccupped sobs, she had apologised for disturbing them so late. Sebastian had told her that there was nothing in the world he liked more than to be disturbed by his daughter. He told her to take deep breaths and calm down. She must concentrate on her driving and get to them safe. She promised that she would. Laila leant over Sebastian's shoulder and shouted into the phone that she would warm the milk for some hot chocolate.

When Jamilla had arrived, the hot chocolate was ready and waiting. Sebastian put his arm around his tearful daughter and led her into the kitchen, where Laila was buttering slices of thick toast. She put them on three small plates and carried them to the table, where they all sat down for their late-night snack.

"I'm glad you're here," Sebastian had said. "Your mum doesn't let me eat toast usually. The butter's bad for my cholesterol, apparently."

Jamilla had slowly begun to feel better, comforted by the toast, the hot chocolate and her parents' love. When her mum had asked her if she had argued with Robert, she had nodded. That's an understatement, she thought. Where could she begin? How could she tell them what he had done and the terror she had just experienced in his apartment? And Samantha? How could she explain about her? She hadn't even told them that she was missing. But now she was back. She couldn't get her head around the events of the last few days, so how could she explain to her parents what had been happening? She needed time to process her thoughts. She asked them if they wouldn't mind if she went to bed and talked about it in the morning.

"Darling, whatever you want," said Sebastian. "You go and get a good night's sleep and we'll see you in the morning."

She had left them, sitting there at the kitchen table in their dressing gowns and with their worried faces, and had gone to bed. Now, she was wide awake, waiting for sounds of movement so that she could go downstairs. She couldn't disturb her parents any more than she already had.

It wasn't long before she heard their bedroom door opening and her father's footsteps creeping down the stairs. He had always been an early riser. She opened her bedroom door slowly and tiptoed onto the landing.

"You don't need to be quiet," said Laila. "I'm awake." Her bedroom door was open. Jamilla went straight in and climbed into the bed. Laila fluffed the pillows on Sebastian's side of the bed and tucked the quilt around her daughter. "Your dad's making tea, do you want one?"

"Yes, please," said Jamilla.

"Sebastian!" Laila shouted. "Sebastian! Your daughter needs tea, please."

"Okay," came a distant voice from the kitchen.

"What are you smiling at?" asked Laila.

"I thought you'd ring him, or text him or something. I didn't expect you to bellow down the stairs. I could have done that myself."

"Well, there's nobody here but us, so there's no need to be quiet now that we're all awake," said Laila, laughing. "It's nice to see you smile," she said. She stroked Jamilla's hair and kissed her cheek. "When you're ready to talk about what's bothering you, we're here to listen."

So, when Sebastian arrived with three mugs of tea on a tray and settled himself on the end of the bed, she told them what had been happening.

She told them that Samantha hadn't turned up for work on Monday. Alistair had told her and Robert that Samantha had left him, albeit just for a short time, because they had been arguing. Sebastian nodded and said that he had heard the way Alistair spoke to her, particularly when he thought nobody else could hear him. It was disgusting. But she hadn't left him, Jamilla explained. She had been kidnapped and had been held hostage in a huge house somewhere in the countryside. She started crying then and Sebastian put his tea down and ran into the bathroom, coming back with the toilet roll to mop up her tears.

She told them that the whole time, Alistair had prevaricated because he thought he knew best. For whatever reason, he didn't want to ring the police, so poor Samantha had been kept as a prisoner since Saturday night. She must have been terrified, thinking she was going to die. Or worse.

Jamilla answered her shocked parents' questions as best as she could through her tears. Yes, she was all right. Well, she's alive at any rate. She's in hospital now. Robert phoned for an ambulance. She had been dumped in the car park at the back of chambers and Alistair had received a phone call, telling him where she was. No, he didn't know who had done it. She was a bad way, battered and bruised and she had a huge cut on her head. Yes, they will be keeping her in for a few days. No, she doesn't know who had taken her or where she had been held. Alistair said that someone must have drugged her. She had a vague memory of leaving her friends on Saturday afternoon and then she woke up in a strange house with a lunatic. Yes, Alistair said she could describe the man and she would be giving a more detailed statement to the police today at some point.

"You're not going to work today, are you?" asked Sebastian, when she had finished her tale and there were no more questions. "You're in no fit state."

"No," said Jamilla. "I told James to clear my diary until Monday. I don't have any court hearings until next week."

"That's good," he said. "You need to stay here and rest." He patted his daughter's hand.

"I'd like to see Samantha, if she's allowed any visitors," said Jamilla.

"Why don't you both go and see her tomorrow?" said Laila. "Your dad's having lunch with your Aunty Elsie, so maybe you could go and have lunch with them, and then see Samantha afterwards."

"Yes, that sounds like a plan. She will probably be overwhelmed by visitors today. Her family and stuff," said Jamilla. "I might not be much company for you and Aunty Elsie, though, Dad. I can't seem to stop crying."

"That's understandable," said Sebastian. "You've had a shock. Elsie would love to see you, but only if you feel like it."

"They're going to The Midland for afternoon tea," said Laila.

"That's nice," said Jamilla, forcing a smile.

"Well, I might change the plans, I don't know…" said Sebastian.

"No, you will not," said Laila. "It's Elsie's favourite place. You can't let some idiot…"

Sebastian mouthed at her to be quiet.

"What's going on?" asked Jamilla. "Dad? I saw you telling Mum to be quiet. What aren't you telling me?"

"I didn't want to worry you, that's all," said Sebastian. "It's something and nothing, but until it's sorted, well…"

"He's had a couple of death threats..."

"Death threats? What the hell!"

"Laila, please. You're going to frighten the girl to death. It's not as bad as it sounds.," said Sebastian. "It's connected to a client who I saw in Manchester Prison last week. He's on remand and said that if I didn't get him out, then I'm a dead man. But he's still in there, so he can't get to me. I've told the police and it's okay now."

"Wow," said Jamilla. She sipped at her tea. "That's not nice. You must have thought he was serious though, for you to call the police?"

"Well, yes, but there's nothing to worry about. Like your mum said, I can't let some idiot dictate my life. Okay, so who wants breakfast?"

Jamilla finished her tea and held out her mug to Sebastian, who took the empties downstairs, promising to make some more tea. He told Jamilla that he still hadn't perfected the art of a good poached egg, so it would have to be fried or boiled.

The telepathic look between Laila and Sebastian said that they agreed that they wouldn't tell their daughter about the other death threat, from the man who had turned up at the house and put a knife to Sebastian's throat. It was dark when Jamilla had arrived last night, so she hadn't noticed the tiny scratches on the front door, left after her dad had scrubbed away the red paint. And she didn't need to know that the same man had shouted at her dad in the supermarket car park. She had enough to worry about.

As he went downstairs, Sebastian told himself that he needed to get a grip. Crime happened every minute of every day, but most people weren't unaware of it. His job and Jamilla's job meant that they were exposed to more than their fair share. He couldn't let that cloud his judgement of Manchester. He couldn't get to the stage where he was frightened of going out. Feel the fear and do it anyway. Isn't that the title of a famous book, or a saying, or something? Just because he had received death threats didn't mean that they would be carried out. He was going to be perfectly safe. He would enjoy his lunch tomorrow in The Midland and he wouldn't let Jay Harris or Harris' brother ruin it.

But Samantha being kidnapped? That was a whole different level. That must have been terrifying for her. He hoped that Manchester wasn't turning into the crime capital of the UK. He had never heard of someone being abducted off the street like that. Over the years, he had worked on many cases where people had done terrible things to each other. Stabbings, vicious assaults and all kinds of violence. He had long since accepted that was how some people settled feuds. The parties were known to each other, more often than not. In most cases, both sides were somewhat to blame. But being abducted by a stranger was rare. If this was America, this was the sort of crime where the FBI would get involved, wasn't it?

Poor Samantha.

Nobody was safe these days. If it wasn't for Laila pushing him to go about his normal business, he'd love to cancel his lunch at The Midland tomorrow. He didn't feel like going back into town. He'd much rather drive to Elsie's house and have lunch in a quiet country pub. But this wasn't about him. It was about his sister and he would man up and take her out for her afternoon tea.

As Jamilla made her way downstairs, followed by her mum, she decided that she didn't want to tell them about Robert and the trouble he was in and the fact that a huge angry man had kicked his door down last night and terrified the pair of them. She couldn't bear to think about it, never mind talk about it.

Chapter Forty
Thursday

Chambers was quiet. The laughter and chatter that could be heard coming from the kitchen on a normal morning had been replaced by whispered gatherings and muted conversations between the few people who were there. Alistair was spending the day at Samantha's hospital bedside. James had told Robert that Jamilla wouldn't be in until next week. She hadn't told him herself, but he wasn't surprised that he hadn't heard from her.

Samantha being found in the car park yesterday afternoon had been a shock to everyone, and would be a topic of conversation for a long time. But Robert couldn't face it. He decided that his need for solitude was greater than his need for coffee and so avoided his colleagues in the kitchen. He went straight into his office, where today's brief was waiting for him.

He had a few hours to read it and make himself acquainted with the evidence before his conference this afternoon with the solicitor in charge of the case. This was what he had been working towards; what he had been studying for all these years. An opportunity for him to work on a case without supervision. If only he could concentrate for more than two minutes without his mind wandering. If only he could summon up a modicum of enthusiasm.

He closed the door (sod the open-door policy) and sat down at his desk. He looked across at Samantha's empty desk. In no time, she would be back at work, he told himself. They would laugh together and drink coffee and discuss their cases and everything would go back to normal. Hopefully. He tried not to think about what she had just been through and who had given her the cuts and bruises he had seen. They had no proof that Frankie was involved. He had denied it when Alistair had asked him. What a bastard! He wondered whether Alistair was prepared to tell the police where he bought his cocaine and have Frankie investigated. Probably not. If he was Alistair, he would keep quiet.

But he couldn't think about that right now. He had work to do, and he had to get on with it. Without Alistair here, this was his time to prove himself and secure himself a permanent place in chambers. This was the start of his career and he had to tread carefully. So much in his life was turning to shit. He had to protect his career.

He pulled at the pink ribbon that tied the papers together and began to read. The Crown versus Harry Blackman. Mr Blackman was the owner of a small estate agency in Manchester. He had been accused of sexual assault of two of his female employees and the rape of a woman who had instructed the agency to sell her house. The brief defence statement filed on behalf of Mr Blackman informed him that all sexual encounters with the three women were consensual. That's bollocks, thought Robert, as he put the defence statement to one side. Unless this guy is a classically handsome millionaire philanthropist who works with children's charities or animal shelters, who can cook, who worships his mum and also loves watching rom-coms on a Saturday night, then there's not a hope in hell that he would have three women throwing themselves at him within the space of a few weeks. How could this idiot expect the jury to believe that he went to someone's house to do a valuation and the owner just happened to be feeling randy and asked him for a shag? A complete stranger. What are the chances of that?

Robert picked up his phone from the corner of the desk. For the second or third time that morning, he checked the volume and checked that it wasn't on silent. There was no message from Jamilla. He had left her a voicemail and numerous messages. He knew that expecting a reply was wishful thinking. After last night, she wouldn't want to see him ever again. He couldn't blame her. He wouldn't want to either if he was in her shoes. Even so, the most condemned man deserved a defence, didn't he? If she would just give him five minutes to explain.

He told himself to put her out of his mind. Just for today, he needed to concentrate. For the next hour, he read the instructions from the CPS and the statements from the victims. He tried to view the evidence with emotional detachment and made pencilled notes. The Crown Prosecution Service had instructed Alistair to advise them on the evidence. This afternoon, the solicitor would expect to meet with someone who knew what he was talking about. Someone with experience and knowledge. He couldn't let Alistair down.

Yesterday Alistair had told him that he would trust him implicitly to give the right advice. Robert had thanked him and told him that he would do his best and that Alistair didn't have anything to worry about. He told him to concentrate on Samantha. Look after her and give her my love, he had said, as Alistair and the barely conscious Samantha were whisked away in the ambulance. He had stood on the edge of Deansgate, with Jamilla by his side, and watched as his friend and office companion were driven to safety. Where Samantha had been for the past four days, he didn't know. He was just relieved that she was safe. He had hugged Jamilla close to him, and told her that he loved her. She said she loved him too, and had reached up to him and kissed his tear-stained cheek.

She had gone home with him then, clinging to him for security. They had ordered take-away Indian food and sat side by side watching television, waiting for it to arrive. After the delivery had been dropped off, Jamilla had taken the paper bag and had given herself the job of dishing up. She complained that Robert always gave her too much. It was over-facing to have all the food on the plate at the same time. She liked to have small portions and then go back for seconds. Robert had laughed and said she was weird but left her to it.

When the sudden knock on the door came, he had assumed that it was the delivery driver returning with something he had forgotten to drop off. But as he walked past the window towards the door, squeezing between the edge of the corner sofa and his giant Areca palm plant that his mother had bought him as a moving-in gift, he saw the delivery man cycling away outside. His view from the tenth floor of his apartment building still amazed him, even after almost a year of living there, and it was habit for him to look out of the window at the slightest opportunity. The ever-changing view of the tiny people and vehicles down below was constant entertainment.

The second, more forceful knock came too soon after the first one to be polite. The hair on the back of Robert's neck rose in anticipation. Of what, he wasn't sure. But what he was sure of was that he shouldn't open the door without the safety chain. Trying not to let Jamilla see (one of the disadvantages of open-plan living), he fastened the chain and opened the door a crack. The first thing he saw was the enormous black boot as it pushed into the space between the wall and the door. Robert immediately pushed against the door, trying to close it. Two heaves were all it took to break the ridiculously ineffective safety chain. Robert would have to send an email of complaint to the management company about that.

"Nice place," said the man. His heavy boots clomped across the living area, straight towards Jamilla in the open-plan kitchen. It was the cowboy gangster. The one who had collected the money from him outside chambers last Friday afternoon.

"Curry? Not cheap that, is it?" He spooned a mouthful of jalfrezi into his mouth. A drip of spicy tomato sauce rested on his chin. "Thought you had no money?"

Robert wanted to shout at the man to stop eating his food and to get out of his apartment. He wanted to tell Jamilla that there was nothing to worry about, she was safe, he could handle it. He wanted to tell her that this was a case of mistaken identity. The man was looking for another man in another place. But he didn't. His silence fell between him and Jamilla, like an invisible barrier that neither of them would be able to navigate around.

He had watched Jamilla's face. His beautiful Jamilla. He had never seen her look so petrified. She glanced at the door, and he knew that she was looking for an escape route. More than anything, he wanted to take her hand and lead her to the door and tell her to go home. But the exit was blocked by a six-foot-three giant of a man. He hadn't seen him before.

"Just a little message from Frankie," said the cowboy. He chewed on another spoonful of curry and ripped a corner off the garlic naan. He waved the naan in the air like a conductor's baton. "Because as you know, Frankie likes to give his messages in person."

Robert studied the man and wondered what his chances of tackling him were. He might have a chance, he thought. He was good at rugby, and he wasn't small himself. He would have to take him by surprise and while he was down on the floor, Jamilla could spray something in the other man's eyes and make good her escape. There was kitchen cleaner in the cupboard under the sink. A spray bleach type thing that would hurt like hell if she could manage to get it in his eyes. But the sudden punch to the stomach unbalanced him. Before he knew it, he was on the floor and Jamilla was screaming.

That's good, that's good, he thought. The screaming will attract the neighbours. But the door-stop man closed the door behind him, rushed over to Jamilla and grabbed her from behind, forcing his grubby dirty hands over her mouth.

"I can pay him tomorrow," Robert managed to say, as he got to his feet. "Five o'clock, like we agreed."

"Don't take the piss by asking for more time then," said the man. "Frankie doesn't like people taking the piss out of him."

And I don't like people barging into my apartment and wrecking my evening, thought Robert. He looked over to Jamilla. Her silent tears and almost imperceptible shake of her head told him that this was the end. She had been pushed to her limit. Being burgled and attacked by strangers was one thing, but Jamilla now knew for certain that Robert knew his attackers and for that, she would never forgive him.

After dipping the naan bread into the curry again and shoving it in his mouth, the man spotted Robert's Longines silver watch on the coffee table. Without a word, he walked over to it, slipped it on his wrist and strode over to the door, nodding at his companion to follow him.

"That curry's good," he said, as he opened the door and walked out.

"Jamilla, are you okay?" Robert ran over to Jamilla and tried to hold her, but she held her arms outstretched in front of her, so he couldn't get close. Then she picked up her handbag and her jacket and followed the men out of the door.

Robert wasn't surprised when he arrived at chambers this morning and James told him that she wouldn't be in. Maybe it was for the best. Right now, he could only deal with one thing at a time. His mind was becoming too full, too over-whelmed. In order of priority, he would deal with this brief, then he would ring his best friend Lucas and ask him for a loan and after that, he could salvage his relationship with Jamilla. If there was anything left to salvage.

Just as he formulated the action plan in his head, he remembered that he had never asked the man not to hurt Jamilla. He knew that she would never forgive him for that.

Chapter Forty-One
Thursday

The plain clothes policewoman knocked gently on the door to Samantha's private room in Manchester Royal Infirmary and peered through the small gap in the curtains. Alistair beckoned her in. He would have liked to open the door for her, but he was frightened of letting go of Samantha's hand. He sat on the right side of her bed, nearest to the window, the left side being occupied by a saline drip stand and frequent nurses, who popped in with their concern and sympathy and scribbled notes on the sheet of paper at the bottom of her bed. He winced every time he caught sight of the canula in her left hand.

"Hi," said the policewoman. "Is it okay to come in? The doctor said you were awake and feeling better."

"Yes, come in," said Samantha.

"My name's DC Erica Townsend. I'd like to ask you some questions, if that's alright."

"Yes, of course. Alistair, can you get the officer a chair, please."

Alistair reluctantly let go of Samantha's hand. "Come and sit here. I'll stand." He indicated the chair where he had slept last night and had spent most of today. A deep pink high-backed chair with wooden armrests. It was better than the tiny plastic ones in the waiting room of the Accident and Emergency Department where he had waited for what seemed like hours last night.

"I'm sure you can find another chair from somewhere," said Samantha.

"No, honestly. I need to stretch my legs," he said.

The officer smiled her thanks and sat down in Alistair's chair. She rested a notepad on the edge of the bed and held a pen in her right hand, ready. "Thank you," she said. "Let me start by saying, if you feel dizzy or tired or anything, please let me know and I can take a break. I can even come back later. Whatever you feel. Is that okay?"

"Yes," said Samantha. "But really, I'm fine. I've just got a bit of a bump on my head that's all. My headache's much better now. I'm hoping to go home later."

"I'm not sure about that, darling," said Alistair, standing at the bottom of the bed and holding onto the bedframe. "Let's see what the doctor says when they do the evening ward rounds. I'd rather you didn't rush out." He didn't want to add that, if he had his way, she would be kept in the hospital for weeks, until he had figured out what to do about Frankie. He wanted to tell the police officer that he knew who had abducted her, or at least who was the brain behind the brawn. There was no doubt that Frankie needed to be stopped, sooner rather than later. But how could he tell them without implicating himself? Frankie wouldn't go down alone. That was not his style at all.

"So, let's start at the beginning, Samantha," said DC Townsend. "Can you tell me as much as you can about what you remember from Saturday?"

"That seems so far away," said Samantha. "Honestly, my friends and family are all I've thought about all week. I thought I'd never see them again." She wiped the tears that were streaming down her face with the edge of the hospital blanket. Alistair gave her a tissue from the box on the table tray at the end of the bed.

"You went out with a couple of friends in Manchester, is that right?"

"Yes, Chloe and Laura. We had some lunch and a drink, but I was meant to be going to my sister's house in the evening with Alistair, so I didn't stay that long. I can't remember what time I left them, but it wasn't long after lunch."

"And were you intending to drive home?"

"Yes, my car was parked in the car park behind chambers, at the back of St. John Street. One of the perks of working in town." Samantha smiled and tried to stem the flow of tears, pushing a scrunched-up tissue in the corner of her eyes. "I can't say for sure what happened next. It's so blurry. I remember walking down Deansgate and then I have a vague memory of being dragged into another car. I think he put something over my mouth, because I blacked out."

Alistair patted her feet underneath the hospital's waffle blanket. DC Townsend scribbled down what Samantha was saying.

"What was the first thing you remember when you woke up, after blacking out?" she asked.

"Well, when I woke up, it was early morning. It was the strangest thing. I didn't know where I was. I thought it must be Laura's house, because she had recently moved, so that's why I didn't recognise it. I assumed that someone had spiked my drink and my friends had put me to bed."

"Were you in bed?"

"Yes. I could see my clothes on the floor in the bedroom. He had folded them up."

"The bastard," said Alistair. "Sorry, sorry. I didn't... sorry." He waved his hand at the officer, trying to dismiss his sudden burst of emotion.

Samantha smiled at him through her tears. "He didn't do anything to me. Not in that way. It's okay."

"Sorry," said Alistair again to DC Townsend.

"Don't worry, you're bound to be emotional too. When terrible things happen to crime victims, it affects the whole family."

"Do you want to go and get us some coffee, Alistair?" said Samantha.

Alistair nodded and left the room with instructions to bring back two cappuccinos plus a black coffee for himself. DC Townsend told him that there was a Costa Coffee on the ground floor. She knew that would keep him away for at least fifteen minutes, which would give her time to speak to Samantha on her own.

"I can understand that he's upset," said DC Townsend. "It isn't easy for men to hear that their wives have been mistreated by someone else, especially in a case like yours. He must have been very worried."

The officer had read the statement that Alistair had given to her colleague yesterday evening. He had said that he had no idea who could be behind this, and he hadn't received any request for a ransom, he had assumed that his wife was having some time on her own, after they had argued.

It was baffling. This didn't seem to be the usual kidnapping. Who kidnaps a person and doesn't ask for money in return for their loved one's safety? It didn't make sense. She was sure there was something more to this story. Kidnappings were generally carried out for money, or for revenge or for a sexual motive. But in this case, none of those seemed to fit. No doubt the truth would rise to the surface of the muddied waters in due course.

"Well, one good thing has come from this, I suppose," said Samantha.

"What's that?"

"My husband is showing me how much he truly loves me. I've not had this much affection from him since our honeymoon."

DC Townsend smiled. "Well, that's something," she said. "Samantha, while he's out of the room, can I ask you the delicate questions? Get them out of the way."

"Yes, of course."

"Did the man who abducted you assault you in any way sexually?"

"No, he didn't," she said. "It's hard to explain what he was like. I wouldn't say that he was gentle with me, because he absolutely wasn't. He did punch me a couple of times, and he shouted and swore at me. But it's almost as if he didn't want to. Like he was following orders."

DC Townsend nodded. "It's possible that he was," she said. "Did you see anyone else, or did you hear him talking to anyone else?"

"Yes, I heard him on the phone a few times. That's how I managed to escape - well try to escape. He was distracted on the phone, and I ran downstairs and found an unlocked door. He was shouting at the person on the other end of the phone, saying that it wasn't the deal that he agreed, or something like that."

"Did you have any understanding of what he meant by that?"

"Yes, well I'm guessing, but on the first day, or maybe the second day, I can't remember now, when I asked him whether Alistair had been told about me being kidnapped and whether they had asked him for any money, he said that it didn't work like that, and they would tell him when they were ready. I don't understand, because isn't the point of being kidnapped that they tell the family and get money?"

"Yes, usually," said DC Townsend. It was as though Samantha had read her thoughts. This situation was extremely odd.

Samantha told the officer as much information as she could about the man's appearance, about his 'Emma' tattoo and about the car that had been parked outside the house. She described the rooms that she had seen in the house and as much of the courtyard as she could remember. She couldn't tell her where the house was, other than it was surrounded by fields and close to a churchyard. She could remember being thrown into the boot, but she kept drifting in and out of consciousness, because it didn't seem long before the car came to a stop, and she was pulled out and thrown to the floor. Then soon after that, Alistair had found her.

"When you were put in the boot of the car, did anyone help him, or did he manage it alone?"

"No, there was someone else there," said Samantha, nodding. "I wasn't fully conscious at all times, I don't think. I had given my head a good crack on the floor, but I know that two people picked me up."

"Are you sure?" asked the officer.

"Yes. One at my head and another at my feet. I can't remember what they looked like though, sorry. I can just remember black clothes and a black baseball cap. He must have been a lot smaller than the other man, though."

"What makes you say that?"

"Well, I'm not a big woman by any means, but he seemed to struggle picking me up. I know they say that a dead weight is heavy, but…"

"Could it have been a woman?"

Samantha was shocked that DC Townsend would consider that a woman would be involved in a horrible crime such as this, but she said that it would explain why the man seemed to soften as the days went on. He had given her some books and more cups of tea and asked her if she was warm enough. That seemed to make sense. He must have been taking orders from a woman.

DC Townsend shrugged and said she was thinking about the woman not being as strong as the man, rather than the fact that she was exhibiting a caring side. But it was another line of enquiry for them to consider.

Alistair returned to the room with a bag full of cookies and muffins and two cappuccinos, which he left on the table. He gave Samantha a kiss on her cheek and said that he would drink his coffee outside. He would take an opportunity to get some fresh air and have a walk in the hospital garden. He left the room as quickly as possible. The last person he wanted to speak to was another police officer. Especially after the text message he had just received from Frankie on his burner phone.

I take it your wife was delivered safe and sound. As long as our arrangement continues, she will stay safe. Will be in touch.

Chapter Forty-Two
Thursday

Frankie opened his front door to Jake. Wordlessly, he turned his back and walked into the living room. Jake followed, closing the door behind him.

"I thought you wanted a fucking job," said Frankie. "Thought you needed the money."

"I do, I do," said Jake.

"So why did you take her back before the job was finished?"

"She…"

"It wasn't your call to make!" shouted Frankie. "That was my decision, and I wasn't ready for her to be taken back."

"But, like I said, she had a head injury. It needed looking at."

"You need your fucking head looking at. If you weren't family, Jake, I swear to God, I'd punch you into the middle of next week. For fuck's sake!" Frankie stared out of the window, shaking his head in disbelief. "How much did she see of the house?"

"Just the bedroom and then the kitchen, that's all."

"And the fucking boot room and the fucking yard at the back! That house is in my name, you fucking moron."

"Well, yeah but..."

"Shut up!" said Frankie. "Don't speak another word. I don't want to hear it. If you want your money, you need to finish the job, then you can have it. First of all, I want the car back. Take the plates off it, put the original ones back on and then leave the keys with me, right?"

"Right, yes," said Jake.

"There's a screwdriver in the kitchen. Then ring your missus and tell her you'll be home tomorrow. There's a suit in the guest bedroom upstairs and a gun in the bedside table. It's loaded with six bullets. You'll spend the night here and then make your way into Manchester tomorrow." Frankie took a photograph of Alistair out of the inside pocket of his jacket. He unfolded it and handed it to Jake. "He's your target. He works at Whites Chambers on St. John Street. He knows too much. I can't trust him. Finish him off and then you'll get your money."

Chapter Forty-Three
The Day of the Shooting - Friday

Jamilla was surprised when she looked at her phone and saw that it was almost eight o'clock. She hadn't slept that well for weeks. Now that Samantha had been found safe, it was as though her body had finally agreed to stop producing cortisol by the bucket load and replace it with sleep inducing and extremely welcome melatonin.

There were three missed calls from Robert and dozens of messages, which she refused to read. Some of them, as long as essays, no doubt declared himself a changed man, or at least on the path to being a changed man. Jamilla had had enough. She wasn't interested in what he had to say. She deleted the unread messages and blocked his number.

She opened the bedroom door and was immediately comforted by the smell of smoked bacon floating up the stairs from the kitchen. The siren of the smoke alarm that followed made her smile. Domesticity. Safety. Family. That's what she needed this weekend. She knew that if she went to her own house, there was a high likelihood of Robert appearing uninvited on her doorstep. She couldn't bear to see him. He wouldn't have the balls to turn up at her parents' house.

Last night, her dad had suggested they could call at her house on the way back from lunch this afternoon and she could pick up anything that she needed for the weekend. That was a great idea, she had told him. Right now, she didn't want to be alone. She wanted to be here. She knew that her parents would be happy for her to spend as much time as she wanted with them. Her short-term plan was to turn off her phone and be cosseted by her parents, until work dragged her back into the real world on Monday. By which time she would be refreshed and ready to face it.

In the kitchen, her dad was wafting a tea towel in the direction of the open back door.

"Burning something, Dad?" she said, giving him a kiss and a hug.

"Not at all. What made you think that?" he said, laughing.

"Nothing," she said. "I like my bacon well done anyway."

"And well done it shall be. Fried egg?"

"Yes, please."

"Your mum's in the shower. It will be ready in a few minutes. Why don't you pour yourself some tea and I'll give you a shout when it's ready."

Jamilla knew that he meant he would rather have the kitchen to himself, to concentrate on the timings. He wasn't the greatest cook in the world. She poured some tea from the teapot in the middle of the table and went through to the living room. She curled up in the corner of the sofa and sent a message to Samantha.

How you feeling this morning? Can't wait to see you later x

Immediately the reply came. *Been up since the crack of dawn. Why do nurses start their day so early? Might be coming home later, so will let you know x*

Jamilla was looking forward to seeing her. Selfishly, she had hoped to be able to see her in hospital, where she could speak to her privately, without Alistair hanging around like a bad smell. Although, she was unsure what she would say to her. She couldn't lie. She didn't want to lie. Samantha would know if she was lying, there was no doubt about it. But what would she tell her about what Alistair had been doing all week? That he had been seen talking to Frankie a couple of times in court? That wasn't exactly proof of any wrongdoing, was it? Suspicion wasn't enough. How would she explain why he hadn't called the police and why nobody had come to her rescue? The poor woman had had to fend for herself and make her own escape because her feckless husband hadn't done the right thing.

What on earth had Alistair been up to? What had he been thinking? She couldn't understand why he had been so reluctant to report Samantha missing. He should have called the police on Saturday afternoon when she hadn't come home. At the very least, he should have scoured the length and breadth of Manchester, checking every hotel to see if she was there. His complacency was astounding. Even when he got the text from Samantha saying that she was with Olivia Stevenson, he still didn't ring the police.

He was up to something. She was sure of it. She knew that he was involved with Frankie, in some capacity. She just had to prove it. Barristers had conversations with dodgy-looking guys all the time at court, but what she had seen was different.

She wasn't a hundred percent sure, but the more she thought about it, the more convinced she was that she had seen Frankie give Alistair some cash. That's what he had dropped onto the floor. She had seen the colour drain from Alistair's face and he had reached down and picked it up, quick as a flash. That would explain the fifty-pound note that he had given her to cover the cost of the Uber the other night. Who had cash these days? And who had fifty-pound notes? Criminals, that's who.

On Wednesday morning, she had fully expected Alistair to tell her that he had spoken to the police the night before. She couldn't believe that he hadn't. What kind of prick does that? He knew that his wife was in trouble, and he did nothing about it. Why? Because he was in it right up to his neck. Maybe he had become a drug runner for Frankie. Maybe he sold cocaine to his friends and neighbours for him. Whatever it was, her gut was telling her that there was something sinister going on between them.

Alistair himself had thought that Frankie was responsible for kidnapping Samantha. Although, having 'a few cross words', as he had put it, seemed a tenuous reason. Alistair must think she's stupid if he thinks she believes that. No doubt the police will uncover the truth sooner rather than later.

Jamilla had an appointment to speak to someone called DC Townsend later. They were due to meet at chambers after her lunch with her dad and Aunty Elsie, so she had a good few hours to think about how much she should tell her. At the moment, it was all supposition, fuelled by her intense dislike of Alistair. Maybe it would be better for her to keep her thoughts to herself, for now.

"Breakfast is ready," shouted her dad from the kitchen.

She smiled as she got up and took her tea into the kitchen. She was looking forward to this kind of treatment carrying on for the rest of the weekend.

Chapter Forty-Four
Friday

Robert faced Friday morning with somewhat less apprehension than he thought he would. He no longer dreaded the visit from Frankie's men at five o'clock, now that his bank balance was a little healthier than it had been this time yesterday. He knew that he could rely on Lucas. He hated asking him for money, but he had no choice. He couldn't have asked his father again. When he spoke to his friend, he had blamed his problematic finances on the fact that he was self-employed. He only got paid when his bill had been settled by the instructing solicitors, he had explained, which could be months after he had done the work. Lucas had told him that it wasn't a problem and had transferred two thousand pounds into his account while they were still chatting on the phone.

    Robert had said that usually it wasn't an issue, but for some reason, he hadn't had any money for months. He laughed and said that at least he had something to look forward to when the money eventually reached him. He said it would be like having six months wages all in one go. Lucas had called him a lucky bastard. Robert had forced a laugh. That was so far from the truth that it didn't bear thinking about.

    Deceiving his best mate had brought a lump to his throat.

"How's Jamilla?" Lucas had asked.

"Great," Robert had told him. Another lie that slipped off his tongue, melting into the warm air like ice cream. He didn't want to explain that she would probably never speak to him again. How could he begin to tell someone that his home had been burgled by two heavies and that he and Jamilla had been assaulted? That would be bad enough in itself, but if any of his friends ever found out that the visit had been brought about by Robert's own self-inflicted stupidity, he would never live it down. His self-respect, his reputation would be in tatters.

By the time he arrived in chambers, he had done what he was becoming used to doing, what he did best - he had put his own personal crisis to the back of his mind. Dealing with one problem at a time was the only way for him to cope these days.

"Hi James," he said, as he pushed open the door to chambers. "Got any plans for tonight?"

"As it happens, I'm free, mate," said James. James had been single for the past two months and never liked to turn down an opportunity to go for a drink after work. "Are you inviting me out on a date?"

"Absolutely. Just casual, mind you. Don't expect me to snog you at the end of the night. I'm not that kind of bloke. You'll have to wait for the second date for that treatment."

"Gutted!" said James, laughing. "I'm on an early finish tonight, so can be done by half five."

"Perfect," said Robert. "See you then." By then, his weekly debt would be paid, and he could relax a little. Until next week.

"What are you two gossiping about?" said Alistair. He sauntered into chambers with his usual swagger and arrogance. Robert would ordinarily be irritated the moment he saw him, but he was glad that Alistair was beginning to get some of his old self back. "Don't tell me, I'm not sure I want to know. Here, I've brought you some breakfast." He handed a brown paper bag to Robert and gave two to James. "Just a salmon and cream cheese bagel to say thank you for sorting out yesterday. There's one there for Imran. I couldn't leave him out."

"Thank you, Mr Mallory," said James.

"Thank you," said Robert. "There was no need, really. I enjoyed doing the conference."

"Did everything go all right?"

"Yes, fine. No issues at all."

"Okay, good," said Alistair. "Let's get to work then. There's a list full of hearings this morning."

Robert rolled his eyes towards James as he followed Alistair towards the lift. The old Alistair was still there, bright eyed and bushy tailed it seemed.

As they ate their breakfast in Alistair's office, Robert asked him how Samantha was, and Alistair told him what she could remember of her ordeal. Neither of them mentioned Frankie and Robert didn't ask whether he was at the other end of the phone call that Alistair had received to alert him of Samantha's whereabouts. Robert didn't know the extent of his involvement with Frankie, but presumed that it was in connection with cocaine. No doubt Alistair would tell him about that in his own time. Or maybe not. It would be his call.

As they had waited for the ambulance to arrive on Wednesday afternoon, Robert had wanted to ask him a million questions. He had wanted to tell him that he knew Frankie and that he had become involved with him, too. He wanted to tell someone who would understand what a massive mistake it was to cross paths with such a dangerous man. But Alistair had enough on his plate. His focus then was Samantha, not Frankie. Robert would bide his time.

Knowing Alistair, he would have formulated a revenge plan already. He wasn't the type to let someone walk over him and bully him. Frankie was a gangster, yes. He had gained his fortune through organised crime, that was true. But Alistair was a clever man. His power was his intelligence and he would undoubtedly use it to bring about Frankie's downfall. Whether it was now or at some point in the future, he was sure that it would happen. And when it did, Robert was planning to be right by Alistair's side.

Chapter Forty-Five
Friday

Alistair was thankful that his morning's list of court hearings wasn't particularly taxing. There was nothing that he had to concentrate on too much. Friday was known as the mop-up day, when the court dealt with sentencing hearings, bail applications and hearings to fix suitably convenient trial dates. This Friday was no different. Robert sat behind Alistair in Court Three, listening and learning and passing him the necessary paperwork. It crossed Alistair's mind to allow Robert to conduct one or two of the hearings, but that would have meant that Alistair's thoughts were free to run wild, galloping unchecked all morning. For the moment, he needed to keep them on a tight rein; controlled and manageable.

He knew that he would have to deal with the problem of Frankie at some point, but now wasn't the right time. He wanted Samantha out of hospital and fully recovered, before he could think about anything else. One thing was for certain, the status quo between him and Frankie couldn't continue. He wouldn't allow it. He wasn't going to work for him any longer, he would make sure of that. But how he guaranteed that Frankie accepted his decision, he wasn't sure. Frankie wasn't a man who would take no for an answer. The text Alistair had received yesterday was proof of that. But he couldn't continue to live under Frankie's cloud.

He wanted Frankie to be punished for what he had done to Samantha. But, in reality, that could never happen without alerting the police to the fact that they had been working together. If Frankie was arrested, Alistair knew that he wouldn't go down alone. He would tell the police everything. Yes, Alistair could deny everything, of course. He could deny that they had ever met. Frankie who? He had never heard of him. But life wasn't that simple. The evidence was out there. Telephone calls and texts, number plate recognition and the fact that Frankie's house was littered with security cameras recording every visitor would lead to both of their downfalls. Frankie would tell the police whatever they wanted to know about Alistair. Collateral for a lighter sentence.

As the judge delivered the sentence to the last defendant in the court's list, Alistair pushed his run-away thoughts back down and tried to concentrate. Living in the moment had always been something he had struggled with. Right now, it was imperative for the survival of his mental health.

Finally, the morning's work was done, and he and Robert could make their way back to chambers.

"Wow, that weather's taken a turn for the worse," said Robert, as they reached the main door of the court building. The blue sky from earlier was now completely obliterated by white-grey rain clouds, covering everyone with fine drizzle. They sheltered for a moment under the canopy that ran down the side of the building. "Have you got an umbrella?" he asked Alistair.

"No. It looks like we're going to get wet."

Robert looked up at the sky, trying to decide whether to rush back to the warmth of chambers, where he could enjoy his sandwich and a coffee in the kitchen, or whether to walk up to King Street, to the White Company to get Jamilla a small gift and in doing so, get absolutely soaked. He couldn't afford one of their beautiful cashmere shawls, which he knew she would love. But he had enough for a candle or a body spray. If he did decide to walk to King Street in the rain, when he got back to chambers, he could take his jacket off and hang it over the back of his chair to dry, but his trousers would be wet all afternoon. And would his journey be worth it? Jamilla was highly unlikely to accept any peace offering from him, despite the self-sacrifice that had accompanied the purchase.

But he loved her.

"If you don't mind, I'm going to take a little diversion down King Street. I need to get Jamilla something and I know she likes the White Company," he said, deciding to take a chance.

"Had another row, have you?" asked Alistair.

Robert studied Alistair's face for a sign that he was being supercilious and conceited, but all he saw was genuine concern and the slightest hint of friendship. If Julia and George, their colleagues from chambers, hadn't appeared right at that moment, he would have opened up to him about the loan he had from Frankie and the trouble he was having paying it back on time. But the moment was gone, taken from him by friendly greetings and talk of the inclement weather. He said goodbye and left Alistair to walk back to chambers with them. Julia and George each had a large black golfing umbrella, despite the fact that neither of them played golf.

A few minutes later, James pulled open the heavy wooden door leading to chambers, just as they all arrived back. He stepped to one side and allowed the group to enter, on his way out to buy his sandwich.

Julia hadn't stopped talking the whole way back, telling Alistair about her defendant and the weight of the evidence against him. He didn't mind. He was happy to keep his mind occupied with other people's mundane conversations. For a second, it made him forget that his wife was in hospital, having just been kidnapped by a gangster who wouldn't set him free from his villainous clutches.

As George, ever the gentleman, shook his and Julia's umbrellas at the door and placed them in the tall umbrella stand, Alistair pressed the button for the lift. It arrived immediately and they all stepped inside. Alistair was aware of the man in the black suit who had followed George and then pushed himself to the back of the lift. He was going to ask him what floor he wanted, but the man had his head down and Julia hadn't finished her incessant chatter. He pressed the button for the second floor. The man could sort himself out. He seemed to know where he was going, as he hadn't asked for any directions.

When the lift door opened, Alistair told Julia and George that he would drop his bag in his office and would see them in the kitchen in a few minutes, if either of them had time for a coffee. They both said they did. They turned left out of the lift. Alistair turned right.

The door to Sebastian's office was half open and Alistair could hear Sebastian and Jamilla's voices as he approached. He would rather have avoided Jamilla. Her ever-present un-spoken accusations were something he would rather leave for another day. But he couldn't be rude. He would just pop his head around the door and say hello to Sebastian. He didn't need to stay for long. He would tell him he was busy, as no doubt they were too. But he couldn't walk by without speaking to him.

"I thought I heard a familiar voice," he said, as he knocked and pushed open the door.

"Alistair, how lovely to see you," said Sebastian. "You remember my sister, Elsie? She's come to meet me for lunch."

"Yes, of course," said Alistair "It's nice to see you again." He crossed the room, sending a quick smile in Jamilla's direction, and held his hand out to Elsie, who stood up to greet him.

"I hope your brother is planning to take you somewhere nice," said Alistair.

In the seconds that followed, Alistair's world revolved in slow motion. He was vaguely aware of the fact that Elsie hadn't replied. She wasn't meeting his gaze, as she shook his hand. She was looking to her right, towards the door. What was that expression on her face? Disbelief? Horror? It seemed to be both. Alistair couldn't understand why. Her mouth opened in a scream, but he couldn't hear anything. He turned his head, anxious to see what she was staring at. The man in the suit, the man from the lift, was standing in the doorway.

His right hand was held aloft.

He was pointing a gun at them.

Someone screamed.

Someone shouted.

A phone was ringing somewhere.

A loud bang.

Then Elsie fell to the floor.

The blood pooled around her as she lay still.

Chapter Forty-Six
Friday

Imran, head to one side, held the phone between his ear and his shoulder. He knew that Miss Kershaw was upstairs somewhere, but she wasn't answering her phone. He would normally re-arrange her diary and then give it to her a fate-accompli, but she had mentioned that she wanted some time off next week, so it was only polite to check with her first. But if you didn't answer your phone, you didn't get to choose. He was too busy to mess about. This morning had been hectic and neither he nor James had had time to stop for lunch. Thankfully, the salmon and cream cheese bagel that Alistair had bought him for breakfast had managed to go some way to sustain him. When things had quietened down, he had allowed James to go and get his sandwich first. James was the type to eat one more sandwich than a hungry pig at a buffet and he wouldn't have been able to last much longer without food.

As Imran chatted to the young solicitor, laughing and flirting, which he did with everyone, he thought that he heard something that sounded like a gunshot. Was it coming from upstairs? Or was it a car back-firing outside? The soul-piercing screams followed a second later.

In the time that it took for his mind to comprehend what was going on, the double doors to the stairs at the side of the lift flew open. A tall thin man in a black suit ran into the reception area. Imran could hear the screams louder now that the door was open. He didn't know what had happened up there, but he knew from this man's crazed and frightened expression that he was somehow involved. The man stood for a second, as though he had forgotten where the exit was. Sweat ran down his face.

Imran dropped the phone.

He had to stop this man before he got to the door.

"Oi, what's going on?" he shouted.

He ran out from behind the long reception desk and reached the door in a couple of strides. He held his arms outstretched, with his back to the door. He was ready for any altercation that may be forthcoming. He prayed that somebody upstairs had called for the police. They would be here soon. They weren't usually far away from court. Whatever happened, he knew that he couldn't allow this man to escape.

The man stopped in front of him. Inches away. Imran could see his bright blue eyes, surrounded by dark eyelashes. He had a vision of the man's mother gazing into the same eyes as she held him close as a baby. What would she think of him now, if she knew what he had just done? A mother's pride and joy.

The man then raised his right hand and pointed a gun directly at Imran's forehead.

Imran took a deep breath and stood tall. He didn't want to die, but he would take his fate like a man. He didn't want his wife to spend her retirement alone, going on cruises as a single passenger, eating dinner with strangers and pretending to be happy and enjoying herself. He didn't want her to cry alone in the house at night, when the rest of the family had gone home with her assurances that she was fine. He didn't want his daughter to grow up without him. He knew that his brother would look after them both. He would give a speech at his daughter's wedding. But it wasn't the same.

He was lucky that he would be so missed. He had been blessed and now his time was up. There was nothing he could do to stop it.

He closed his eyes and waited for the bullet that would propel him from this world into the next.

When he heard the front door open and felt the cool wind rush into the reception area, he prayed that it wasn't James returning too soon with his sandwich. Please let there be a long queue in the sandwich shop. Please keep James safe. He is too young to die.

He waited for the sound of his colleague's startled voice, but when it didn't come, he opened his eyes, slowly and reluctantly.

The reception was empty.

The gunman had gone.

Chapter Forty-Seven
Friday

When the ambulance arrived at chambers for the second time that week, James directed the paramedics up to the second floor where their patient was waiting.

He had returned, carrying his expensive but worth-every-penny sandwich, just half a minute after the gunman had left. He found a distressed and shaken Imran sitting on the floor by the door, crying and garbling something about a man in a suit with a gun who had managed to get upstairs. James was about to sprint upstairs, ready to face whatever carnage the man had caused, but he was stopped by Alistair, who ran into reception, his chest heaving and out of breath. He told them that he had already called for an ambulance and the police.

"Where's the first aid box?" Alistair had shouted.

James told him there was one behind the reception desk. He ran behind the desk to fetch it.

"What's happened?" he asked, as he handed the large green box to Alistair.

"It's Sebastian's sister," said Alistair. "She's been shot."

As Alistair ran back upstairs with the box, not bothering to wait for the lift, James had helped Imran to his feet. He held his arm under his elbow and directed him to the first chair at the end of the row under the window, facing their desk.

"I'm going after him. Stay here!" he said as soon as Imran was settled in the seat.

"No!" shouted Imran. "You're the one staying here. What do you think you're going to do, tackle him to the ground? You don't know which way he ran. He will be half way down Deansgate by now."

"I can find him. Let me go!" said James. "We can't just let him get away."

A tearful Imran had clung tightly to his jacket sleeve. "There's CCTV all over the city. He won't get far. Even if he gets away today, they'll catch him tomorrow."

James wasn't sure that would be the case, but Imran had reminded him that their whole profession was possible because of bungling criminals who had been caught. He needed to have some faith in the justice system. James surrendered to the wisdom of his older colleague and settled down next to him. Imran needed him now. He had gone very pale. Where was that bloody ambulance?

James peered out of the window. He couldn't see a blue light.

"We won't be able to hear anything with the door shut," he had said. That wasn't strictly true, but his adrenalin filled body was incapable of sitting still. He had propped the front door open with the old wooden triangular shaped doorstop. He listened and waited. He couldn't hear anything yet, except for a group of four on the other side of the road, talking and laughing too loudly. He had wanted to shout over at them to be quiet. They were dealing with an emergency over here. Have some respect! But they weren't to be blamed. They didn't know that someone's life had been shot to smithereens only minutes before. They carried on, oblivious to the tragedy unfolding across the road. How many times had that happened to him, he wondered? How many times had he walked past a house where someone had just died? How many times had he overtaken a slow-moving black car that was taking people to a funeral?

Life went on for the lucky ones.

It was a good sign that Alistair had darted downstairs for the first aid kit, wasn't it? he thought, as he waited. That must mean Sebastian's sister was still alive. Injured, yes, but not dead. First aid kits are obsolete objects for dead people. Blankets and plastic sheets are for dead people.

He knew that Sebastian loved his sister. She was a sweet lady, from what he had seen. She had been to chambers quite a few times to meet Sebastian for lunch. Sebastian would be devastated if anything happened to her. And Jamilla. She would be, too.

"It's here, it's here," he had said, as he saw the ambulance screech around the corner from Deansgate. It stopped in a parking bay outside the door. The driver cut the engine but left the blue lights flashing. He watched as two paramedics, weighed down by heavy bags of lifesaving (he hoped) equipment ran towards him.

That was twenty minutes ago. They were still upstairs. What were they doing up there? Alistair didn't say that anyone else had been shot, did he? Everything was a blur. He couldn't quite remember. He wanted to go up and help, but he knew he would just get in the way; he wasn't trained in first aid. He knew he would faint at the sight of any blood.

The police had arrived within a few minutes of the ambulance. Two police cars were creating a roadblock outside. Someone was waiting with a roll of blue and white tape.

Outside, having returned from his relationship-saving shopping trip, Robert pushed his way through the gathering crowd, but was stopped by the uniformed officer at the door.

"I can't let anyone in or out," said the officer. "You need to stay back."

"I work here," Robert said. "What's going on?"

"You need to stay back, sir." The officer ignored his question and continued to block the door.

"James, James, what's going on?" Robert shouted over the officer's shoulder to where he could see James in reception.

James raised his index and his pinkie fingers, to indicate that he would ring him, and Robert watched as he took his phone out of his trouser pocket. Robert picked up on the first ring and James explained to his friend what had happened. He said that Elsie was being looked after by the paramedics in Sebastian's room and that Sebastian and Jamilla and Alistair were with her. Robert had no idea that Jamilla was in the building and begged and pleaded with the officer to let him through, but the officer stood firm. His instructions were that nobody was to pass the threshold. His boss would have his guts for garters if he went against orders, he told him.

Robert had no option but to wait. Apparently, the fact that his girlfriend might need him wasn't enough. If she was his wife, things would be different, he couldn't help thinking. A legal contract and a piece of paper seemed to stand for something in times of emergency.

He was in the process of sending a message to Jamilla when the paramedics appeared. Elsie was stretchered between them, bundled up in a red NHS blanket. Sebastian was carrying a saline drip attached to her arm. Within seconds, Elsie was wheeled into the waiting ambulance, along with her brother. Jamilla quickly followed, carrying her handbag - the one that Robert had bought her for her last birthday - and another smaller one, which he assumed was Elsie's. He called out to her. Whether she heard him or not, he wasn't sure. She ignored him and ran past, straight to the ambulance and jumped inside. The back doors were closed, the paramedics boarded, and the ambulance drove off.

Robert finished typing his message to Jamilla, simultaneously wiping tears from his eyes.

The police officer guarding the door let him into the building, making it clear it was against the rules, and then began his job of tying the tape to the closest drainpipes and lampposts.

Whites Chambers was now secure and the painstaking job of finding the culprit could begin.

Chapter Forty-Eight
Friday

"Hi, are you awake?" asked Jamilla as she opened the door to Samantha's hospital room later that day. "I'm sorry I've not brought any grapes." She forced a smile.

"Yes, come in, come in," said Samantha. She pushed herself into a sitting position and rested her head on the pillow. "I wasn't expecting you until after your lunch. Weren't you planning on having an afternoon tea at The Midland?"

Jamilla burst into tears. Sitting on the edge of Samantha's bed, she hugged her friend tightly, sobbing into her shoulder.

"Aww, don't worry about me," said Samantha. "I'll be all right. I suspect I'll be discharged later today. Tomorrow morning at the latest. The doctors haven't done their final round of the day yet, but I'm okay."

When Jamilla's tears continued, Samantha tried to reassure her that her face looked worse than it was. The bruise had faded loads already. She would be back to work in no time. She stroked Jamilla's hand as she perched on the edge of her bed. She wanted to ask her about Robert, as she suspected he was the real reason for her tears. Although Jamilla loved her and they were close friends, Samantha knew that this unexpected outpouring of grief wasn't for her. Not a hundred percent, anyway.

Eventually, Jamilla sat up. She went into the ensuite bathroom and wiped her eyes and blew her nose.

"Now, do you want to tell me what this is really about?" asked Samantha, when she returned.

Jamilla, dabbing at her sorrowful, red-rimmed eyes, told her that she and Robert were finished. She told Samantha about Robert's loan from Frankie and about the men who had burst into his apartment and had threatened them both and stolen Robert's watch. He could drown in his own problems, as far as she was concerned. She never wanted to see him or talk to him ever again. She was thinking of changing chambers, so that she didn't have to look at him on a daily basis. Samantha nodded, held tightly to her hand and told her to cross one bridge at a time. Samantha said that, although she loved Robert as a colleague, she agreed that he wasn't good enough for her. It was clear that his drinking had been gradually getting out of control for months. It wasn't funny turning up for work with a hangover. It had stopped being funny a long time ago. He was too old for that kind of behaviour.

Then Jamilla said that there was something else she wanted to tell her. Something awful had happened at chambers this afternoon. She said that she didn't want to worry her, but she would find out about it soon. It would be all over the news. There was no avoiding it. Between more tears, she told Samantha about the man who had turned up at chambers with a gun. She said that he had managed to get upstairs without being questioned and had stormed into Sebastian's room and had shot her Aunty Elsie in the arm.

"Your Aunty Elsie! What the fuck! Is she okay? I mean, is she…"

"She's alive, yes, she's going to be fine. She lost a lot of blood but…"

"Who is he? Have they caught him?"

"No, but I'm sure they will catch him."

"I hope so," said Samantha. "Bloody hell. Poor Elsie." She had wanted to stay strong for her friend, but she had been on the brink of tears ever since she had been released by her captor two days ago. They flowed freely now. Jamilla handed her a tissue.

"I'm sure she'll be okay," said Jamilla. "Fortunately, he didn't get her in the chest. Her arm will heal, given time."

"I've never known anything like this before," said Samantha. "It's been a bizarre week. What's going on, Jamilla?" Jamilla shook her head and shrugged. "Is it the same man who kidnapped me, do you think?"

"No," said Jamilla. "Why would you think that?"

"Because maybe he came to chambers to kill me. He clearly just got the wrong person."

"No, don't be silly. Aunty Elsie is years older than you, and you weren't even there."

"But he wouldn't know that, would he? Maybe he just panicked. Maybe he saw you and he thought that you were me."

"No, I don't think so. I mean, yes, we both have dark curly hair, but my skin is much darker than yours. He spent four days with you; he will know what you look like. Don't worry. He wasn't after you."

Samantha nodded. "What did he look like?"

Jamilla shrugged again. "I don't know. I only got a second's glance at him, then it was over, and he disappeared. White guy, skinny and tall, that's all I can say."

"That could be him," said Samantha. "He must have gone back to kill me. Oh my God!" Her hands shot to her mouth and her eyes flicked between Jamilla's face and the door at lightning speed. "Are we safe in here? He could get to me…"

"Hey, calm down, you're safe. There are a million skinny white guys out there, that doesn't mean it was the same man. My dad thinks he was after him actually. He's had some death threats last week from an unhappy client."

"Oh my God!"

Alistair's sudden appearance prevented Jamilla from explaining what her dad had told her while they waited for

Aunty Elsie to be treated. Sebastian had apologised for not telling her sooner, but he hadn't wanted to worry her. He explained that in addition to the death threat from his client in prison, he had also been attacked by someone who the police thought was Jay Harris's brother. The same man had daubed red paint on the front door, threatening to kill him. Her dad said that the threat had worried him, and he had taken it seriously, but to the extent that he thought the defendant's brother would become a nuisance to them, a stalker. That was all. He never thought in a million years that someone would turn up at chambers with a gun. Jay Harris and his brother were clearly more connected to the criminal underworld than he had first given them credit for.

Alistair rushed over to the other side of Samantha's bed. "I'm so sorry that it's taken me so long to get here," he said. "I've been talking to the police. Has Jamilla told you what has happened?"

"Yes, she did," said Samantha. "I'm so glad you're here."

He gathered Samantha up into his arms. Jamilla had never seen him so affectionate. The hug went on for longer than she was comfortable with and just when she was about to get up and leave them to it, her dad appeared.

"Samantha, Alistair, hi," said Sebastian. "Sorry for barging in, but Aunty Elsie is awake. I've just spoken to her. She knows who shot her." Sebastian sounded slightly out of breath, as though he had rushed from the A&E Department to impart this breaking news.

"She knows him?" asked Jamilla. "How?"

"He's one of her new neighbours. His name's Jake. She hasn't known him for long, she said. In fact, she doesn't really know him at all, but she knows his wife, Emma. I have spoken to one of the police officers and told him all about it. They're going to send someone over to his house right away."

"Emma?" said Samantha. "You said his wife is called Emma?"

"Yes, that's what Elsie says."

"That was the name that was tattooed on the man's arm. The man who kidnapped me."

"Really?" said Sebastian. He didn't believe in coincidences, but he couldn't see how these two events were linked.

"Tall skinny bloke, about six foot two, three?"

Jamilla and Sebastian both nodded.

"It was you!" screamed Jamilla. "He wanted you!" She jumped up off the bed and backed into her dad. Sebastian put his arm around her shoulder. She pointed at Alistair. "He wasn't after my dad at all. He was after you."

"We don't know…"

"Yes, we fucking do, Alistair. This was the same man who kidnapped your wife because of some vendetta. Is he working for Frankie? Don't answer me, because I fucking know that he is. You bastard! Now, because of you, my aunty is lying in a hospital bed. If he wasn't such a shit shot, she could be lying in the morgue right now."

"Alistair?" Samantha dropped his hand and waited for an explanation. She waited for the words that would save their marriage, that would assure her that her husband wasn't involved in something that he shouldn't be. She wanted him to tell her that she hadn't just spent four nights in captivity because of him. "Is this true? Is this connected to Frankie?"

"Who's Frankie?" asked Sebastian.

"Frankie is the man who sends the orders," said Jamilla. "Isn't that right, Alistair?"

Chapter Forty-Nine
Three Days Later - Monday

Report from Manchester Evening News
Monday 22nd May 2023

The police investigating last week's shooting at Whites Chambers on St. John Street have now found a body. The body has been identified as belonging to Jake Bradshaw of 34 Calder River View, Lancaster. The police are not looking for anyone else in connection with his death.

Mr Bradshaw's body was discovered by a dog walker in Rivington Park. He had a fatal gunshot wound to the head. A small handgun was found at the side of his body. A signed suicide note was discovered in his car.

A police spokesperson says that the handwriting and the signature on the note have been identified by his wife as likely to have been written by Mr Bradshaw. Forensic tests have yet to be carried out.

The police are unable to release the full content of the suicide note at this time, but our reporter can reveal that the note admits that Mr Bradshaw was responsible for the recent kidnapping of Manchester barrister, Samantha Mallory, and the death of Frankie Byrne of 47 Manchester Road, Chorlton. Mr Bryne was found dead by his wife last Friday afternoon at his home address. He had been shot in the head at close range. Mr Bryne was known to the police and was suspected of running an organised crime group responsible for the importation of hundreds of thousands of pounds worth of cocaine and other Class A controlled drugs. A subsequent search of Mr Bryne's property revealed a large quantity of drugs and a number of handguns.

Mr Bradshaw was Mr Bryne's cousin and was believed to have been working for him at the time of his death.

Samantha Mallory, currently recuperating at home following her ordeal, said that she was shocked by the two deaths. She went on to say that she could now put this terrifying episode behind her and get on with the rest of her life. She said that she has no idea why she was targeted and kidnapped by Mr Bradshaw. Both Mrs Mallory and her husband are successful lawyers and a police press statement states that the kidnap was likely to have been financially motivated.

Mr Bradshaw's wife, Emma Bradshaw, is being questioned by the police in connection with her involvement in Samantha Mallory's kidnapping.

Chapter Fifty
Monday

Samantha closed the door behind the reporter and went back into the kitchen. Alistair was stacking the dishwasher with the dirty coffee cups and side plates.

"I don't know why you have given them the time of day," he said, without looking up. "They're not interested in you. They just want a story."

"I wish you'd leave the dishwasher," said Samantha. "I can do it when you've gone." More than anything, she wanted to slam the door of the dishwasher closed on his fingers. She wanted to cause him exquisite pain, which he could wrap up, along with his freshly pressed shirts, cashmere jumpers and matching socks which were waiting for him in the suitcase in the middle of their marital bed, and take it with him. "Do you still have The Guardian app on your phone?" she asked.

"Yes, why?" Alistair turned his back on the dishwasher, took his phone out of his pocket, opened the screen and scrolled through his apps, as though about to proffer evidence.

"So why do you read a newspaper if you hate journalists so much? How do you think they get their stories if people like me don't speak to them? Honestly, Alistair, you're so bloody pompous. All the world is wrong except you. It must be amazing being you." She pushed passed him, stabbed the dishwasher's on button and closed the door.

"I was just…"

"I don't care what you were just," she said. "Anyway, have you finished your packing? Because if you haven't, I'll get out of your way until you're finished."

"There's no need for that. I thought we were going to be amicable about this."

Samantha ignored the hurt puppy-dog look in her husband's eyes. She didn't want to be taken in and duped into thinking that he cared about her. He clearly didn't. Someone who had made lies and deceit their closest allies had no place in her life. No place in her heart. Jamilla had been right all along; Samantha deserved better.

On Friday, when Jamilla had guessed that the gunman had meant to shoot Alistair and that his connection with Frankie was more than he had admitted to, Samantha had dropped his hand like a hot brick and told him that she didn't want him anywhere near her. Now she knew the truth, Samantha wasn't sure which was worse, the fact that Alistair had lied to her and had become involved with an organised criminal gang, or the fact that he hadn't made a scene at the hospital and hadn't begged for her forgiveness. Sebastian had opened the door and Alistair had meekly walked out.

He had told her that he was sorry the next day when they talked and he had told her the whole truth, or what he said was the whole truth, but the lack of earnestness meant that the apology had fallen flat. It lay between them, as lifeless and unmoving as their marriage had become.

Jamilla had hugged her in the hospital and said that she could stay with her for the time being, until she found a place of her own. But Alistair liked to play the role of a gentleman, if nothing else, and he insisted that Samantha should go home, and he would book into a hotel. When she had been discharged from hospital later that evening, it was Jamilla and Sebastian who had taken her home, not her husband. They had collected a pizza on the way and had stayed with her until late, chatting and eating and they hadn't left her until she had persuaded them that she was tired, that she was absolutely fine and that she would take a long bath and go to bed. She hadn't cried until she was sure that they had gone. Then with her head in her hands, she had sobbed and sobbed until she was exhausted.

On Saturday morning, when Alistair's message arrived, asking if he could explain, she had reluctantly agreed. She wanted the truth, knowing that it would inevitably hurt her. As she waited for him to arrive, making a pot of coffee that she knew he loved, she thought that she might be able to forgive him. She wanted to. She had loved him so much, surely that much love didn't dissipate so quickly? She told herself that he had simply made bad choices but that didn't mean he was a bad husband, did it? Don't they say that the truth shall set you free? But uninvited flashbacks of her four days in captivity, using the bathroom while a thug stood guard outside, being without her friends and family and being scared witless, all because of Alistair, meant that she could never forgive him.

He had perched on the edge of the sofa in the living room, sipping the coffee that she had made for him, when she realised that their marriage was over. She asked him to tell her the whole truth about his relationship with Frankie. Annoyance had flashed across his face, which Samantha chose to ignore. He wasn't used to being questioned. She silently waited for him to confess. To what, she wasn't sure.

"It wasn't a relationship," he had said, making speech marks in the air with his forefingers. "He was someone that I bought cocaine from, I told you that."

Samantha took a deep breath. "You did tell me that, yes, but tell me the rest. There has to be more to it."

"There isn't," he had said. "There really isn't."

She looked deep into his eyes, seeking the truth or the hidden lies, whatever she could find.

"You must have upset him."

"Why must I?" The annoyance was beginning to turn into anger. He glared at her.

"Because why would he send one of his minions to kidnap your wife if everything between you was hunky dory?" Samantha tried not to shriek. She knew he didn't like it when she became emotional. She didn't want him to storm out. She needed the truth. "Were you dealing drugs for him?"

"No," he said, looking her straight in the face. He appeared to be telling the truth, but he was a trained showman. He had had years of preaching to unsuspecting jury members, getting them on his side, persuading them that his words were the truth. "Jamilla said that she saw him giving you money in court."

"He didn't give me money."

"Is Jamilla lying?"

"No. She didn't see the whole thing, that's all." He paused and took another sip of his coffee. "Okay, I'll tell you everything. You won't like it, but I don't want there to be any lies between us." He stretched out an upturned palm, expecting Samantha to take his hand, but Samantha sat back on the opposite sofa, her arms folded and out of reach. His arm fell to his side. "He did ask me to sell drugs for him," he said. "He tried to give me that roll of money in court, the one that Jamilla saw, but I wouldn't take it. He was trying to say that that's what I could have, if I started working for him."

"Jamilla saw you pick it up."

"Yes, of course, I picked it up, but I gave it back to him. I did."

"And what was the kidnap all about?"

"I don't know." Alistair put his coffee cup on the side table, sat back and folded his arms.

"Don't fucking mirror me, Alistair. I'm not falling for it. And wipe that stupid smile off your face. This is serious."

That's when he apologised, albeit with words and not with warmth. He shrugged and said that Frankie was a vindictive and nasty man, and he could only assume that the fact that he kidnapped Samantha was just to show his power. He said that he obviously hadn't meant to hurt her, because he had released her. She was here, wasn't she, safe and sound? No harm done.

Samantha had stood up then and asked him to leave. She told him that as soon as she could, she was going to file for divorce. She didn't want to talk to him anymore. Alistair hadn't argued. He had simply collected his car keys and had driven off, to where she didn't know and didn't care. As he had reached the front door, she told him that she would pack his clothes and he could collect them another day. He had agreed without resistance.

She wanted to tell him that the fact that she was here 'safe and sound' was not because of Frankie's philanthropy, but because she had put her own life on the line and had tried to escape. Jake, for all his faults, had been good enough to see that she needed hospital care and had taken her back to Manchester, but he hadn't taken her to a doctor or to the hospital, he had dumped her in a back street like an unwanted pet. But she didn't say that. She needed to save some ammunition for the divorce petition.

Now, she picked up her car keys and her phone from the worktop. "I'm going out. I want you gone by the time I get back. And you can leave your key in the bowl." She marched down the hall, grabbed her handbag from the hall table and slammed the door behind her.

*

Jamilla settled herself on her parents' sofa, slippered feet up on the footstool. "What shall we watch?" she asked. She pointed the remote control at the television screen.

"Something light and fluffy, please," said Laila.

"The Great British Bake Off?"

"Yes, perfect. I haven't seen the last series at all."

Jamilla found the program and then paused it, waiting for Sebastian to join them. A minute later, he appeared carrying a wooden tray with four cups of tea and four slices of homemade cake. Laila baked when she was stressed.

"Ooh, I don't think I can eat a slice that big," said Elsie. She was sitting on the sofa closest to the window, as she liked to see the comings and goings outside. Her left arm was bandaged from the shoulder to the wrist and was resting in a sling.

"Rubbish," said Sebastian. He put her tea on the small table next to her and placed the cake plate on her knee. He handed her a fork. "You know you can't resist Laila's coffee and walnut cake."

"I can't, you're right," she said, digging into the sponge with her fork.

They ate in silence for a few minutes. Laila looked from Jamilla to Sebastian and back again, occasionally wiping the odd tear. Jamilla laughed, squeezed her hand and told her not to be silly; they were all alive and well. She had nothing to worry about. Laila laughed too.

"Are you going into work tomorrow, Jamilla?" asked Aunty Elsie.

"Yes, in the afternoon, that's all. So at least I don't have to battle with the rush hour traffic."

"And will you be coming back here, or are you going home?" She asked the question that Laila and Sebastian hadn't wanted to know the answer to. They both wanted her to stay with them as long as possible. Last night, they had talked about moving the wardrobes out of one of the bedrooms, to make more space, so that she could move back home permanently, if she wanted to.

"I'm going to have to go home soon," said Jamilla. "If I stay here much longer, I won't get in any of my clothes."

"I know what you mean," said Aunty Elsie, patting her stomach. "Your mum's cakes are better than any that you see on the Bake Off."

Jamilla found herself blinking back tears. She wanted to go back home and reclaim her old life as an independent young woman with a career, friends and a busy social life. But she knew things would be different for a while. Samantha wasn't ready to go back to work yet, but chambers wouldn't be the same without her. She didn't want to see Alistair and she certainly didn't want to see Robert. She was enjoying her time with her family.

"I'll just stay for another week or so," she said.

Laila gave her a huge hug.

THE END

Character Studies

Samantha Mallory

Age – early 30s

Physical Description – Unruly, dark curly hair. Pretty.

Personality – Quiet and reserved. The complete opposite to her husband. She has low self-esteem, caused, in the main, by the way her husband treats her. She is kind and gentle and a great friend, who is always happy to lend an empathetic ear. She thinks that Alistair is too good for her and she is constantly striving to be better, although she is perfect. She worries that it is only a matter of time before he strays into the arms of another woman.
Drinks skinny latte.

Partner – Married to Alistair. They have been together for ten years. They met at university. They now live in Altrincham.

Family Background – She has a sister called Beth who is living with a female partner, Sarah. Her parents are very proud of her. She was educated at Altrincham Grammar School, where she won a scholarship for gifted pupils.

Alistair Mallory

Age – early 30s

Physical Description – He thinks he is better looking than he actually is. He wears a Tag Heur watch and a pin-striped suit to work. He drives a Jaguar F Pace.

Personality – A cocky, arrogant twat. He is good at his job and reasonably intelligent, but he has a massive superiority complex and walks around Crown Court wearing his wig like a crown. He hasn't been unfaithful to Samantha, but he kissed Jennifer Maxwell at the Christmas party and showed no remorse.
Drinks black coffee and tea with milk.
He works for the Crown Prosecution Service, prosecuting criminals.

Partner – Married to Samantha.

Family Background – His parents are both wealthy and he went to a prestigious private school in the south of England. He went to Durham University, where he met Samantha.

Sebastian Thomas

Age – 58

Physical Description – A good-looking, smart gentleman. Tall and Black.

Personality – He has been a barrister for 35 years, mostly defending criminals. He is an old-fashioned gentleman and struggles to keep his chivalry at bay at work. He wants to open doors and pull back chairs for his female colleagues, but knows that he mustn't. He works at a mahogany desk and has a dark green leather chair.
Drinks strong tea.
He is disillusioned with the profession and wants to take early retirement.

Partner – He lives in Knutsford with his wife Laila, who is an author and screen writer. They have a daughter, Jamilla, also a barrister.

Family Background – He is the child of parents who emigrated to the UK from Jamaica. They bought a farm and became successful, so were able to send Sebastian and his sister to a private school. He studied law at Oxford University.

Jamilla Thomas

Age – early 28

Physical Description – Blessed with curves. Sexy and confident.

Personality – She is feisty and confident. She is intelligent and ambitious, but her friends and family are just as important to her as her career.
Drinks coffee at work and Prosecco at home. Loves an espresso martini.

Partner – Been dating Robert for seven or eight months. She loves him and is willing to help him overcome his gambling addiction, but she won't take any nonsense from him.

Family Background – She is Sebastian's daughter and has been brought up in Knutsford but now lives in her own house close to Manchester city centre.

Robert Brierley

Age – early 27

Physical Description – Dirty blond hair. Keeps himself fit by playing rugby and going to the gym, but isn't overly muscly.

Personality – He is a trainee barrister. He's immature and too rich. He has money from his parents and a well-paid job, but he has nothing to show for it. His Porche is leased, his flat is rented and he goes overdrawn at the end of the month. He keeps making mistakes and makes bad decisions. Gambling addict.
Drinks coffee and too much alcohol.

Partner – He is dating Jamilla, but their relationship is on the brink.

Family Background – His parents are wealthy and live in Alderley Edge in a large house. He went to a private school and has pressure from his family. He is expected to do well in his career. He now lives in a posh apartment in Castlefield, Manchester.

Elsie

Age – 63

Physical Description – Smartly dressed, especially when in church. Her dark hair is now almost all grey.

Personality – She is kind. She feeds the bird every day in the churchyard, often on homemade scones and cookies. She has lost some of her sparkle since her husband died. Her best friend is Jean.

Partner – Married to Stanley but he died just over twelve months ago. They don't have any children. Stanley is buried in the graveyard and she visits him every day and chats to him.

Family Background – She is Sebastian's sister, so also the daughter of parents who emigrated from Jamaica. She now lives in a Lancashire village, where she is retired. She used to be a solicitor. She loves books and has been an avid reader since childhood, when her mother would encourage her reading by taking her to the library and buying her new books for the house.